About the Author

Michelle was born in South Africa, where she lived for forty years. After sadly being widowed, she moved with her son to the south of England, where he finished his education. Michelle now lives between the UK and South Africa and travels extensively. She is an avid reader and loves spending time with nature. The original Box from St Helena was given to her as a precious childhood gift and was the inspiration for this tale.

The Box from St. Helena

Michelle Elvidge

The Box from St. Helena

Olympia Publishers
London

www.olympiapublishers.com
OLYMPIA PAPERBACK EDITION

A CIP catalogue record for this title is
available from the British Library.

ISBN: 978-1-80074-408-0

First Published in 2023

Olympia Publishers
Tallis House
2 Tallis Street
London
EC4Y 0AB

Printed in Great Britain

Dedication

For my beloved parents and those strong women who
touched my life, enabling me to create and embroider this
tale.

Acknowledgements

Thanks to: Mienke, Cheryl, Noel, Diane, Patsy and Fettes for their advice and endless patience. Mark and Elizabeth for their enduring encouragement. David, my partner, who took me to
St Helena Island and supports me in every way.

St HELENA

By a Prisoner of War 1902

FOREWORD

St Helena Island

St Helena Island is a small volcanic outcrop in the South Atlantic Ocean and part of the 'British Overseas Territory' of St Helena, Ascension and Tristan da Cuhna. (British Overseas Territories Act 2002).

The island was discovered on 21st May 1502 by Galician navigator Joao da Nova, who was sailing in the service of Portugal. He named the island 'Santa Helena' after Helena of Constantinople, whose Saint's Day falls on 21st May and is still celebrated as the island's National Day.

The island became a Dutch and then a British possession. It was an extremely important port of call prior to the Suez Canal being opened and had approximately one thousand ships per year calling at the island.

St Helena also has a darker history from when it was a place of quarantine; trading and holding slaves there before the abolition of the Slave Trade.

Currently, there is a small population of a few thousand inhabitants, mainly descended from Africans, mixed-race Africans and Europeans (known locally as Coloureds), British Settlers, East India Company employees and labourers from Southern Asia, East Indies, Madagascar and China. After the Great Fire of London in 1666, some Londoners came to St Helena, which may have contributed in a small way to the local English dialect.

After his defeat at Waterloo, Napoléon Bonaparte gave himself up to the English, hoping to end his days as a country gentleman in a manor house. Instead, he was exiled first to Elba Island and then after his escape and recapture, to the inhospitable island of St Helena in 1815. There he spent the last six years of his life until he died in 1821 at the age of 51.

In 1890, the Zulu king, Dinuzulu kaCetshwayo, was banished to the island after his capture by the British, as punishment for leading his Zulu army against the British Empire's occupiers in Zululand, South Africa. He fathered seven children, one of which was a daughter, Princess Dinuzulu (also known as Maglan Noden), whose mother was a local woman.

The island was also used as a prisoner of war (POW) camp during the South African War of 1899 to 1902, since the POW camps in the Cape Colony were becoming overcrowded and vulnerable to attack by Boer forces. Some 5,866 prisoners were shipped to St Helena in 1900 and were held in Deadwood Camp, Broad Bottom and High Knoll Fort. Some POWs were given permission to work as household servants, cooks and grooms. Others were even allowed to live in the residents' homes in Jamestown. Sporting equipment was forwarded to the camps from sympathisers in the Netherlands, including eight rugby balls and six soccer balls. Prisoners subsequently founded a club for rugby and soccer which helped with the boredom the prisoners endured, getting rid of some of their energy and frustrations. Some of the prisoners went on to play excellent rugby on their return to South Africa.

St Helena is located in the South Atlantic Ocean, 1200 miles (1,950 kilometres) from the south-west coast of Africa and 2500 miles (4000 kilometres) from Rio de Janeiro in South

America and occupying 47 square miles (122 square kilometres) of land, measuring about 10 by 5 miles (16 by 8 kilometres).

This story begins in Jamestown, the capital city of St Helena, which lies within two extraordinarily deep crevasses facing towards the wharf. This is where, on Ladder Hill, the famous Jacob's Ladder was built in 1829. This ladder has 699 steps and was originally used to enable goods to be moved from sea level to the top of the hill and down again when necessary – particularly manure from stall fed animals. This was carried in carts on the funicular railway at the side of the steps to the top of the hill, and used as fertiliser for the land on that side of the island.

St Helena is home to exotic fauna and flora, the beautiful heart-shaped waterfall and barren cliffs dropping down into the turquoise blue sea. The highest peak is Diana's Peak which provides stunning views across the island.

The island is intersected with deep valleys – or guts as they are known locally – which slope steeply towards the coast, exposing different coloured sands. There is relatively little level ground, and the island has just one black sand beach named Sandy Bay. On the higher ground, bush and semi-tropical vegetation abounds. The only inland waters are small mountain streams which sometimes dry up in the summer months. Jamestown tends to be sunny and slightly humid, whilst the higher areas in the centre of the island can experience chilly, misty rain.

St Helenians are commonly known as 'Saints'.

Coloured People

The term 'Coloured', derived from the British era, refers to the many people of mixed descent living in Cape Town. The definition includes people of different religions and language groups, wealth and education. They felt rivalry from the black people, particularly over employment, and were rejected by the white community. This segregation permeated across the country.

The use of the 'Coloured' can be very derogatory, but at the time it was acceptable in South Africa and St Helena.

"No child should be punished for the accident of their birth."
-    President Lyndon B. Johnson

PART I

Chapter 1
Jamestown, St Helena Island
(1900)

Elsie woke to a loud rattling at her front door. Was that the strong wind howling and causing the noise, or someone knocking?

There was the noise again. Elsie's heart was beating almost as loudly as the urgent and insistent banging at the door.

"Please, help me, ma'am! Please open! I won't harm you," called out a deep and distressed voice from the other side.

Who was this man needing her help in the middle of the night? Was he to be trusted?

The knocking came again, "Please, ma'am! I am bleeding."

Elsie leapt out of bed and slipped her housecoat over her nightdress. Lighting the paraffin lamp, she moved silently towards the front door and stood there listening quietly. She could hear his laboured breathing through the wooden door.

"What do you want?" asked Elsie in a trembling voice.

"Argh! Please, ma'am. I have been stabbed and need a dressing on the wound, then I'll be gone."

Elsie hesitated to unlock the door as she was all alone in the cottage. His heavy guttural accent gave him away as one of the South African prisoners of war. She was also concerned about her reputation. Her neighbours may hear the noise and be peeping through their curtains to see a prisoner at her front door. Fearing he would knock loudly again, she opened the door slightly, keeping her right foot jammed against the back of it as a feeble precaution. She held the lamp out to illuminate the man's face and then glanced down to see him holding his right arm above the elbow. Blood was seeping between his fingers and dripping on the ground. He had a large, felt hat pulled low on his forehead and was otherwise surprisingly tidy and clean for a prisoner.

"Come in and I will see if I can stem that bleeding, but know that I can scream loudly for my neighbours if I need to," she warned him. "You will have to leave as soon as possible as there are eyes everywhere. Surely you should be at Deadwood Camp?"

"Thank you, ma'am," he said, removing his hat as he entered her cottage, following her through to the kitchen where he sat at the table without being invited to do so. He looked exhausted and afraid. He had piercing blue eyes and blonde hair.

Elsie added a small log to the dying embers in the stove and blew hard on them to encourage the flames. Placing the kettle of water to boil, she turned to see the man sitting at her table watching her intently. Elsie felt very anxious under his stare, but composed herself.

"Well, show me the wound then and perhaps I can clean it up and dress it with some clean rags."

The man tried to remove his brown-coloured jacket, wincing at the effort. Elsie helped him and gently rolled up the right sleeve of the khaki-coloured and now blood-stained shirt. She gasped when she looked at the wound as there was a broken knife blade buried in the flesh.

"I am not a nurse! I think you need to see the camp's Medical Officer for this."

"No. Please, ma'am. It's complicated. There has been a disagreement between the prisoners as some of us wish to return to South Africa and our families there, whilst the others want to continue with this war. It is best the authorities don't know about this or I could be incarcerated up the hill in High Knoll Fort for being involved in prisoner disputes. Can you please try to remove the broken knife and could you also clean my wound. Then I will leave quietly. I promise."

Elsie began to wonder why she had opened the door. She thought it best to do as he asked as quickly as possible. While the water heated on the small stove, she opened her late father's old toolbox that had a hammer, pliers and a few old, rusty wood files in it. She poured some vinegar over the old pliers in the hope of cleaning them a little before she approached the patient, who was looking extremely anxious and rather pale.

"Look away!" commanded Elsie, moving the lamp closer to his injured arm. Pinching the broken knife blade in the pliers, she pulled it out of the flesh. Blood spouted from the wound. The young prisoner slumped in the chair he was seated on and slipped down on to the floor.

Elsie froze, staring at the blood pooling next to the unconscious man. On gathering her composure, she quickly started washing the wound with the just-warm water mixed with vinegar, before dressing it with some clean rags. The man started moaning and, opening his eyes, looked up at Elsie's nervous expression.

"Thank you, ma'am. Please can I have some water to drink and then I will leave," he croaked in a deep whisper.

"But where will you go? There is no escaping this island.

Not even Napoleon managed that," she said with a wry smile.

The young Boer seemed quite breathless, grimacing in pain as he struggled to sit up. He looked even paler than when he had arrived at the front door.

Slowly, taking pauses as he endured the pain in his arm, he tried to explain to Elsie the reason for his difficult situation.

"Argh, ma'am, I have to return to the camp 'cause my friends are counting on me to help create a 'Peace Camp' for those no longer wanting to fight the British. The other Boers in the Deadwood Camp are calling us 'joiners and traitors,' I suppose like collaborators. You know, we came here by ship from Cape Town in April and now long to get back home to our land and families in South Africa. Those British soldiers are burning our farms and houses and the poor womenfolk and children are being sent to concentration camps, so they can't support the remaining Boer fighters with food and guns anymore."

Elsie handed him a cup of water into which she had stirred two spoons of her precious sugar.

"Drink this and then you had best return to the camp without being caught."

"May I ask your name, ma'am, as you have been so kind and nice to me?"

"Elsie. And yours?"

"Luke, ma'am. Luke Viljoen."

He stood slowly, holding on to the table and swaying a little before moving towards the front door and letting himself out.

"I owe you, Miss Elsie. Thank you," he said, before disappearing into the windy night.

Elsie could not quite believe what had happened. Whilst she wiped up the congealed blood from her kitchen floor, she asked herself if she had just been dreaming. Then she noticed that he had left his hat behind. Why had Luke knocked on *her* cottage door for help? Had she seen him somewhere before? She did not recall seeing such a handsome Boer on the island. He had seemed to be quite interesting too.

Elsie sank down into the chair Luke had been sitting on and carefully picked up his hat, noticing the bloody finger marks from when he had removed it on entering her cottage. She took one of the rags and started cleaning and buffing the hat.

Sleep was over for the night as she played the event through her mind again and again.

Chapter 2
Elsie's early life

Elsie was born in 1881 on the island of St Helena and was the daughter of a schoolmaster, James Baker who was from Portsmouth in England, and her mother Joanna, who was a local Saint. Elsie's mother had been born into a local family of mixed-race descent. Her parents met and fell in love soon after her father's ship docked in Jamestown, where he had been appointed as the local schoolmaster. Within weeks of meeting, they had married, and Elsie was born some ten months later. Elsie recalled her mother as a very attractive woman with mahogany-coloured, curly hair that she always kept neatly braided with a pretty ribbon that secured the braid from unravelling.

James Baker had been struck by her poise and beautiful smile when he first saw her. He doubted he would ever find such a lovely woman again. A dapper man of medium height, James thought he may only have this one chance of finding such a delightful wife. Despite clashing religious views – James, being Church of England and a keen admirer of Charles Darwin – theirs was mostly a happy home. He even secretly treasured a well-thumbed copy of Darwin's *The Origin of Species*. Elsie's parents had been married in the Catholic Church, where she had later been baptised on her mother's insistence. Even though Joanna had been a practicing Roman

Catholic, James insisted that Elsie be raised as an Anglican, which was deeply hurtful to her mother. Elsie had never truly understood her parents' religious differences as she felt that God loves us all, regardless of our colour or creed. Elsie believed that one should be honest, respectful and obedient, no matter the church of worship. She had chosen to keep this view to herself though, for fear of fuelling another religious argument in the cottage, which offered no room for escape, especially since the differences in her parents' religious views would clearly never be resolved. Even as a child, their arguments had made little sense to her, and she had inwardly raged at both of them for each insisting their personal religious view was the correct one.

Elsie's life was mostly very happy, although she remembered quite vividly the horror in 1890 when a large rockfall occurred in Jamestown and demolished fourteen houses, killing nine people and injuring many of her friends. The next year, a fountain was erected in the main street to commemorate this sad day. She and her friends regularly went to drink from the fountain, and it became a meeting point for many of the Saints.

Elsie's mother, Joanna, had learnt to make lace from her own mother and she earned a small amount of money selling delicate collars and trimmings to the foreign visitors, and to the women in the bigger houses on the island. She treasured the very prized, red rose bush planted next to the front door which James had brought with him from England. In the small backyard, she had planted rows of onions, tomatoes, peppers and leafy, green vegetables.

James Baker, being a schoolmaster with an enquiring mind, was a mine of information and spent many hours reading to Elsie until she was accomplished enough to do so by herself.

They used to take long walks together, exploring the fascinating island and learning about the birds and the plants. James believed that if you gave a child an enquiring mind, they would have the desire to educate themselves.

Elsie never forgot the first time she identified a wirebird, which her father told her was a gift from God to the Island, as it was found nowhere else in the world. She did, however, question her father's actual belief in God as he seemed so intrigued by Charles Darwin and his evolutionary theory. With him being the schoolmaster though, Elsie suspected that he may well have found it necessary to feign religious belief for the sake of his reputation, or out of respect for the Christian community.

James Baker often teased Joanna knowing she would have a fiery reaction when he quoted Napoleon.

'Religion is excellent stuff for keeping the common people quiet.'

The world appeared to be a very big place when Elsie looked at her father's globe of planet Earth. St Helena was a tiny little speck, moored in the middle of the South Atlantic Ocean and very far from England, where Elsie dreamed of visiting one day.

Her father often told her bedtime stories of his childhood in England and would sing a funny little ditty to her when he came to tuck her up in bed, which always made her giggle and feel totally loved:

'Night, night in sweet repose. Lie on your back and you won't squash your nose.'

Then he would kiss her on the forehead and snuff out the candle next to her bed.

Elsie loved going down to the docks when the ships came in, to see the foreign people arriving and listen to the different languages spoken. There seemed to be a cacophony of men, animals and chickens making their presence known. She would stand next to the wooden gates at The Arch – the entrance to Jamestown from the wharf – fascinated by the sights and sounds that the arrival of a ship brought to the island.

Her father taught at the Garden House School, where Elsie also attended. It was in a wooden building with a corrugated iron roof at the back of lower Jamestown gardens. Some of the children of Jamestown attended most days, unless their parents had jobs for them at home. Her father did his best to teach them all to read, write and do arithmetic in the mornings. Only those students smart enough, who had been given permission by their parents, could return in the afternoons to learn more interesting things like English literature, geography, world history and biology. There was also time set aside to teach divinity and singing. Joanna used to come into the school once a week to teach the girls needlework and knitting. The local carpenter sometimes came to teach some craftwork to the boys. Elsie loved school and absorbed the fascinating information like a sponge.

Sometimes her father would take the afternoon scholars up the 699 steps of Jacobs Ladder leading up the slope from the harbour to explore the higher ground, finding different plants like the cabbage trees and enjoying the views from the top of the hills. They used to spot whales, dolphins and turtles in the exquisite turquoise sea below. He taught the children how to climb the ladder with a backward swing of the legs to prevent muscle ache. This nearly always developed into a race to the top, making for great fun and good exercise. Some of the boys were brave enough to slide down the ladder, wedging their shoulders on one handrail and using their feet as brakes on the other. There was a local saying that one may break one's heart climbing the steps and one's neck sliding down.

The tracks creeping up the sides of both Ladder Hill to the west and Munden's Hill to the east were in poor condition. Donkeys pulled carts carrying goods and people up and down these dirt tracks of volcanic ash which often collapsed or were sometimes washed away when it rained.

Education was only provided until the age of fifteen and when Elsie herself turned sixteen years old, her father suggested she start helping him in the school by teaching the younger children. She was so pleased that her father thought her grown-up and clever enough to help him teach. That same year, there was a huge storm that engulfed the island for two days. Huge hail stones had crashed down and it had been dangerous to go outside for fear of injury. Elsie, her father and some of the pupils had taken refuge in the school until the storm passed as it would have been too dangerous for those students who lived a couple of miles away, to walk through such inclement weather.

Elsie had grown as tall as her father and had inherited her mother's beautiful thick, mahogany-brown, curly hair. She had large, almond-shaped, hazel-coloured eyes surrounded by long lashes that almost touched her very high cheekbones. Her skin was fine and a softer tone of brown than her mother and her exotic features made one notice her. Not everyone would have said Elsie was beautiful, but she certainly was a striking young woman with excellent bone structure and a natural poise. Before she started teaching at the little school, her mother presented her with a couple of delicate lace collars she had made for her to wear as the new teaching assistant. Elsie's father continued to share his knowledge of this world with her and there was always such excitement when new books arrived on the ships from America, England and Cape Town.

The little family enjoyed their evening meals together around the small table in the cottage kitchen, taking a cup of delicious local coffee together before retiring for the night. The meals prepared by Elsie's mother were simple, but spicy and nourishing. The family's favourite supper was tuna fishcakes.

When Elsie and her father took their walks together, they would often gather the wild watercress growing alongside the mountain streams. He told Elsie how he also used to collect watercress next to the chalk streams in Hampshire when he lived in England. They sometimes picked angelica on Diana's Peak and wild mint to make tea. During November, they collected mushrooms in Sane Valley near Napoleon's tomb. One of the greatest treats Joanna used to make was a dessert of fried local bananas flamed with rum. Joanna often expressed concern that Elsie would never find a husband as she had not learnt to cook even the simplest meal or keep house and would rather be reading and learning.

Elsie continued to teach at the school with her father and felt that she was really making a difference to the lives of the local children.

When she was nineteen years old her father and mother both contracted a very bad influenza, probably brought to the island by an infected passenger arriving on a visiting ship. Elsie closed the little school and did her best to nurse them, trying to reduce their raging fevers with Balm of Gilead infused in boiling water. Sadly, they both quickly succumbed to pneumonia and death came rattling through their chests within a day of each other.

The shock of losing both her parents, leaving her totally alone in the world, was overwhelming for Elsie.

She arranged for her father and mother's funeral services

to be held in the Church of England and the Catholic Church respectively, and they were laid to rest together in the cemetery surrounding St Paul's Cathedral up on the hill outside of Jamestown.

Elsie knew that despite her grief, the children of Jamestown were waiting to return to their lessons. She braced herself and, within a week, she opened the little school again. She found it easier to be with the happy children and her days were fulfilled as she continued her father's work. She did so miss her parents and particularly the wonderful stimulating discussions she used to have with her father.

There was the issue of keeping the cottage clean and having to start cooking meals for herself. Elsie sometimes regretted not listening to her mother. She should have shown more interest in the domestic side of running a home. How difficult could it be to keep the little stove alight and cook a meal? Elsie burnt many meals and often went to bed hungry, having been so engrossed in reading and preparing her lessons that she had failed to pay attention to the pot boiling dry.

Not long after Elsie's parents had so suddenly passed away, news came that the island was to accommodate some of the Boer prisoners of war from the South African War that had started in the October of 1899. Prior to the arrival of the prisoners, Governor Sterndale of St Helena published the following proclamation:

'His excellency expresses the hope that the population of St Helena will treat the prisoners of war with that courtesy and consideration which should be extended to all men who have fought bravely for what they consider the cause of their country, and will help in repressing any unseemly demonstrations which individuals might exhibit.'

The prisoners discovered from this proclamation that they

might anticipate courtesy and respect. On their arrival at the harbour, they were marched up through Jamestown. Neither a jeering sound nor rude remark was heard from the crowd of local 'Saints', who had congregated to see them pass on their way to Deadwood Camp which had been prepared for them. In fact, the islanders seemed to be in a state of suppressed excitement. Some of the men arriving looked quite weak as they made their way through the town, whilst others were happy and relieved to be on dry ground. It took them about three hours to struggle up the steep tracks for the six-mile trek going east to the POW camp.

The men were accommodated in canvas tents, and later, some in the huts they built for themselves from old biscuit and paraffin tins. Additionally, some wood and iron huts had arrived in one of the cargo loads and these too were utilised to shelter the prisoners. With the onset of boredom, some started carving model carts, boxes, pipes and walking sticks. Others were given permission to work as household servants, cooks and grooms, and were even allowed to live in the homes of those they worked for.

Of course, there was little to no chance of escaping from St Helena - not even Napoleon Bonaparte had found a way of leaving prior to his death. Some tried and many talked about and planned their escape, although none was ever successful.

The POW'S of war were well looked after, and were provided weekly with fresh and preserved meat (biltong), bread, vegetables, sugar and coffee.

Friction developed between the prisoners, and the camp commandants had to split them up with Deadwood Camp holding those who wanted to continue to fight the British, and Peace Camp for those who wanted to return peacefully to South Africa. Broad Bottom camp on the west of the island

31

was later established after quarrels had developed between the prisoners from the Free State and Transvaal regions – two neighbouring provinces in South Africa. The more daunting punishment was High Knoll Fort, which was a place of high security where recalcitrant and insubordinate prisoners were incarcerated.

Elsie continued to teach her pupils, who thought it very exciting to have had the population of the island more than doubled by all these interesting men, although they were forbidden by their parents from going anywhere near the camps. This provided a very thrilling dare and an exciting adventure to some of the braver and more adventurous children, who thought of many ways to sneak visits and chat to the men at the camps. Naturally, the men missed their own families hugely and the children's happy little faces were a real treat. In return, the prisoners often gave the children the toys they had carved from the wood that had been cut down from the dwindling forests.

Elsie did her best to teach and explain to the children the extremely complex reasons for the men coming to the island and the politics leading to the South African Boer War. She said that they were mostly good men, who wanted to govern themselves in South Africa rather than have their laws enforced by Great Britain.

Little did she know that there was one POW amongst them, who would change the direction of her own life forever.

Chapter 3
The School Building

Late one afternoon, Elsie was preparing lessons at the school after all her pupils had left for the day. The weather was warm and the humidity high with not even a slight breeze in the air. She suddenly became aware of a very quiet sound like paper rustling and, on closer examination, noticed that a few of the wooden floor planks and wooden walls of the schoolhouse were loose and sounded hollow when tapped. She feared that this was evidence of a dreaded termite infestation. Elsie's heart sank with this realisation. Certainly, the termites gnawing at the timbers would be making the building unsafe for her pupils to inhabit, as they devoured the wood of the school building.

What was she to do?

What would her beloved father have done?

She went to bed that night and tossed and turned for hours, worrying about the fate of her little school and whether she could continue to hold lessons for her pupils and, if so, where? Suddenly, as though by divine intervention, the obvious thought came to her… She would write a letter to the governor of the island and ask for his help and for some suggestions as to how she could keep her school going.

Elsie got out of bed at once, lit a lamp and covered her shoulders with her housecoat as there was a chill in the air. She could hear rain gently tapping at her windows as she sat at her kitchen table writing a letter to Governor Sterndale, that she would have delivered to him first thing in the morning. She introduced herself as the daughter of the late schoolmaster, James Baker, explaining that she had taken over the teaching at Garden House School in Jamestown after her father's passing, although she thought he probably knew that already. Elsie implored the governor to assist in arranging for the school to be rebuilt, as she had discovered a termite infestation in the current schoolhouse. She ended her letter by asking for an appointment with the governor to discuss further some of the ideas she had.

When the first young pupil arrived the next morning for school, she gave the little boy the letter to deliver to Plantation House, the governor's residence, with a promise of half a penny on his return. It was, after all, a good distance out of Jamestown, up Jacob's Ladder and through Half Tree Hollow to the area of St Paul's where the governor resided.

Elsie continued teaching her pupils for the next couple of weeks with no response from the governor. Several times she even questioned the boy who had delivered the letter, to check that he had done so.

Then, out of the blue, an invitation addressed to Elsie was delivered asking her to come to Plantation House for a meeting with the governor himself. The meeting was scheduled for the following afternoon. Suddenly, Elsie did not feel as confident as she had when she sat down to write her original request to meet with the governor and to present her ideas regarding the rebuilding of the schoolhouse.

The next day she took great care with her appearance before she set off, walking some three steep miles south of Jamestown to Plantation House for the meeting with the governor. She was wearing her Sunday best and carried a notebook in her father's satchel. She had the points listed that she wished to raise with him, as she was sure that once in his presence, she would forget to mention one of her vital suggestions.

Plantation House was set on the northwest facing slope at the head of Youngs Valley. It was a grand and imposing building of two stories, with sash windows either side of the central projecting porch where one entered the house.

Elsie felt like a little girl again and quite overwhelmed at the thought of having to present her case for a new schoolhouse to the governor. She called upon her father to give her guidance and strength and immediately felt more confident. Pulling her shoulders back and standing taller, she knocked calmly at the front door of the governor's residence.

The door was opened by a member of the household staff and, from the personal greeting she received, she was obviously expected. Elsie was led through to the grand reception room where huge portraits of British royalty hung. In the centre of this room stood a large round, wooden table with brass inlay and a fragrant arrangement of flowers picked from the gardens surrounding the house. She followed the member of staff down a passage where the portraits of all the previous governors hung. Elsie was asked to wait in the anteroom that was at the end of the passage. Here sat a secretary at a large desk, typing at a remarkable speed. This anteroom had no windows. It was quite dark and rather formal. The walls were painted a dark green and had severe-looking, red upholstered chairs. Elsie wondered how the secretary managed to work in such a gloomy atmosphere.

Suddenly, the large door creaked open, and Governor Sterndale entered. He had a spectacularly large, white moustache that curled back against his cheeks, and a neatly trimmed beard. Elsie stood as he entered and realised that she

35

was slightly taller than he was. He asked her to follow him into the library next door.

There were so many books stacked neatly on the shelves that after her meeting she wished she could have had a couple of hours there alone to enjoy the tomes. The musty smell of old books and the log fire burning in the hearth permeated the room. Elsie was fascinated by the colourful patterns woven into the beautiful oriental carpet on the wooden floor. A small library ladder with tapestry covered risers stood next to a bookcase in one corner. The governor sat in one of the two throne-like chairs next to the fireplace and indicated to Elsie to sit opposite him, on a brown leather upholstered chair with inset buttons.

"Good afternoon, Miss Baker. Thank you for coming to Plantation House. May I also extend to you my condolences on the passing of your parents? So sad… So sad."

"Thank you, sir."

"Now, now. Onwards and upwards, Miss Baker."

"Yes, sir," replied Elsie, frowning, and thinking what a thoughtless comment that was.

"About the school… You mentioned in your letter that you had some ideas about the possible rebuild. What exactly do you have in mind, Miss Baker?"

"Sir, I was wondering if it may be possible that some of the Boer prisoners could be called upon to help build a new brick structure with a corrugated iron roof, as this would surely be an excellent use of their time and the task would be making good use of a skilled labour force? Obviously, the old schoolhouse would need to be demolished first."

The governor stared at her intently and Elsie began to wonder if she had a smudge on her face, or if she had been too bold? After what seemed an age, he placed his hands on his knees saying, "Hmmm… And where do you propose to hold lessons whilst this 'possible' refurbishment is taking place?"

"Ah," replied Elsie eagerly. "I thought that the children could be taught lessons on weekdays at the back of St James' Anglican Church across the square? Of course, until the new building is complete."

Again, the governor stared at her and by now she was even more convinced that she had gone a step too far. After what seemed like another period of endless contemplation, he finally asked her to meet him and the Anglican minister at St James' Church in Jamestown the following afternoon.

On Elsie's departure, he mumbled something about admiring her courage and suggestions about the rebuilding of the new school. Inwardly, Elsie thought she might burst with joy. She knew how proud her beloved father would have been of her, and secretly believed he was spiritually guiding her. However, she thought it best to keep such ideas to herself.

The following afternoon, Elsie cancelled lessons and headed across the square to St James' Anglican Church for her meeting. The church spire was very tall and cast a dark shadow across the entrance. She shivered a little with nerves and pushed open the groaning, heavy church door. She noticed that the beautiful stained-glass window played colourful patterns across the altar. She had begun to think that perhaps her suggestion of using the church for lessons was too bold an idea, although, she believed it to be a good one. On arrival at the church vestry at the back of the church, the governor was already drinking tea with the reverend, and they invited Elsie to join them. The reverend's wife poured her a cup of steaming hot tea and offered her a shortbread biscuit.

Governor Sterndale opened the conversation regarding the rebuild of the schoolhouse. "Miss Baker, I have informed the reverend here about the essential rebuild of the schoolhouse due to the termite infestation. We have to take precautions or the whole town will be consumed by these little blighters, hey?" he chuckled at his own joke. "Thought the best solution would be to use the back of the church to house the school during the week, until the new school is built." The governor clearly thought that this suggestion would carry more weight coming from him rather than Elsie.

The reverend did not look overly impressed at this notion.

The governor went on. "We have to improvise and live as 'Saints' here on St Helena, eh?" he chuckled again, and the reverend seemed at a loss for words.

The governor informed Elsie that he had already met with POW commandant to recruit suitable prisoners with some building experience and others to demolish the old school building. This would all start happening the following week as the governor agreed that the current school-building may no longer be safe for the children to use, what with the termite infestation having taken hold. There was also concern about the possibility that these termites may spread further into the town.

Elsie thanked both men most sincerely as she truly thought she would have had to beg and plead to make them see her point of view. She could hardly believe her luck, and least of all the smile and wink she received from the reverend's wife on her departure from the vestry. Perhaps there were more 'Saints' around than she thought!

Elsie arranged with the governor for some of the prisoners of war to help with moving books, blackboards and cupboards to the back of the church, with the reverend insisting that every item entering his church be carefully examined for any insect damage in order to prevent any further spread of the termite infestation. It was found that many of the school desks had evidence of termites and, as a result, they were welcomed as firewood in the POW camp.

Elsie soon started her lessons at the back of the church and had to ensure that the children always behaved quietly and respectfully, as the reverend seemed to appear on a regular basis to check on their behaviour. The children sat on some of the back benches with their writing slates on their laps whilst Elsie wrote on a blackboard placed on an easel in the aisle.

In the meantime, the demolition of the old schoolhouse had begun. Elsie felt sad to see the rubble littering the site. She treasured so many wonderful memories of her father's teaching days there, where he had shared his knowledge.

Some of the prisoners had previous experience of dealing with termite infestations in their farmhouses and barns in South Africa and it was therefore soon discovered that there were a couple of subterranean termite nests under the foundations of the old schoolhouse. They mixed borax powder and powdered sugar together to create a termite poison. The termites carried this back to their nests where the other termites also ate it. This mixture was sprinkled around the area several times and even poured down into the nests through pipes to make sure that the mixture was consumed by as many termites as possible. The new concrete foundations of the schoolhouse were laid some weeks later when the building supplies arrived by ship from Cape Town and they were sure that there were no more termites in the nests.

Every day on her way home, Elsie walked past the school building site to inspect the progress. The prisoners always greeted her most courteously. These men all looked much the same to Elsie in their khaki clothes, wide-brimmed felt hats pulled low over their bearded faces. Their foreman, who was also a prisoner, spoke English with a very strong, guttural voice and a South African accent, but he was always available to answer Elsie's questions and heed her suggestions. A couple of guards were posted close by and kept a beady eye on the men too. The building emerged out of the foundations at a rapid rate and the progress was most satisfying for all involved.

Within a few months, the school was almost ready for lessons to take place once again. It was now a double-storey building with a covered veranda corridor upstairs, connecting the classrooms. The outside walls and roof of the building were clad with corrugated iron sheets. The walls were painted white and the roof, a bright turquoise green, with the window frames the same colour. The inside walls of the school were painted a pale blue. Elsie felt that the correct atmosphere had been created for enhancing learning, logic and serenity. She was delighted with the result and, before the day arrived for the official opening of the rebuilt schoolhouse, she ordered a new, blue dress to be made by the dressmaker for the occasion. She attached to it one of the delicate lace collars that her late mother had so lovingly made for her. She also ordered a matching blue ribbon for her hair from Solomon's General Store.

The day of the official opening of the school building turned out to be a wonderfully happy occasion. The governor arrived in his full, formal uniform and the Anglican minister arrived in his fine robes. There were prayers said by the minister and a speech from the governor praising Elsie's foresight at having requested and planned the rebuilding of the school. Even some of the POW labourers had been allowed to attend, standing under one of the large, shady Ficus trees in front of the school building. Some of the prisoners had been given the task of making benches and long tables for the children to sit on and study. There were even new blackboards at the back and the front of the classrooms.

When the governor declared the school officially open, the school children gathered standing in rows according to their height – with the shortest children in the front and the tallest at the back. They sang 'God Save the Queen' at the top of their voices, and everyone joined in, apart from the Boer prisoners who did not share the sentiment expressed in the anthem. However, they respectfully stood to attention under the watchful eye of their commandant.

When everyone had left, Elsie went inside and, after unpacking some of the boxes that had been carried back from the church, she stood in the middle of one of the classrooms gazing around her. How proud her father would have been of her for instigating the building of the new school. She felt his presence strongly as she locked the door leading to the gardens next to the castle. She placed the shiny keys in the pocket of her new blue dress and walked home with a spring in her step up the hill to her own cottage on Napoleon Street.

Elsie was thrilled at the prospect of lessons beginning again in the new school, as the children had been somewhat subdued since teaching had commenced at the back of St James' Church. She had also managed to enlist another teacher to assist her, which would make life a great deal easier for her and enable more of topics to be covered.

The ships that docked sometimes had old newspapers on board and Elsie asked the harbour master to save them for her as they were good reading material for the children. There was always great excitement to read the newspapers from Britain.

Around this time, the sad news was announced by the governor that Queen Victoria had passed away on the Isle of

Wight on 22 January 1901 at the age of 81. Her eldest son succeeded her on the throne and became King Edward VII.

It was about a fortnight later that the prisoner, Luke, knocked on Elsie's door asking for help and, on departing, forgot his felt hat on the table in her cottage.

Chapter 4
The Felt Hat

The 'vilthoed' (felt hat) hung on a hook of the hat rail next to the front door of Elsie's little cottage. She often looked at it, replaying the strange events of that evening and puzzling about why Luke had knocked on her door that night. She had wondered how the wound on his arm had healed. A few times Elsie had even tried the hat on and posed in front of her little age-misted mirror to see how she looked, laughing at herself as she replaced the hat on the hook at a loss about what she should do with it.

Elsie did not have to wait too long to find out as, when she got home from teaching her lessons a few days later, there was a note pushed under her door. It was written in tiny lettering on the back of a label that had been carefully removed from a can of bully beef.

'Dear Miss Elsie,

Meet me tonight at at the waterfall at 8 and please bring my much-missed hat.

Luke.'

The cheek of asking the schoolteacher to run around after a POW, even though some of them had helped to rebuild her schoolhouse! She had a good mind to send one of the pupils, but that would be opening herself up to local gossip as to why she had one of their hats in her cottage in the first place. How annoying of this man!

Elsie's major concern was not to be seen by the other Saints in the town whilst walking with a 'vildhoet.' She popped the hat on her head and, on looking in the mirror, had an idea. She would wear some of her late father's clothes which she had not yet had the heart to give away and pass as a man under the cover of dark. She opened her father's wooden chest that still held his belongings and was immediately overcome with the familiar smell of him. It almost felt as though he had stepped into the cottage, and she gasped as tears welled in her eyes. How she missed her parents. She lifted out a tweed jacket, a pair of trousers and a shirt. There was also a flat cap that she would tuck into the jacket pocket to wear on her return home, needing to tuck away her long plait.

After eating some bread and cheese for her dinner, Elsie changed from her normal attire into her father's clothing. This may have been one of the most daring things she had ever done in her life. Living on a small island did not bring too many exotic adventures!

Of course, the trousers were far too wide in the waist. Elsie took her father's belt and hammered in a new notch with a nail she found in his old toolbox. She dampened her hair so there were no stray tendrils creeping out from under the hat, where she had tucked her braided hair away. As soon as it was dark enough outside, she set off with her father's walking stick and the little knife that he used to carry for taking samples of plants on their walks. At least Elsie felt she had a little protection walking out in the dark, walking stick in one hand and the knife in her other hand tucked in a pocket. She tugged the hat low over her forehead and, before setting off, she peeped out of the windows of the cottage to ensure that no one was about. She strode confidently and purposefully along the path following The Run that led to the waterfall from Nosegay Lane. The Run had been built with the purpose of channelling the water flow through the town and carrying sewage down to the sea using the flow of water which cascaded over the Heart Shaped Waterfall. It was getting darker by the minute and Elsie was glad of the walking stick to support her on the steep and uneven surfaces. She smiled to herself as she felt a bit like a walking mushroom with the large hat pulled low down on her forehead.

On reaching the approach to the waterfall path, it dawned on Elsie that she was somewhat vulnerable and had no idea of precisely where she would find Luke. Besides, she thought it may be easier not to talk to him. What if it was all a setup? Elsie looked around her and could see and hear no one, so she quickly decided to hook the felt hat on a branch of a gumwood tree next to the path. She did this and replaced the hat with the flat cap she had brought along, carefully tucking her long plait away under the cap. Her heart was pounding in her chest and, feeling the panic rising, she started running back down the path towards Jamestown. In her hasty retreat, Elsie tripped on some roots of a tree and cried out as she fell on her knees. She felt a sharp pain shoot up the wrist of the hand that she had used to break her fall. The walking stick had rolled out of reach and the flat cap fell off her head with her long plait tumbling free.

Before Elsie could recover herself and replace the flat cap, she felt a strong hand at her elbow lifting her back on her feet. She gasped in fright and immediately recognised Luke as he whispered to her in his South African accent.

"Sorry, ma'am, I didn't recognise you dressed in that disguise. Are you all right after falling like that? You came down pretty hard."

"Fine… I'm fine, thanks! I must be getting home. Your hat is on a branch of that tree behind us," she replied sharply, brushing him aside.

"I know, I watched you put it there. Thank you, but I really wanted to see you again to say how much I appreciated your help that evening when I knocked on your door. You were mean with those pliers removing the blade, but the wound has healed nicely."

Elsie suddenly felt bad that she had not asked how he was after the injury, but of course it would never do for her to seem too interested. However, she was more than a little curious about how he was getting on with the split in sentiments amongst the prisoners.

"What has happened about the other prisoners who feel you are collaborating with the British?" she asked.

"Ah, it is still a problem but, as I told you before, there is some talk of moving us – the collaborating guys – to another camp called Peace Camp. In the meantime, I need to watch my back. But hey, ma'am, aren't you hurt from your fall?"

With that, Luke gently took her hand and examined it by carefully twisting it from side to side. Elsie winced a little, but thankfully it seemed that nothing was broken.

"Do you have a hankie in one of those pockets?" asked Luke, looking at her get-up with amusement.

Elsie felt deep inside the pockets and unearthed a handkerchief that was still pristine clean, or so it seemed in the starlight. She handed it to Luke, and he folded the fabric to bandage it around her wrist as a support. As he was doing so, she felt a tingle of delight at his touch. He seemed kind and genuinely concerned about her. Physical contact was something of which she had little experience, and it surprised her how empty it left her feeling when he took his hands away after tying the handkerchief around her wrist.

"Thank you," she whispered. "Don't forget your hat again."

Luke walked back to collect his hat and, putting it on his head, instructed Elsie to, "Take care of that wrist and rest it for a few days. I should probably go now as I need to sneak back into the camp without the guards seeing me. You are a brave and trusting lady. I have seen you before... around the schoolhouse when I was there helping to rebuild it. I'd seen you walking to your cottage so that is how I knew where you lived."

With that he gently took her bandaged wrist and kissed it. "Now I have kissed it better like my dear ma used to do." With that he quickly disappeared through the trees on the side of the path.

Elsie stood for moment to gather herself as there was now no trace of Luke. She wished he had stayed a little longer. Common sense prevailed and she thought it best to start heading back home. Feeling a sense of loneliness, she kept to the shadows as she made her way back into Jamestown. The lamplighter had already done his evening rounds, so Elsie avoided the pools of light beneath the lit streetlamps.

A few days later, she found another note neatly written on another scrap of paper pushed under her door. It was again from Luke, asking her to meet him at a ravine known as the Devil's Punchbowl near Napoleon's tomb, on the following Saturday afternoon. She was quite excited – although a little concerned. Firstly, that he had been outside her cottage to deliver the note and, secondly, that she should take the chance of meeting him in the daylight. However, when the morning came, she carefully did her hair in two braids that she looped at the nape of her neck, securing them with pretty ribbons. She wore a straw hat to protect her face from the sun and slung her father's leather bag across her shoulder.

Elsie had packed a small lunch for two, plus a couple of apples that she had managed to buy for an inflated price from the local market. The apples had arrived on a ship from Cape Town and were always a treat. She set off for her walk to the ravine, not attracting any attention as the Saints were used to seeing her wandering off into the hills like she so often had done with her father.

It was a beautiful day with a gentle breeze blowing up the valley from the sea, which certainly made the walk more enjoyable. On arriving at the ravine, Elsie again had no idea where she would find Luke and so decided to enjoy the scenery and the ambience of the area. She settled herself at a good vantage point under the shade of a large ebony tree next to an area where white arum lilies and ferns grew in abundance, and started to read the book that she had also packed in the leather bag. It was not long before she heard someone making their way towards her and she sat quietly before she saw one of the townsfolk approaching.

"Good afternoon, ma'am. How's you be?"

"Good afternoon, sir. I am good thanks, and yourself?"

"All fine. I saw you wandering up the hill for a walk, just like your poor pa used to do in the before days. You always busy reading and learning. Too much 'wordification' for the likes of me," he chuckled. "I'm going up to Diana's Peak and coming back afore sunset. Care to join me rather than sitting here on your ownsome?"

"Thank you, but I am enjoying the lovely day and the views here. I, too, shall head down to home before sunset. Do enjoy your hike," replied Elsie, fearing that the gentleman may read the guilt in her face.

"Don't be leaving it too late as the weather can quickly turn scruffy. Bye, then."

She watched him disappear along the path and hoped he had not been suspicious of her sitting alone at the ravine. Lost in reading her book, she did not hear Luke arriving. Suddenly, there he was, leaning against the ebony tree under which she sat. She thought it extraordinary that she had not heard him approach.

"Hello! I didn't hear you approaching. Did you fly in?" Elsie said with a smile.

"No, but I had climbed this very tree to wait for you and quietly slithered down when I thought the coast was clear. Lots of practice from the war of hiding in wait, but this is far more pleasant."

Luke sat down next to her and took her wrist that he had bandaged after her fall when they had previously met. "Looks like I did kiss it better then?" he said a little cheekily.

"I suppose you could have," she replied coyly.

They easily and comfortably started chatting about the current atmosphere in camp.

"By the way," Luke said, "us 'loyalists', who sort of collaborated with the British, have now been relocated to Peace Camp, which is next to Deadwood Camp. Some of the other prisoners who don't agree with us call us 'traitors.' All they think about is independence, but at what cost to our families, hey? There really is a bad atmosphere between us now and some guys have even had a 'ducking' at the latrines! Sis! That is revolting!" Luke paused for a while to think about what he had witnessed and what might happen to him sometime, then he continued explaining to Elsie about life in the camp. "Most of the prisoners from the Free State have now been sent to the new camp at Broad Bottom, but I am probably going to remain at Peace Camp. The biggest problem in the camps right now is that everyone is getting so bored. We play some cricket and football, and also lots of rugby, which helps get rid of some of our energy and frustrations, especially when you tackle a guy you don't really like! A few well-aimed kicks in the scrum make you feel so much better, but not the guy getting kicked," he laughed.

"Really?" replied Elsie, a little shocked as she had never witnessed a rough rugby game and failed to understand why kicking someone would make one feel better about oneself.

Luke continued, oblivious to her slight horror.

"Also, there are various societies like debating, of which I am a member. There is even a non-smoking society, but I am not a member of that! I like the odd bit of tobacco when I can get it, which is mostly on the black market. Some of us are practicing woodwork when we can get hold of a piece of wood. You know the governor has now forbidden that any more trees be chopped down on the island?"

"And, quite rightly too," agreed Elsie slightly haughtily, thinking how furious her father would have been to see the deforestation of the island.

"Some of the prisoners of war are making napkin rings and small wooden boxes. Actually, I am trying to make a small wooden box myself which is a slow process as I have never learnt carpentry before and certainly not on such a small scale, but it is keeping me occupied."

"I would love to see this little box you are making one day," Elsie added, trying to sound enthusiastic.

"I have also requested to work in the governor's garden and am hoping I will be chosen to do so soon. Friends have told me about the large tortoises that originally came from the Seychelles and that now live in the grounds. Apparently, the oldest one is called Jonathan! Imagine how nice it would be to have pet tortoises."

"Ah yes, that's true. I saw them on the lawns of Plantation House a few months ago when I went to see the governor about rebuilding the schoolhouse. I do so enjoy the new school building and not having to worry about the termites. The brick building is also much quieter inside than the old wooden school and one can hardly hear any of the noise from the town square, so my pupils seem to be less distracted and much more focused."

Elsie went quiet and when Luke asked if she was all right, she replied, "I do miss my parents, particularly my father's guidance. It has been quite difficult and lonely for me since they both died of the flu that was brought to the island."

Luke gently placed his hand over hers and they sat together in silence, both lost in their respective thoughts.

Luke, fondly remembering his own parents, told her in an emotional voice, "My pa was killed in South Africa during the Boer War. He and I were in the same unit, fighting together. He was shot right next to me, and I held him in my arms as he died." Tears rolled freely down his cheeks and disappeared into his beard. "We had to keep moving though, so I quickly buried him in a shallow grave.

"Now my mother has been forced to leave the farm with my two sisters. I am almost certain that the British have burnt down the family farmhouse. Probably the barns and sheds too, to stop them assisting the Boers with food and guns. I am really worried about my family as they may have been sent to a concentration camp like so many others have."

Luke again went quiet and squeezed Elsie's hand. The physical contact delivered comfort and thrilling sensations to both.

He explained that the farm was in the Free State province, where there had been a lot of fighting between the British and the Boer soldiers.

Luke continued, "Those British soldiers were not used to the heat and harsh sun. Some of them really suffered and got heat stroke. The Boers called them 'red necks' as a result of the sunburn. We were not too sorry for them though," he chuckled.

"I feel so helpless here on St Helena and really want to get back to the farm. Maybe I will be able to try and build it up again. My family needs me now. I am also thinking about what has happened to the Black labourers and their families that were living on the farm. Poor buggers! They are totally dependent on working there. The farm had been quite successful with a dairy and butchery attached. Those bloody redneck British have more than likely taken the animals, burned the house and scorched our veld by now!"

Luke's facial expression softened as he spoke so fondly of his home and family. Then, at a glance, he seemed to age as his brow furrowed over the concern he had about his family's predicament. Just as quickly, his blue eyes would twinkle with laughter, then again look like a brewing storm as the conversation ebbed and flowed. He had the most expressive eyes that she had ever noticed before.

Aware of how angry and emotional he was becoming, it occurred to Elsie that a change of subject could be helpful.

"How do you manage to get out of the camp as often as you do?" she asked with a cheeky grin.

Luke gave her a wry smile. "One of the local guards is a sympathiser of the 'loyalists.' He and I have an arrangement. He gives me a pass from time to time, I share my biltong ration with him. So, he is a little lenient on my comings and goings.

I sometimes feel like a caged animal though, with the frustration and worry about my family. It can make me feel quite crazy."

And so, over the next weeks and months, Luke and Elsie continued to meet either by prearrangement, or she would find a little scrap of paper pushed under her door asking her to meet with him at a certain time and place. They seldom met in the same spot for fear of being seen together and creating a noticeable pattern.

Each time, Elsie longed for the next meeting a little more as she enjoyed Luke's company and listening to his stories about South Africa. It sounded so exciting and vast, and nothing like the friendly and peaceful St Helena.

The more time she spent with Luke, the more handsome she thought he was. He frequently told her how beautiful she was, which no one had ever said to her before. Elsie always made sure she looked her best when meeting Luke, although she only had a few gored skirts and linen blouses to make the best of her appearance. She also had the lovely blue dress that she had had made for the opening of the new school building which she now wore to church on Sundays.

They continued to meet whenever Luke could escape the camp, which also had to be when Elsie was not teaching. They planned to find each other at the green meadows near Mount Pleasant, in the shady trees of Geranium Valley near Napoleon's burial site, and they even hiked up to Diana's Peak, which was the highest peak on the island and afforded stunning views of St Helena. Taking in the 360-degree view, they felt as though they were totally free and on top of the world. Elsie told Luke that her father used to say that St Helena would always belong more to the South Atlantic than to Britain.

Another time they hiked all the way to Sandy Bay Ridge

and watched the sea rolling onto the beach far below. Around them, the island appeared to wave and shimmer as the breezes played with the rolling acres of flax plantations. Elsie shared the knowledge that her father had passed on to her of the plants, insects and birds they came across during their walks.

They once found the remains of an old Chinese joss house dating back to the time when the Chinese labourers from Canton Island lived on St Helena from 1810. To get there, they walked past the bottom of the Governor's House towards the old 'Butchers Graves' and through a grove of huge Indian bamboo, where the white birds called 'fairy terns' were hovering above their heads, almost reflecting the white arum lilies that decorated the sides of the path. They sat on one of the large bamboo trunks that had fallen across the path and marvelled at this magical place.

One evening, Luke had suggested that Elsie meet him at the pool at the bottom of the Heart Shaped Waterfall. It had been a very hot day and by the time Elsie got there she felt she was glowing, so she removed her shoes and stockings, and sat on one of the rocks next to the shallow pool at the bottom of the waterfall. She dangled her feet in the beautiful clear, cool water. There had been good rains on the island that year and the waterfall was running quite strongly. The spray from the falling water cooled the air, creating a mist that settled on her. The beautiful, white fairy terns hovered and settled in the trees above her like little angels. She waited a long while for Luke but, although always a little concerned about his sneaking in and out of the camp, she felt sure he would turn up sooner or later. After the sun set and the darkening sky started revealing the stars so clearly visible, she felt as if she may be able to reach up and touch them.

It was getting late, and Elsie had thoughts of heading back

home. Clearly Luke was unable to come and meet her this time. As she was reaching for her shoes, she heard him emerge from the surrounding trees wearing only his undershorts. He came up and kissed her on the cheek before flopping down to lie in the shallow cool water. Elsie was very embarrassed as she had never seen a man's bare torso before, not even that of her father who had always been so discrete!

"Sorry I am so late. There was a new guard on duty, and I had to be very careful to wait until he was distracted before I left the camp. I was worried you would leave so I ran all the way here. Man, it is so hot! I thought a wallow would cool me down." Luke sat down beside her and told her that he and his sisters always went to swim in the river on their farm in South Africa during the hot weather.

"Hey, why don't you come and lie in the water now, with me?" asked Luke.

"Oh, I couldn't. What would I wear?" Elsie laughed.

"Your underwear will be fine. Come on, it's so lovely and cooling."

It did look tempting and so Elsie, telling him to look away and giggling, set her inhibitions aside along with her blouse, skirt and petticoat. She knew Luke was watching her and when she was just in her chemise, drawers and knickerbockers she quickly went to join him lying in the pool. The cool water was quite delicious on her body, and she was thrilled and excited as she splashed water at Luke in a playful manner.

Luke decided to climb higher on the slippery rocks to get more of the waterfall spray to splash on him. He gave Elsie a hand up to come and join him. She almost slipped, but he grabbed her around the waist to stop her falling. They both froze as they felt the tingling of their touching skin. Elsie felt a warm glowing sensation between her legs that was certainly a new experience and quite marvellous. They stayed like this, mesmerised by the glowing feelings of their bodies so close together and by the stunning waterfall creating the swirling misty veil around them. The full moon had risen, bathing them in a warm glow. The setting could not have been more perfect.

With Elsie still clinging to him, Luke helped her back down to the rocks. They sat there together, holding hands and wondering what next as their bodies ached for more contact. Luke took Elsie in his arms and kissed her. He started gently, but pushed his tongue between her lips searching deeper into her mouth. Elsie was startled at first and, although it felt exciting, she also felt extremely inexperienced. She had no idea how to respond, if at all, and began to feel breathless. She pulled away and Luke looked at her smiling, "Your first kiss?" Elsie smiled and nodded. Luke smugly said, "Glad it was me."

"I should get dressed and wring out my wet underwear. I'll go behind that tree and change," replied Elsie. As she started to get up, Luke kissed her again and this time with even more passion. Elsie pulled away and started to feel a little anxious. At that moment, she so wished she had spoken to her mother about being intimate with men, but it was now too late. She had no idea what was right or wrong. She questioned her intelligence as a schoolteacher and wondered how she knew so little about human sexuality. She doubted she would be able to find much written on the subject.

She gathered up her clothes and shoes and went behind the tree to remove her underwear to wring it out before she got dressed again. Luke remained sitting on the rock.

While she was standing with not a stitch of clothing on her beautiful curvaceous body, Luke appeared beside the tree and stood watching her. She tried with little success to hide behind the flimsy chemise she had wrung out.

"Don't hide from me, Elsie. You are a beautiful woman and I want to watch you dress."

Feeling she should object, but secretly enjoying the admiration in Luke's eyes, Elsie continued to wring out her knickerbockers and drawers. Luke stepped closer and took her in his arms and started kissing her neck. Elsie gave a little shriek of delight and the most incredible sensations darted though her body and seemed to end in a hot nucleus between her legs. She was a little shocked at her responses to Luke's touches and felt herself start to shake with excitement and desire. Luke laid her down on top of her skirt that was lying on the forest floor on a bed of wild nasturtiums and continued to kiss her neck, then slowly moved lower to take one of her large, dark brown and very pert nipples in his mouth whilst teasing it with his tongue. He moved to the other nipple and Elsie thought she may explode with desire. Then Luke was on his knees and his tongue moved down from her nipples to her navel that he tickled with his tongue. Suddenly, he was kissing that warm place between her legs, and she could hear his breathing getting heavier. She thought her soul was beginning to quake.

Without hesitation, Luke had turned her over on to her tummy and he pulled her hips up to meet his as she supported herself on all fours. She felt him hard against her buttocks and he reached forward holding both her breasts in his hands and started kissing her neck again. There was so much happening. Elsie felt her body was out of control and her mind suggesting that she should tell him to stop, but the sensations were so new and thrilling, she found herself unable to even try and halt him. Luke held her hips and she felt his large manliness against her, and he was again feeling and probing her warm, now very wet place with his fingers. She felt exquisite pain as he forced himself inside her and she cried out in shock and surprise at the sensation. Luke did not seem to hear her as he continued to plunge inside her. With the rhythm growing faster, his breathing sounded like a man running a race. How long was this going to continue as the initial exquisite pain began to feel like a crude invasion of her body? She tried to pull away, but that seemed to make him pound harder into her. Finally, Luke cried out her name and collapsed like a dead weight on top of her. She felt she could hardly breathe under his weight before he rolled away, lying next to her. They lay there in shocked silence listening to the gentle sound of the waterfall. Soon, she heard Luke breathe as if he was asleep, so she rose and quietly got dressed and made her way back through the forest to her little cottage as quickly as she could by the light of the full moon. At least the lamplighter would not be around as he never lit the streetlamps when the moon was full and bright. She sobbed all the way, feeling overwhelmed and somewhat frightened by the experience.

When she was undressing to put on her nightdress, she discovered blood and a sticky, strong-smelling substance in her knickerbockers and immediately went to wash them clean.

She climbed into her bed with a whirlwind of emotions and questions in her head.

Had she consented, or had she just not objected?

Had she enjoyed or endured?

Did she or did she not want more?

Is it always like this for all women?

Had he made love to her, or had he been thinking of another woman. Or, God forbid, even an animal?

Why did he take her so strongly and forcefully from behind?

Why had he not faced her and looked at her during their

love making?

Did he love her or was there just no one else?

Was his roughness in ignorance or was he uncaring?

He sounded quite possessed during the act.

Elsie lay in the darkness of her little cottage feeling used.

Was that it?

Was that really love making?

Then her worst thought arrived.

Had he not respected her because her skin colour was darker than his?

She had heard that some South Africans were racists, but surely this could never be the case with Luke, as he had told her she was beautiful and clever on many an occasion.

Her hands wandered down between her legs where she felt sore after the forceful invasion of her very private place. She gently started rubbing the area, which seemed to soothe the bruised feeling. The sensation was rather pleasant, and Elsie could not help but continue. Her excitement grew as the rate of her rubbing increased and, without warning, her body exploded into a million stars bursting and tingling. She heard herself involuntarily cry out as a wonderful warm feeling took over her body, radiating from somewhere deep inside her and she fell into a deep sleep.

When she woke the next morning, she realised she had overslept and missed the Sunday morning church service, about which she was pleased as she felt so ashamed of what she had experienced the night before and unsure how she would have faced the reverend or the other parishioners without looking as though she was hiding something. Thoughts flooded back of how the evening had evolved and Elsie was wracked with guilt at her forward behaviour of undressing down to her underwear. That must have caused

Luke to treat her like he chose to. Next the most frightening thought crossed her mind.

This is how one gets pregnant. She had seen the goats fornicating in the fields.

Why had she not thought about this earlier?

She had found an old rubber douche amongst her mother's things when she was tidying her wooden chest and assumed her mother must have used it for contraception, although her mother had never mentioned such things.

Not knowing what else to do or whom to turn to for advice, Elsie immediately made up a solution of water and vinegar to use on herself. Oh, why had she not had a conversation with her mother on how to deal with these matters? Although, her mother may well have only explained these things prior to Elsie getting married. The vinegar-water stung her inners and she began to weep, feeling terribly used and sorry for herself. Hopefully this was not too late.

Elsie stayed indoors all day and vigorously cleaned her little cottage and did her laundry with vengeance, pummelling it as though it was Luke. She was so angry with him and wondered what thoughts he was having.

Was he remorseful of how rough he had been with her? Or was that how things were done? Surely lovemaking should be gentler.

The experience had somehow felt carnal and lewd to her, with none of the romance she had dreamt of and read about in romantic novel writings.

She wondered when she would hear from Luke again, if at all. Sadly, Elsie did not think she would have the courage and certainly would be too embarrassed to explain to him how disappointing their intimacy had been for her. Anyway, she could not let it happen again as she knew she was dicing with pregnancy and an unmarried, pregnant schoolmistress would never do in Jamestown. She could not bear the disgrace, or the disappointment of the governor, the reverend and his wife. She could never explain that she had secretly been meeting a prisoner.

Chapter 5
Fever on the Island

The week passed with no note from Luke. Then came the news that enteric fever had broken out in the camps and the prisoners of war were forbidden to move about on the island. The camps were all put into total lockdown. The prisoners of war who worked in the governor's gardens and everyone connected with the camps could potentially put the whole island at risk. There were even rumours that any prisoner seen out of the confines of the camp could be shot on sight.

The fever gripped the island with fear. The source of the illness was unknown, but the doctor on the island warned that it was possibly carried in contaminated food and water, ordering that all consumables be boiled before consumption. The officers' quarters in Jamestown were fitted up as a Boer hospital for those prisoners who were very ill.

Those who contracted enteric fever started to cough and rose-coloured spots appeared on their chests in the first week. During the second week, they were too tired to get up and developed a higher fever, delirium, and a distended abdomen.

Many of the men slowly returned to health, whilst some developed overwhelming infections and others contracted pneumonia.

Death seemed to be looming over the island and no one felt safe for the next few months.

Elsie felt helpless but could not offer assistance in any

way, other than pray that no more souls would succumb to this dreadful illness. She had noticed on odd days that she too was not feeling that strong and sometimes had to leave the room whilst teaching the children, as she was overcome with nausea. However, she had developed neither a cough nor the rash, so took heart that it was not the dreaded enteric fever.

She still had heard nothing from Luke during this time and was anxious and concerned that he may be ill, or even dead. There was no way she could enquire about his wellbeing or even go near the camps. She reminded herself that he had always seemed resourceful when he needed anything. Possibly that was it, and she would never hear from him again. Part of her was relieved at the thought as she would not have to face him and discuss what Elsie believed was strange and disrespectful behaviour towards her, and not how she thought the experience of making love should be. The haunting emptiness thereafter had left her feeling disappointed and wronged. She had seen how giddy and excited brides seemed to look. Well, that was all spoilt for her now and it was her fault for allowing it... or had she?

Within the next couple of months, the enteric fever passed but took with it many innocent souls, both in the camps and some of the Saints.

Elsie by now, was having serious thoughts and concerns that she was more than likely pregnant and was completely at a loss as to what she could do about it. She felt the need to confide in someone, to at least share her news and get advice. Her main concern was to uphold both her reputation as the schoolmistress and her late parents' good name on the island.

One afternoon after school, she decided to chat to the reverend's wife, who always smiled and greeted her warmly. Perhaps she would have some idea of what to do and Elsie hoped that, at the very least, her secret would be safe with this kindly woman who was not likely to gossip like any of the women on the island

Elsie left her cottage with a trembling heart and, knowing she had no one else to turn to with the truth, she set off towards the church rectory. She stopped and hesitated several times, questioning whether any good could possibly come of her confession. On arriving at the rectory, she knocked on the door and was at once welcomed in by the reverend's wife, Jane, who assumed Elsie had come to see her husband about something relating to the school.

In a whisper Elsie said, "It is you I need to speak to, ma'am."

Jane told Elsie to sit in the small front parlour and went off to make tea. Elsie was trembling and about to leave when the door opened, and Jane entered carrying a tray. They waited for the tea to draw and chatted about the weather and Jane said how brave she thought Elsie had been to have suggested the rebuild of the school, and that she did not know many women who would even have thought of the idea.

Elsie sat nervously playing with the keys attached by a thin chain to her skirt belt and, without understanding her emotions, she suddenly burst into tears.

"Oh, my goodness, my dear, whatever could be upsetting you so? Please, tell me and perhaps I can help you?" said Jane reaching out to take Elsie's hand.

Elsie continued to sob and tried desperately to swallow the huge ball of pain she felt in her throat as she tried to control her emotions and breathe normally. She slowly calmed herself down with the realisation that she now had no choice but to confess her state.

"Ma'am... I believe myself to be pregnant, which is

indeed a truly shocking and unacceptable state for an unmarried, Christian schoolmistress to find herself in. It is all my fault, and I should not have been so foolish and careless. I just don't know where to turn as I am so afraid and ashamed. I came to you, ma'am, to ask for your advice. Please, help me" she implored as she began to sob loudly again.

Elsie fully expected to be told to leave the house immediately, but instead Jane said, "Now start at the beginning and tell me all about it, so I can see what we can do."

Where to begin…? Elsie felt that she had been taken for a fool and possibly the loneliness she had experienced so acutely after both her parents died had clouded her judgement. She went on to explain how Luke had arrived, injured and distressed at her door late one night – that she should probably not have opened the door, but that was not the Saints' way. Elsie explained how Luke had forgotten his felt hat after she had cleaned and dressed his wound, how she had met him thereafter and he had made her feel beautiful and intelligent. She just never thought of the consequences of unabashed love and passion. Jane listened intently and at no time appeared to be shocked by Elsie's tale. In fact, she smiled as Elsie explained about the excitement of meeting at various beautiful and romantic spots on the island. Elsie thought it best not to go into too much detail of the very warm evening at the waterfall when she behaved so boldly. She explained neither about her sitting in her undergarments in the pool with Luke, nor exactly how one thing led to another.

They both sat there in silence for a little while and then Jane asked, "Does this man, Luke, have any idea that you are with child?"

"Oh no, ma'am, I have not seen him again since the fever gripped the island. And, with the curfew that has been very,

very strictly in place, there has probably been no chance for him to leave the camp."

"Well, he has to be told and must take responsibility for his actions."

"Oh, ma'am, I am not sure that is possible as he should never have left that camp and I fear he would get into awful trouble if I exposed him. Surely that would not help either of us?"

"My husband visits the camps a few times a week and provides pastoral care to some of the prisoners, although we do not like to see or call them as such. You see, these men were defending their land and families as most good men would do. It is not our place to judge them. Well… nevertheless, I am asking your permission to put your position to my husband and suggest he informs Master Luke Viljoen of this predicament. I can assure you that he will be most discrete, as will I. The child you are carrying is one of God's children and we need to do what is best for the child, whilst trying to keep your reputation intact."

"Thank you, ma'am. I am so sorry to have burdened you with my problem."

"In my opinion, a child is always sent for a reason. You do not burden me. I could merely be a conduit to ensure God's will be done. Now, leave this with me for the moment and I will see what we can do once I have spoken to my husband."

"But surely he will be horrified that the schoolmistress is pregnant and not married?"

"I think not, Elsie. We have seen and helped many in far worse situations. Off you go and I will come and see you when I have something to report."

The days passed, and Elsie heard nothing more. She sat up in the evenings sewing herself an apron with a very gathered waist and a pleated bib. She was hopeful that this would disguise her expanding waistline and of course, sensibly, would keep the chalk dust off her skirt.

Elsie still took her walks to enjoy the countryside, remembering all her father had taught her about the fauna and flora of this beautiful island. Her thoughts transported her back to the times she had shared with him, and she felt his presence when she walked alone, enjoying the views. However, she was also saddened by the spoliation of the countryside and the cutting down of trees by the prisoners for fuel and for their wooden carvings. Thankfully, this practice had recently been forbidden by the governor. She could sometimes hear the men playing rugby or singing if the wind blew their cries or melodies down the valley. Were any of them Luke's voice?

When as she was locking up the schoolhouse one day, Jane appeared at the door and suggested they take a walk. They wandered down towards the wharf and, once through The Arch, Jane started to report her findings, or at least those of her husband.

It appeared that the reverend had called for Luke during one of his pastoral care visits to Peace Camp and informed him of Elsie's condition. Initially, he denied ever leaving the camp unescorted by the camp guards. The reverend reminded Luke that as a God-fearing man, he should double-check his conscience. They had sat in silence for a while and then Luke finally admitted that he had once been intimate with Elsie. The reverend suggested he do the honourable thing by marrying Elsie and, when he one day got back to South Africa and was a free man again, that he should send for her. Luke said he would do this once he had returned to the family farm to assess the situation. He needed to speak to his family and plan for Elsie and the expected baby to join him. The reverend advised

Luke that he would quietly make arrangements for Elsie and Luke to be married in order to protect Elsie's reputation on the island and for the sake of the unborn child.

Elsie was very shocked that the arrangements seemed to have surged ahead with no consideration of her feelings or opinion. Anger initially raged through her like a poison, but she thought of her unborn child and her so-called sanity prevailed. Yes, she probably had no option but to go ahead with a marriage to a man she realised she hardly knew. It seemed that the decision had been taken out of her and Luke's hands and, in fact, he had not even asked her to marry him.

Had their situation been different, Elsie wondered what a real romantic marriage proposal would have felt like. This certainly did not feel exciting or even the right thing to be doing.

How could she possibly promise 'until death do us part,' and that she would 'honour and obey him'?

Why, oh why had she lost control that night at the waterfall?

Could a moment of their passion and her naivety end up being a lifetime sentence?

Elsie knew that whatever the future held for her, the small foetus growing within her belly had to be her priority from here on in. She reluctantly commented to Jane that she felt that she had no other options and that she would go ahead with the marriage for the sake of the child and her reputation on St Helena. In fact, the marriage had already been arranged for the following morning at St Paul's Cathedral, which was up on the hill away from Jamestown. It was also out of the general view of any local gossipers as the reverend had felt that discretion was called for. Elsie's parents had been buried side by side in the cemetery surrounding St Paul's Cathedral, so at least she felt that they would be near to her on her wedding day.

Elsie could hardly sleep that night. She felt as though her life was balancing on a precipice with her future so unknown. Her child gently stirred, which reminded her that this was no longer just about her. Responsibility had come unplanned, and she vowed that, regardless of what life presented to her from hereon, she would be the best and most devoted mother she could possibly be. She could hardly imagine holding her own child in her arms and feeling its need and love.

The next morning, Elsie dressed carefully and braided her hair in two long plaits looped over her ears before entwining and pinning them in a chignon at the nape of her neck. She wore her navy-blue, long skirt with the waist recently extended by sewing in a triangle of fabric at the back to allow for her growing waistline; a snow-white blouse untucked; and one of her mother's beautiful lace collars. Having found a long cloak in her mother's old trunk, she draped that around her shoulders. On leaving the house, she noticed a couple of beautiful red rosebuds in the small front garden and picked them to tuck into her chignon. She knew how her mother would have disapproved of her state but believed she would still have loved her regardless. Her father would have soldiered on and loved her child unconditionally as he was never one who cared for reputations and what he regarded as inconsequential, man-made rules on how one should live. Oh, how she missed them and particularly today, as she walked up the hill on her own to St Paul Cathedral to marry a man about whom she knew so little.

On arriving at the cathedral, Luke was already there with a guard from the camp. Jane was waiting for her at the entrance to the cathedral. She took and squeezed Elsie's hand and led her down the aisle before sitting down in the front row, with the guard on the opposite bench behind Luke. Elsie looked up at the curved trusses in the roof and the white walls inlaid with memorial plaques of those gone before. The tall stained-glass windows let in gentle-coloured beams of light. The ceremony was short and to the point and there were no rings to exchange, but they held hands when they took their vows, and the marriage was witnessed in the marriage register by Jane and the camp guard.

Before Luke was escorted back to the camp by the guard he whispered to Elsie, "You look beautiful!" and she was sure he had tears in his eyes when he was led away.

As Elsie walked alone back down the hill to her cottage, she felt as if she had stepped out of a weird dream.

Had that just happened?

Was she now really Mrs Luke Viljoen?

She was sure no other bride had ever walked to and from her wedding unaccompanied. When she got home, she gently sobbed to herself, regretting that she would never know the joy of a real wedding like she had seen some of her friends on the island experience. People would find out that she was now married as the notices had to be posted in the local newspaper and the parish church noticeboard. She would hold her head high and say she was very happy with the situation. She planned to tell anyone who asked that, when the war was over, she would be following Luke to South Africa. She hoped people would be forgiving and believed they would soon have something else about which to gossip. Now was her turn and she would weather the storm.

Remembering her mother's wedding ring that she had kept tucked away in a drawer, she slipped it on to her ring finger to prove she was now a married woman.

The news of her marriage quickly spread, and the school

children all started calling her Mrs Viljoen, which she initially thought sounded very strange. Some people seemed a little taken aback that she had chosen to marry a POW but, soon enough, most of the Saints got on with their daily living.

Elsie started feeling more tired as the time crept closer to her delivery. A relief-teacher was taking her classes at Garden House School as it was becoming too much for her in her last trimester. When she lay on her bed in her cottage at night, she realised that she was no longer feeling the loneliness that she had experienced when both her parents had suddenly died. Her thoughts of her future with her child excited her and gave her hope.

The local carpenter, whose children she taught in her school, arrived one day with a lovely little crib he had crafted, and his wife had sewn and cross-stitched the edges of the linen sheets in a pale-green coloured thread. Elsie was delighted with these gifts, and their kind gesture made her feel that her situation could possibly have been accepted by some of the Saints. Jane, always so kind and caring, had knitted a couple of matinee jackets and a few pairs of the dearest little booties on which she had embroidered tiny yellow rosebuds. Elsie thought she should try to knit some baby garments too, but her efforts were a disaster and the result looked as though a cat had toyed with her knitting. Instead, she took some of her savings and went to the general store to buy some of the little baby clothes they had in stock and a few cotton diapers too.

The baby seemed very energetic, and Elsie was constantly aware of it moving and kicking her which brought her huge comfort. She always found herself smiling at those reassuring movements. She realised that her time could be drawing near and really had no idea what to expect. The reverend's wife had some midwifery experience and had said that when Elsie started getting contractions, she should send one of her neighbour's sons to come and fetch her.

When Elsie took her bath in an iron tub in her cottage she was amazed how shiny her stretched belly appeared and she was fascinated by the visible long, slow stretches her baby was making inside her. How she loved this child already. She caught herself chatting and singing to it whenever she was alone.

Her belly grew even bigger and sleeping became increasingly difficult as her back hurt and she was frequently needing to visit the outhouse. Elsie smiled remembering her father saying that the outhouse was ten yards too far in the winter and ten yards too close in the summer, although that possibly applied more to when he lived in England.

One night, as Elsie got out of bed in the middle of the night, she was horrified to find liquid pouring down her legs. She had read that one's waters normally broke at the start of labour. She knocked on her neighbour's door and asked them to send a message to the reverend's wife to say that her baby was coming. Her labour was strong with overwhelming contractions that left her unable to breathe. She thought she was dying when Jane arrived, but she soon calmed her down. The labour seemed endless, and she even prayed aloud to God for it to all be over. Jane talked calmly to her and mopped her brow. Then, after nearly a full day, the final contraction came and Elsie knew she could take no more. Exhausted and no longer thinking logically, she felt the pressure of her baby's head finally emerging between her thighs and Jane helped the little shoulders out with a final push from Elsie. Jane smacked the tiny buttocks to make the baby cry. She cut the umbilical cord, wiped the infant clean and wrapped the beautiful baby daughter in a small blanket before handing her to Elsie.

Elsie wept with joy and relief. "Is my little girl all okay, ma'am? Does she have everything?"

Elsie was assured that her daughter looked perfect and so she was.

"What will you name her?"

"She will be named Katherine Georgina."

This little girl had been born with a caul on her head that the reverend's wife had carefully removed and placed on a clean cloth to dry. There was a suspicion that children born with a caul would have some powerful challenges in their lives and some heavy burdens, but a dried caul could also be sold to seamen, who would purchase a small piece for a considerable price believing that, if they kept such in their purse, it was a preservation against drowning. Jane thought that Elsie could do with the money and would be able to sell pieces of the dried caul to some seafarers in the harbour, although a reverend's wife should not really have thought of or entertained such superstitions.

When Elsie was stronger, post the birth of Katherine, she did discreetly sell some of the dried caul to some very eager customers down at the harbour, and kept a small piece back to give to Katherine one day.

Chapter 6
The Departure

When the notice of the end of the war came in June 1902, the government in St Helena set up the Oath of Allegiance, which the prisoners had to sign before being released back to South Africa. Many did not want to do this and were kept on in St Helena, but eventually all but four prisoners signed and only those four remained.

On 22 August 1902, General Cronje and 994 ex-prisoners left St Helena Island to return to South Africa on a ship called *The Tagues*. There had been a peace agreement between the British and the South Africans and it was time for the prisoners to return to their homes and families, or what remained of them.

Elsie had received no news from Luke and was unsure whether he would be amongst the first to leave or, in fact, whether he was even still alive as he had made no effort to see or contact Elsie since their marriage.

Little Katherine was now three months old and had fluffy blonde hair and bright blue eyes like her father.

Elsie decided to go down to the Square to see if he was amongst those first men to be leaving to return to South Africa. She dressed little Katherine in her best smocked outfit and waited with the many other Saints, who had also come down to the docks to bid farewell to the ex-prisoners. There seemed an endless stream of men walking towards the ship, carrying their few belongings and looking very tatty. Most of them were still wearing the clothes they had arrived in a couple of years ago. Towards the end of the line of men, she caught sight of Luke coming towards the harbour. They immediately made eye contact. On drawing level with her, he stopped to ask how she was and reached out to touch his pretty little daughter's very fair face

"She is a little beauty. What have you named her?" asked Luke.

"Katherine Georgina. That is Katherine Georgina Viljoen," replied Elsie proudly and a little defiantly.

"I am so sorry, Elsie… Goodbye!" said Luke and, looking away, he handed her a small wooden box made from local gumwood with red roses painted on the front and a tiny key for the lock hanging by a piece of string attached to the handle on the lid. Carved out on the lid were the words:

'ST. HELENA ISLAND 1901 K.G.V.'

The initials K.G.V. stood for 'Krijgsgevangene' meaning 'prisoner of war' in Dutch.

Elsie realised that, by coincidence, their daughter's initials were also K.G.V. – Katherine Georgina Viljoen – or perhaps it was not quite by chance. She had given her daughter the same initials as the status of her father when Katherine was born.

With that, Luke continued to walk towards the ship without once looking back.

Elsie stood rooted to the spot staring after him. Her emotions were polarised between wanting to run after him, and feeling such anger that he had walked by with so little to say or explain to her. After all, she was his wife and he the father of her child. Katherine became fractious and needed attention, so Elsie walked back to her cottage carrying her baby and the little wooden box that Luke had handed to her.

A couple of hours later, Elsie heard the horns blasting in the harbour to announce the departure of *The Tagues* for Cape Town and she stood in her little front garden wondering if Luke was one of those on deck looking up into Jamestown. Her situation suddenly seemed so surreal that she was not sure whether to laugh or cry. Sanity prevailed and she hugged her baby and got on with her motherly chores. Whilst sitting in her rocking chair breastfeeding little Katherine, who was an extremely content and happy baby, she wondered what was in the little box Luke had handed her. She decided to look inside it once she had settled Katherine for the night and was herself bathed and tucked up in bed. She placed it next to her bed where it would sit for the rest of her life.

On finally climbing into her comfortable bed that night, she fleetingly thought of Luke heading back to South Africa, probably sleeping on the deck of the ship.

She placed the little key into the lock and slowly turned it to discover what was hidden inside.

There was a folded letter and three very grubby five-pound Bank of England notes.

Elsie held her breath as she carefully unfolded the letter and shut her eyes for a minute before reading it. She instinctively knew that reading this letter would leave her in no doubt about where her relationship with Luke stood. This was a letter that needed to be read slowly and calmly.

20 August 1902
Dear Elsie,

I had hoped to have a discussion face to face but we have been informed that some prisoners are soon to return home to see what remains of our families, farms and our lives in South Africa post the Boer war.

I was informed by the reverend that you had given birth to a daughter, for which I congratulate you. I hope she will bring you the happiness and fulfilment that you deserve. I am sure she will be a beauty like you and no doubt her future education will be a major priority to you.

I admit that we were married in church before the child was born, so she will bear my surname. However, I have to say that from hereon I can never acknowledge you as my wife and, in fact, will have to deny ever being married. In South Africa having a Coloured wife will never be accepted. Besides, my family would simply disown me! I also have concerns that the child will have your skin tone. There would be no place for her in South African society where colonial racism is rife and ever increasing.

With regards to our relationship, I will only remember the happy times we shared on St Helena and the excitement and fun we had. I enclose some bank notes for the child's keep and will try to forward more money, which I will do secretly from time to time via the reverend who married us.

My life will start again on return to my homeland, and I intend to make a huge success of it with nothing to hold me back. I also believe it best that you tell the child, for all our sakes, that I died before her birth.

I made this little box for you and painted the red roses upon it like those at the front door of your cottage. I feel that, in a way, these roses are a symbol of our relationship: the

beauty, the thorns we have had to bear, then the wilting and
dying flowers.

Good luck and I hope another man one day cares for you
in the way that I am unable to.

I leave some of my heart with you always.

Sincerely,

Luke

A single, large tear rolled down Elsie's cheek – it would be the last she would ever allow herself to cry for him. The letter was hurtful and blunt. He had made his choice very clear and now she would make hers in the best interest of her daughter and herself. At just twenty-one years old, Elsie knew her mind and she had a core of steel that would ensure her daughter got the best possible opportunities in life, despite Luke Viljoen.

She folded the letter and put it back in the box on her bedside table, turned the key in the lock and linked the key through the chain she wore around her neck with the crucifix her mother used to wear.

Surprisingly, she felt calm and very sleepy. She was now free to make the plans she wished. Tomorrow would be her new beginning.

PART II

Chapter 7
To Cape Town

On awakening, Elsie fed and bathed Katherine and made her way down to the harbour to find the harbourmaster. The activity in and around the harbour always gave her a thrill: people getting on with the business of unloading and loading the ships; the noisy fishmongers selling their catches; and the fishermen on the quay mending their nets. It was such a vibrant and alive space.

Elsie found the harbourmaster supervising a ship being loaded near the old fishermen's cottages at the edge of the harbour, and she asked him to please advise her when next a small cabin was available on one of the ships departing for Cape Town. She had decided to start sorting out what she and Katherine would need for their lives in South Africa, and she would pack their belongings into the two chests that had belonged to her late father and that had travelled with him from England.

Her plan was to take all the things she no longer needed to the bric-a-brac store in Jamestown for onward sale and she was counting on earning a little from the sales. It was an emotional exercise as nearly every household item or piece of clothing brought memories of her idyllic childhood flooding back. She had grown up with two parents who individually adored her. They may not have always liked each other, but deep down she believed that there had always been respect and love between them.

Elsie made an appointment with the new Governor Gallwey – who had recently replaced the much loved and respected Governor Sterndale – to present her position and ask him to arrange British travel documents for both she and Katherine. She felt sure that if they both arrived in South Africa with British papers, they would be regarded as European. Elsie would be able to live as such in what she had heard was a somewhat divided society. She also asked the governor to enquire if there were any teaching posts that she could apply for, to ensure that she had employment on her arrival in Cape Town.

The governor commented that he was very disappointed that St Helena would be losing her, but that he understood and would support her in her efforts to make a better life for herself and her daughter in South Africa. He also assumed that she would be joining her husband, and Elsie let him think that; but he therefore made no enquiries about finding her a teaching position, as he was aware of the sensitivities that would be involved due to her skin colour. He thought it best for her husband to manage this on her behalf when she arrived in South Africa.

It took some nine months before the harbourmaster came to tell her that a suitable ship that had just docked had a small cabin available for her. She and Katherine would travel to South Africa in a week's time. By now, little Katherine was a year old and starting to walk, which would be a challenge on the voyage. Elsie immediately said that she would take up the cabin and paid the harbourmaster the fare without hesitation. She told him that her two chests would be ready for collection in a couple of days. Despite not having heard of a possible teaching position that she could take up in Cape Town, Elsie decided to travel anyway, as with her teaching experience how hard could it be to find a school to teach at in a growing and developing community?

The week passed far too quickly as Elsie made the final arrangements for her departure from the school, even though she had been teaching less since Katherine's birth. Her most difficult farewell was to Jane, who had really become a maternal figure in Elsie's life. Both the reverend and Jane wished her a happy married life when she met up with Luke in South Africa. Elsie smiled bravely but did not have the heart to tell them the truth. She felt that it may be easier to write to them about Luke's decision once she had settled and was independent in Cape Town, as she knew they would be very anxious about her relocation to a foreign land on her own with a small child.

Part of Elsie felt a little terrified about her bold decision, but there was a spark in her soul that made her feel empowered and independent.

When the ship set sail, the quay was lined with present and past pupils and their parents waving goodbye. The reverend and Jane presented her with a hamper of food for the voyage and, rather surprisingly, some bank notes that they said Luke had forwarded to them for her and Katherine. Even the new governor was there to wish her well. As the ship sailed out of the harbour into the Atlantic Ocean, Elsie felt as small as one of the drops therein, and there was a little sadness in knowing that it would probably be the last time she would see her beloved St Helena.

She already missed the green hills; the white arum lilies; the quaint happy little wire birds; her family cottage; but most of all the Saints, that wonderful group of people unique to St Helena.

The journey was reasonably uneventful, but poor Katherine struggled with seasickness when the swells grew large. Having recently started walking, the lilting of the ship confused the little mite, and she took to crawling again unless she was holding Elsie's hand. It was eight days before they saw land.

Elsie's first sight of Cape Town was early one morning as the sun was rising. There was a large mountain looming above the city with a cloud masking the top of it and not another cloud in the sky, giving the appearance of a white tablecloth draped on top of the mountain. A large star-shaped fort appeared to be guarding the bay. They sailed past Robben Island (meaning 'seal island' in Dutch), then into a very noisy and busy harbour with many ships in the docks. It all seemed so frantic and large compared to Jamestown Harbour. There was an overwhelming stench of fish and sewage mixed together. Animals were in pens bleating and bellowing, and there was even a crate with what looked like a lion in it pacing up and down. Everyone seemed to be speaking a language that was a mixture of Dutch and English. There were large, fat seals basking on the rocks and black and white penguins standing very still as though they were on guard.

Elsie stood on the deck holding Katherine in her arms, watching all the activity of docking. She went to their little cabin to place the last of their belongings in her bag. The two chests that travelled with her had been stowed in the hold and she hoped they had remained dry as some of her most precious items were stored inside, including books that had once belonged to her father. She and Katherine carefully made their way down the gangplank to the waiting port authorities. There were two very stern-looking men who asked for their papers. They seemed rather confused about the papers that the governor of St Helena had issued them. They questioned Elsie over whether Katherine was her child, as she was White and did not look much like her mother. Katherine felt anger rise within her but thought it best to remain calm during this situation. She advised them that her husband was a certain Mr Luke Viljoen, and she was coming to join him as his wife – which was not exactly true but she reasoned that her personal circumstances really had nothing to do with them! When Elsie presented them with her marriage certificate, one man commented to the other that Mr Viljoen's family was in for a big shock. They looked at each other and laughed as they returned her papers and wished her luck.

Confused and fuming, she stood waiting on the quayside for their luggage to be unloaded. There were many carts and wagons waiting for other passengers. She approached a few to see if they would transport her and baby Katherine with their two chests to a local boarding house, but they all replied that they already had fares booked.

By the time the chests had finally been unloaded, Katherine had become very fractious, and Elsie looked about desperately for some means of transport to a safe abode. Everyone seemed to be avoiding her anxious, searching eyes. Eventually, a kindly Coloured man got down from his donkey cart and asked where she wanted to go.

"To a local boarding house for my daughter and me, please," requested Elsie.

The man hesitated and, with cap in hand, he shifted from one foot to the other trying to explain. "But, sister, you are Coloured just like me and your child looks like a White person's child, with the blonde hair and blue eyes. There is nowhere that they will accept you on the White side of town," he said emphatically.

Elsie looked at him in disbelief.

Surely, he was joking… what difference would it make?

"Well, where am I to go? I can't stay here at the harbour."

"Certainly not, sister, not an elegant and well-spoken lady like you. Not the sort of place for a woman to be on your own," he said winking. "Ah! I tell you what… My missis— that is, my wife will know better what to do with you two. Come back to my home in District Six for the night and we can make a plan."

"How very kind of you, sir," replied Elsie, rather relieved.

"No one ever calls me *sir*," he laughed. "My name is Alfie, and who are you?"

"I am Elsie Viljoen and this is my daughter, Katherine," Elsie replied, extending her right hand, to which Alfie gently held her fingers and touched his right elbow with the fingers of his left hand. Elsie was curious at this strange greeting, but thought it not the time to question, particularly as Katherine was now sobbing with tiredness and hunger.

Elsie later learnt that this was a sign of respect and by touching your left hand to your right elbow when shaking hands, you were demonstrating that you did not have a hidden weapon.

Alfie looked at her kindly with his twinkling eyes surrounded by many fine lines. His grey, coarse, curled hair and his slightly Malaysian-featured, light brown face looked like so many of the Saints on St Helena. For some instinctive reason, Elsie felt that she could trust him even though it appeared she had no other choice.

He got one of his colleagues to help him load the heavy chests onto the back of the cart. They were obviously talking about Elsie, but she could not understand a word of what they said.

The donkey cart with its heavy load slowly made its way out of the busy harbour and, finally, little Katherine fell into an exhausted sleep in Elsie's arms. The journey to District Six seemed endless as they steadily made their way up the hill. After passing some very grand buildings and homes, they came to the boundaries of what Alfie explained was the start of District Six, where people of many mixed race lived. Elsie obviously looked confused, and he further explained that the mixed-race people lived in this particular area whilst the White people lived in other, separate districts.

District Six was a bustling area with double-storey, whitewashed buildings supported by buttresses. The main form of transport appeared to be either donkey carts or bicycles. Some people were pushing barrows, plying their wares of vegetables, spices, fruit, wood, fish, cooking oil, chickens, and utensils. It seemed a happy and relaxed place with people laughing, joking and calling out to each other. The contrast with the rest of Cape Town that Elsie had merely passed through seemed immense.

They finally stopped at a narrow double-storey house with a woman sitting outside on a roughly made wooden stool, chatting to another woman, and peeling what looked like potatoes. They both stopped talking and stared at Alfie and his unusual cargo.

"And... who have we here, Pa?" said one of the women, who turned out to be Alfie's wife.

"Long story, Ma, but not for the neighbours' ears. I will explain inside," he replied, looking pointedly to the woman standing and chatting to his wife, who beat a hasty retreat.

Holding the still slumbering baby, Elsie carefully climbed down from the cart with the help of Alfie and made her way up the couple of stairs into the modest home. There was a smell of freshly baked bread and the small kitchen and living room area was spotlessly clean. Alfie's wife introduced herself in whispers as 'Marie' and suggested they put the sleeping little Katherine on a narrow bed behind a curtain in the far corner of the room. Katherine moaned but rolled over in a deep sleep. Elsie explained to Marie that the child had battled with sea sickness and struggled to walk on the constantly lilting ship.

Marie was a large woman with an ample bosom covered by a white apron. She had a multi-coloured scarf wrapped skilfully around her head, and a smile that lit up her whole face and showed her perfect teeth.

Marie started making a pot of tea while Alfie got one of the neighbours to help him carry in the chests from the back of the donkey cart. He said he would join them shortly as he first had to take the donkey and cart around the back of the house to feed and water the animal. The backyard had a shed for the donkey, a small pen or 'hokkie' for the chickens, and a 'longdrop' privy in the farthest corner.

Marie and Elsie continued to chat in whispers about the child and, of course, the elephant in the room was the fact that little Katherine was White – 'Pure White' as Marie would later always refer to Katherine's race distinction, which Elsie found endearing terminology but was not quite true.

When Alfie came inside and washed his hands and face in a bowl of water at the back door, he sat at the table with the women, joining them for rooibos tea and homemade bread with apricot jam. Elsie thought she had not tasted anything quite so delicious in ages or, in fact, ever!

Alfie smiled at Elsie and said, "Think you had better tell Ma and me your tale, so we can try to do our best to help you, sister."

Elsie felt as though she was sitting with her kindly parents again and found herself explaining with great ease that she had fallen pregnant by a South African POW named Luke Viljoen on St Helena Island. Her parents had sadly passed away a few years before this, from a virulent strain of flu that had infected the island from one of the many ships calling at the harbour for fresh supplies. She had no other real family, as her father had been a schoolteacher from England and her mother a local girl with no immediate family either. The Anglican reverend and his wife had been a huge support to her in her hours of need. She explained also how she and Luke had married quietly. Her voice choked a little when she told them that Luke had handed her a letter when he was shipped off the island saying he would deny their marriage in South Africa. He had suggested that Katherine be told her father had died, which Elsie agreed may be for the best under the circumstances.

Elsie told them how she believed that Katherine would have more of a future in South Africa as she was sure she was going to be as bright as a button. She said that she hoped to be able to work as a schoolteacher to pay for their keep and for her daughter's education in Cape Town. Both Alfie and Marie listened intently and accepted her story without judgement on any of the parties concerned. Elsie later realised that nothing in her story was new or shocking to them. She also grew to understand how they were never bitter about their unchosen roles as Coloured people in South Africa and truly tried to live as good Christians. They and their neighbours were remarkably cheerful and humorous people who were always able to laugh at themselves.

Marie and Alfie suggested that Elsie and Katherine should stay with them until Elsie could find some work, and Marie offered to babysit little Katherine until Elsie could afford to make another arrangement. They said she could share the bed with Katherine for the night and Alfie would look for a small crate at the docks the next day for Katherine to use as a cot. Alfie and Marie had a small bedroom and sitting room upstairs that led to a narrow wooden balcony overlooking the busy lane below.

When Katherine woke from her sleep, she was all smiles and seemed delighted to be on stable ground as she explored taking a few hesitant steps by herself again. Marie had warmed some water and poured it into a zinc tub, into which she popped Katherine. The little girl looked so happy and settled splashing the soapy water in the tub. Elsie repeatedly expressed her gratitude to Marie for welcoming them into her home.

That evening they all sat down to a dinner of spicy goat meat and vegetable stew with a slightly sweet sauce and the mashed potatoes that Elsie had seen Marie peeling when she arrived earlier that day. Elsie was astounded at how delicious the food tasted, especially after her own bland cooking since her mother died, followed by the slop that had been served by the cook on the ship from St Helena.

Over dinner Alfie and Marie said that they would make some enquiries at the local convent school to see if Elsie could get some work there. They hesitantly asked Elsie if she was a Catholic and she said she has been baptised in the Catholic Church and that her mother had been a Catholic, but her father an Anglican. Marie looked relieved as she commented that that could make all the difference! They asked if Katherine had been baptised, but Elsie said that she had not got around to doing so, what with her planning to leave the island. Elsie had not wanted to appoint godparents on St Helena whom Katherine would possibly never see again and would therefore have no part in her upbringing. Alfie and Marie looked at each other conspiratorially and said that may be helpful.

Elsie and Katherine snuggled down together that night in the narrow little bed, but that hardly mattered as they were both exhausted and normally slept together anyway, particularly on chilly nights.

Elsie woke the following morning to the sound of someone busy in the kitchen, and there was Marie, making porridge for their breakfast. Alfie joined them and said he had some enquiries to make for Elsie, which he would do after a delivery to the harbour. Following breakfast, Marie handed Elsie a duster and grass broom to get on with the cleaning whilst she washed the breakfast dishes. She pointed Elsie in the direction of the zinc tub outside that was used the night before for Katherine's bath. Elsie was instructed to grate the bar of green Sunlight Soap to use to wash their clothes. Elsie appreciated the direct manner and approach that Marie had to life as she preferred to know exactly where she stood.

With household chores done, they headed to the market area in District Six to buy fresh food for dinner that evening. Elsie was sure that she and Katherine would stick out like a sore thumb, but no one seemed to take much notice, and all shouted friendly, happy greetings to Marie in what sounded like 'kitchen-Dutch' and heavily accented English rolled into one. The sounds and exotic smells of spices and drying fish in the market were thrilling. There was a stall selling beautiful red and green apples, and another cooking delicious-looking street-food over a metal barrel filled with glowing embers. One of the market stallholders gave Katherine a small bunch of grapes. Neither she nor Elsie had ever seen or tasted these delicious little delicacies before. Oh, what joy to have that wonderful, sweet grape explode in your mouth when you bit into the soft juicy flesh.

Marie haggled with the fishmonger, and they came away with some 'smoorsnoek' (smoked snoek fish), for their dinner. The smell was strong and enticing and Elsie already looked forward to dinner time, although it was still only morning.

When they got home, Marie told Elsie that she was going to prepare a dish with the smoorsnoek. Elsie watched as Marie deftly chopped onions and peppers and sautéed them in oil. She added potatoes, spices and water, boiling it to reduce most of the liquid. Elsie was instructed to carefully remove the long thin bones from the smoked fish and flake it. When Alfie returned for dinner that evening, Marie warmed the onions and potatoes gently as most of the liquid had boiled away, then she added the flaked fish, squeezed fresh lemon juice and sprinkled a little lemon zest over the dish. Again, Elsie was astounded at this delicious, tasty food. Little Katherine could not spoon it into her mouth quickly enough which made them all laugh. It had been a long time since Elsie had enjoyed a family meal.

Alfie reported that he had visited the convent and spoken to the mother superior, who indicated that she would like to meet Elsie the next morning. The convent was a walk of two hours or so away from District Six, in an affluent White area. Alfie said he would accompany Elsie there in the morning and Marie offered to mind Katherine.

Elsie hardly slept that night thinking about her forthcoming meeting at the convent. She tried to play as many scenarios as possible in her head and plan her replies to any questions that the mother superior may pose. She decided it would be best to be completely honest and tell her about Luke's request that Katherine should be told that her father had died on St Helena before she was born, and his reasons for this request.

Alfie had returned from the harbour with a crate on the back of the donkey cart, that he scrubbed clean in the back garden after dinner. He thought it would make a nice little bed for Katherine after he had sanded the rough splinters away and painted it white. Marie said that they would find some kapok in the market to stuff a mattress and some Butcher's linen (striped hardwearing fabric) for Elsie to make a mattress cover.

The following morning, Elsie rose early and dressed in her Sunday best. She put on her navy long skirt and white blouse, attaching one of her delicate lace collars, plaited her long hair, tightly rolling it into a bun at the nape of her neck and securing it with hair pins. She was anxious about leaving Katherine as she had never left her with anyone before, but Katherine seemed very at home and happy to stay with Marie.

Alfie and Elsie set off, struggling against the gusts of wind whipping at their clothing. Table Mountain loomed over them and seemed angry, with the swirling and scudding clouds enhancing its dark mood. The walk felt much longer than seven miles to Elsie, as initial journeys so often do. They finally arrived at the convent building in St. Johns Road in the suburb of Wynberg. It was a serene sight with its whitewashed exterior and olive-green railings, with little crosses welded into the filigree leading up a few freshly polished red stairs to the large imposing black front door. Alfie banged three times with the gleaming brass knocker. Elsie tried to smooth her hair, feeling as though she had been pulled through a bush backwards. She may have to think of wearing a secured headscarf in future, like the other women all seemed to do in Cape Town. The door opened and a nervous looking, young novitiate nun with a short veil and a blue habit opened the door. Elsie was slightly comforted to notice that her skin was also not 'pure White' and that she had similar features to herself.

Alfie explained that they had an appointment with the mother superior, upon which they were asked to come in and sit on a wooden bench inside the large front door. Elsie sat nervously on the edge of the bench, listening to the sounds of praying in unison and a beautiful chanting hymn. There was a strange smell of incense, mothballs and boiled cabbage wafting through the entrance hall. She sincerely hoped heaven did not smell like that!

On a table that was flanked by two closed doors leading out of the entrance hall, stood a statue of the Virgin Mary holding the infant Jesus. There was a tall vase of white arum lilies that immediately took Elsie's thoughts back to the valleys and streams on St Helena, where they grew wild amongst the tree ferns, and she suddenly felt the pang of homesickness.

After a while, one of the doors opened and a very tall nun walked into the entrance hall. She wore the black and white habit of the Dominican order. She had a white coif on her head which made her look even taller, secured by a white wimple that came under her chin covering her neck, and she wore a black veil over her head that draped down her back. Her tunic was secured with a woollen belt which held a set of rosary beads hanging down her side. A large silver cross hung around her neck on a thick black cord. There was a long apron-like item that covered both the back and front of the habit which Elsie later learnt was called a 'scapular'. Elsie had the irreverent thought that the nun looked like a tall penguin that she had seen at the harbour when she arrived in Cape Town, but made sure she quickly dismissed the idea as this was surely not the time or place for such cheeky comparisons!

The mother superior introduced herself. She had a beautiful face with porcelain looking skin. Her eyes were a striking blue and Elsie felt they may be able to penetrate deep into her soul. Once they were all seated in her spacious office, facing each other across the large, shiny wooden desk, she told Elsie that Alfie was always doing favours for the sisters of the convent and that he was, himself, a devout Catholic. Mother Superior explained that when he had come asking for the nun's help with Elsie and explained her situation, the very least she could do was to meet her and hear her case personally.

Elsie said that she was hoping to gain employment to support herself and her child, explaining that, although she had had no formal teacher training, she had learnt a great deal from her late father who was a qualified schoolteacher from England. He had come to run a little school in Jamestown on St Helena. Elsie also enlightened the mother superior regarding her personal situation and how kind Alfie and his wife had been to help her out so far. She admitted that she had very little comprehension or understanding of colonial racism, or South African culture in general, and coming to the purpose of her meeting, she eventually asked if it would be possible for her to take up a teaching position at the convent. In response to that question, the mother superior raised her eyes to heaven and closed them, slowly shaking her head.

"Elsie, my dear, if it was up to me, you could start teaching here very soon as you seem to be a level-headed, intelligent young lady with good teaching experience. Besides, you have an excellent command of the English language. However, I doubt the fee-paying parents of the pupils at this exclusive girls' school and the education authorities would accept you as a teacher. I truly am so very sorry."

Elsie sat in stunned disbelief. Surely this racism did not stretch its ugly tentacle into education and the Catholic Church? She realised that her mouth was hanging open in shock and her heart was racing at a furious speed. Alfie spoke up and asked the mother superior if there was any other position within the convent that Elsie could take up?

The mother superior thought for a short while and then replied that they could do with another cleaner in the school as their current cleaner was not well and was not always able to cope with her duties. She suggested that Elsie could come in after three o'clock in the afternoons, Monday to Friday, to clean some of the classrooms, the ablution areas and the school library. The last room to clean, the library, is what made Elsie accept the cleaning job. Elsie hoped that she could look at or even borrow the odd book from time to time. They arranged that she would start at the beginning of the next month on a trial basis.

The mother superior mentioned that Alfie had told her that little Katherine had not yet been baptised a Catholic, and that they should organise this as soon as possible. Elsie was a little taken aback at this suggestion as she felt that this was surely personal business and her decision. However, this seemed shaky ground on which to protest, so she muttered that she would visit the priest to plan for Katherine's baptism. The nun rose and took Elsie's hands in both her own and said, "Bless you, child, for coming to us for help. God has truly guided you here."

Elsie smiled and thanked her for the opportunity and said she would try to clean the school to the best of her ability.

Elsie started what felt to her was a lowly cleaning job at Springfield Convent School, with a feeling of frustration and shame that she was unable to use her teaching ability merely because of the colour of her skin and facial features. However, she stuck at the job with an optimistic vision of possibly one day getting the opportunity to teach again. Mother Superior always took the time to stop and chat to her whilst she was working and enquire after little Katherine.

Elsie wrote to the reverend and his wife on St Helena to advise them that she and Katherine were settled. She told them that she was working at Springfield Convent School in Cape Town but did not mention that she was employed as a cleaner and not a teacher!

With a heavy heart and feeling somewhat insincere, Elsie went to see the priest to make the arrangements for Katherine to be baptised in the Catholic Church. She asked Alfie and Marie to be godparents and they were absolutely delighted and proud to be asked, having no children of their own. Marie made a beautiful christening robe of white lace for Katherine to wear, and, after the baptism service, they celebrated with neighbours and friends back in District Six. The event turned out to be such a happy occasion and Elsie, for the first time, felt that she had been accepted and now belonged in that society.

Marie loved looking after Katherine whilst Elsie went to her cleaning job during the week. At least mother and daughter had most of the mornings together and Elsie would put Katherine down for her afternoon nap after lunch, before walking to work. Marie prepared dinner for them to sit down and enjoy as a family once Alfie and Elsie were home.

Alfie built on a little lean-to room in the back yard of their home, making an adjoining room where Elsie and Katherine lived and enjoyed a degree of privacy. Elsie gave half her meagre income to Marie for their keep. They became a happy little family. Elsie wished for a home of her own again, but there really seemed no chance of this with such a low paid cleaning job at the convent.

District Six was situated within sight of the docks and was so-called as it was the Sixth Municipal District of Cape Town.

It was a lively and musical community made up of former slaves, artisans, merchants and Cape Malay people, plus a small number of Xhosa Black people, Afrikaans Whites, Indians and Jews. Many shopkeepers lived above their shops and if anyone needed anything one could knock on the door and the shopkeeper would come downstairs and sell you whatever was required. On hot summer evenings, everyone slept with their doors and windows open wide. The thieves of District Six protected the inhabitants and committed their crimes elsewhere.

After a few years, when it was time for Katherine to start attending junior grade school, Mother Superior asked Elsie to come and see her one evening after she had finished cleaning. She advised Elsie that Sister Brigid was starting a small school for Coloured children in District Six and that Elsie could work with her there as a teaching assistant. The job would come with a small, very basic cottage, where Elsie could reside. Mother Superior added that Katherine would need to start school and could be admitted as a boarder in the girls' convent, as she was now approaching school-going age. Whilst this was a fee-paying school for the White students, Mother Superior added that there was a bursary available and that the nuns wanted to award this to little Katherine. Elsie was horrified at the thought of not living with her daughter but knew she could never afford the school and boarding fees at the convent school for privileged White girls. Feeling so torn with the offered opportunity of being able to teach again, but not being part of her daughter's everyday life, presented Elsie with a huge dilemma. She knew she could not deprive Katherine of an excellent education because she wanted to spend more time with her. She also felt a huge responsibility to the Coloured children whom she had grown to love and for whom she had great empathy. She believed that the only way forward for these children was a good education, and she would so love to be a part of that. At the same time, not being able to publicly acknowledge her own daughter was deeply painful for Elsie, knowing that she would never be Black enough to be accepted in Black society and surely never White enough to be thought of as Katherine's mother.

Mother Superior had also mentioned that the bursary was financed by an anonymous donor who was offering a full scholarship on merit to a girl at the school, and she felt that Katherine would be greatly deserving. What Mother Superior had not told Elsie was that Luke Viljoen was this donor and that he had secretly traced Elsie and Katherine through the reverend and his wife on St Helena Island. He had sworn Mother Superior to secrecy on the condition that he would pay for all of Katherine's schooling and her boarding expenses. He also made a substantial donation to the new school for Coloured children and to the costs of the cottage being built in the grounds of the school to house the assistant teacher, the post planned for Elsie.

Oblivious to the identity of the donor, Elsie discussed the situation with her now adopted parents, Marie and Alfie, and they too felt that this was an opportunity not to be passed over. Elsie was concerned about she and Katherine not being able to acknowledge that they were mother and daughter. She explained the situation to Katherine, who had grown into a confident little six-year-old. She was very matter of fact about it and accepting of how the situation would be. Katherine had grown into a very pretty child with long blonde hair, blue eyes and fair skin. She adored her adopted grandparents and immediately promised to visit them during her days off from school. Elsie tried to explain to her that things may get complicated with their skin colour difference, but Katherine was determined that she was going to boarding school and that she would smile at her mother and say, 'Good morning, ma'am,' when they met. Katherine seemed thrilled by the conspiratorial idea of no one, other than the nuns, knowing that they were mother and daughter, but Elsie had her doubts. The idea of teaching again and the prospect of her daughter getting an excellent education was, after all, the reason she had left St Helena in the first place, and it would be silly to pass up these opportunities for them to live a better life. At least they could be together as a family during the school holidays in District Six.

Sister Brigid and Elsie worked together teaching the Coloured children at the new school. The children all loved Elsie and felt very comfortable with her as she looked just like them. Elsie felt she was learning so much from Sister Brigid, who had come from Ireland full of wonderful teaching ideas and methods. Alfie was often at the school mending and repairing things. He always brought a parcel of delicious treats from Marie when he visited and said that Marie now had so much time on her hands with Katherine away at school and Elsie living at the new school, that she had even started selling some of her homemade delicacies at the market and was doing rather well with it.

Elsie's little cottage in the school grounds was small but very cosy and Alfie had made a simple bed, a table and two chairs, plus a wardrobe that he had fashioned out of packing cases acquired from the docks. Marie had made a beautiful patchwork quilt for her bed and some curtains for the windows. Always on her bedside table was the little box that Luke had presented to her on his departure from St Helena. Elsie still kept it locked with the key around her neck. She knew that soon Katherine would notice the coincidence of the initials KGV carved on the lid which matched her own initials. Elsie decided that she would tell Katherine that it was a private box and that one day, when the time was right, she would give her the key, although that could expose the lie that she had told her daughter that her father was dead. In fact, for all Elsie knew, Luke could well be dead! She temporarily put this matter on the back burner and decided to deal with it one day in the far distant future.

During the school holidays Katherine would be collected by Alfie to go back to District Six after all the other children had left. He would often take them on outings on his donkey cart to Adderley Street, which bustled with carts and trams transporting people to and from the railway station. Alfie passed as a mere cab driver, and no one seemed to notice them. Katherine always begged Alfie for a few pennies to buy flowers for Elsie and Marie from one of the many flower sellers sitting on the pavements. Sometimes they even went down to the seaside to paddle along the shore.

Katherine took to boarding school like a duck to water and was totally involved in every possible activity from day one. She got into a fair amount of trouble from time to time for talking during classes, and discipline was quite harsh in the form of a steel ruler being wacked across the knuckles of her little hands or the back of her knees. One day she forgot to relieve herself during a break as she was so busy playing hopscotch. She asked the teaching nun if she could be excused to go to the lavatory when classes had resumed and was asked if she was not well. On replying no, but that she had forgotten to go during the break time, the nun refused to excuse her. Katherine eventually had an accident, being unable to control her bladder any longer and she felt the hot urine running down her little legs and forming a very large puddle under her desk on the classroom floor. The nun was furious with her and sent her to sit outside the classroom. After the lesson had ended, she was made to her clean up her mess. Katherine was mortified and even more so when some of the girls laughed at her.

Despite this incident, Katherine proved to be a popular child and was sometimes invited to other girls' homes for the weekends. When asked about her parents, she said her father was dead and her mother was far away, which seemed to satisfy the curiosity of both pupils and parents.

Katherine made very good friends with a little girl named Suzanne, whose father was a professor at the South African College in Cape Town. One weekend Suzanne invited Katherine to come home with her as they would be celebrating Suzanne's tenth birthday and family and friends would be coming for a party. Katherine was thrilled as she had never been invited to a birthday party before. She did not arrive in a party dress as, firstly, she did not own one and, secondly, she did not know a special dress was needed to attend a party. Suzanne's mother dressed her in one of Suzanne's many dresses and she looked even prettier than normal.

Suzanne's parents' home was in the Cape-Dutch style and whitewashed, with beautiful sweeping gables that looked like curling angel wings embracing the large dark wooden front door. It was nestled in a perfectly manicured garden in the leafy suburb of Constantia. The house staff had set out a long table in the shade of an old oak tree. The white table linen was a perfect contrast against the very green lawn. There was a large birthday cake in the middle of the table and each place setting offered the most delicious little cucumber sandwiches, tiny jam tarts and strawberries that had been grown in the kitchen garden. There was also a large glass of thirst quenching, sparkling, homemade lemonade, plus a bowl of multi-coloured jelly.

After everyone had sung happy birthday to Suzanne, it was decided to start playing games and one of these was 'hide and seek'. The children were all playing in the extensive gardens and hiding amongst the plants and behind the large tree trunks. Katherine noticed that one of the French doors leading into the house from a long veranda was open, so she thought she would hide behind the drapes in the room that turned out to be the study and library of the professor. She had not been hiding long when she heard a noise behind her and there stood Suzanne's overbearing father, who had a dark beard and very black eyes staring out under his bushy eyebrows. He launched at Katherine and picked her up, whirling her around the study. Katherine was surprised and shocked. No man had ever had such close physical contact with her before. The professor started laughing and Katherine could smell strong liquor on his breath, just like some of the beggars smelled on the streets of District Six. He asked her if she was enjoying the party and she merely nodded her pretty little head in shock, eager to escape his clutches. Still carrying Katherine in his strong arms, he shut the French door, drew the drapes closed and sat down at his desk placing her on his large lap. He started bouncing her up and down on his knee and asked if she was still having fun. This time Katherine shook her head and asked to leave as she was beginning to feel very uncomfortable and wanted to get back to the party. He ignored her and continued bouncing her up and down, but now closer to this stomach. There was a noise outside and he suddenly pushed her under the desk and told her to be quiet. Then he took her hand and started rubbing it against his crotch.

Katherine felt it getting harder and bulkier. The more she tried to pull her hand away the harder he gripped at her wrist and continued massaging himself. He started undoing the buttons of his trousers and said that Katherine was a very bad girl and look what she had done, as she saw a large sausage thing emerging out of his trouser fly. She had only seen such sausage like things hanging in the butcher's store in the market. He said she had to taste it and Katherine was terrified and started to cry as he forced her mouth over his penis and grabbed her braided blonde hair, moving her mouth up and down at a furious rate. The large bulk of the penis smelled and tasted awful and was making her want to choke and be sick as it seemed to be going down her throat. He started to moan, and she tasted a disgusting acrid liquid in her mouth that she spat on the floor as she pulled away from him. He started laughing again saying she was a little minx and a very wicked child. He said that she was far too bad to be at a convent. He threatened to tell the nuns and priests about what she had done but added that he would forgive her and keep her secret because she did not have a father. Katherine heard Suzanne calling her and he grabbed her hand and marched her out of the study back into the garden saying that Katherine had been hiding there.

Katherine was stunned and terrified that everyone would know what had happened. She felt dirty and still had the horrible taste of Suzanne's father in her mouth. She was confused and not sure why she had been accused of being a wicked child or why she should be forgiven for not having a father.

That night she lay in one of the twin beds in Suzanne's bedroom and hardly slept for fear that the awful professor would come and find her again. She thought of asking Suzanne if her father did such nasty things to her too with his foul sausage thing, but thought better of it, in case Suzanne thought she was telling untruths. Katherine wondered if that was what fathers did with their daughters and felt sorry for Suzanne as it was a very horrid and terrifying experience. She also, for the first time, felt grateful that she did not have a father, if that was what daughters had to do with them. She decided that maybe she was wicked and a minx after all, and so had better not tell Elsie what had happened as she may be furious that her daughter had behaved badly as a guest in the home of a professor.

She also vowed never ever to eat a sausage in her life again.

Chapter 8
Cape Town Life

Elsie found it very difficult to not be able to acknowledge Katherine as her daughter in public and could not wait for the school holidays and some weekends, when they could go back to District Six for a Sunday lunch with Marie and Alfie.

One day, when they were walking together towards District Six, Katherine burst into tears for no particular reason. Elsie asked her what was wrong and was so torn at not being able to put her arms around her little girl to comfort her, as they were on a public street and could not be seen doing so for fear of the repercussions. In between sobs, Katherine said that she had to go to confession in church on Monday morning to confess her sins, but that she couldn't think she had committed any bad deeds. Elsie was furious and felt familiar anger surging through her in the same way it had when her parents argued about religion on St Helena, when she was a young girl. How could children possibly be accused of being bad and having to confess things that could not be *evil*? She was also angry that the penance would more than likely be to say 'Hail Mary' prayers. Trying to suppress her anger, she explained to Katherine that she believed that all children were good and that only the adults could be bad. It infuriated her that innocent children were being forced to confess their sins to a priest! Elsie suggested to Katherine that she say to the priest that she had not sinned, rather than make up some fictitious story as some of Katherine's friends had taken to doing. Katherine seemed to think that this was a good idea for the moment but was concerned that the priest may not always believe her in the future. They laughed at the situation and enjoyed their private little joke together.

Elsie battled to let her anger subside at the thought of children, and particularly her daughter, being forced to tell their inner most secrets to a stranger hiding in a dark confessional box. Surely the sacrament of Holy Communion should be delayed until the teenage years, when one could make a more informed decision about confession and the receiving of communion. Forcing small children to dress up like little brides and grooms to take their First Communion surely lost their focus, although this may have appeared angelic to their parents. Elsie doubted that many children even understood or appreciated the event. Was the Catholic Church not just netting them before they got away? And, if they did stray, their Catholic guilt would haunt them for doing so?

Then again, Elsie did respect the values and opportunities that the Catholic Church had given her – and Katherine by association – but she struggled and questioned some of the teachings and rules.

She would never know the real reason for her daughter's anxiety about going to confession. Katherine was deeply troubled by the memories of what she had been forced to do to Suzanne's father and they still made her feel ill, and bizarrely sometimes guilty. She was still confused as it felt more like the professor had been the bad person rather than her, so she therefore decided there would be no need to confess this to anyone. The disturbing memories of the horrid smell and actions of Suzanne's father haunted her at unexpected times.

Suzanne and Katherine remained good friends, but

Katherine never disclosed to her friend what had happened in her father's study on her tenth birthday and never accepted any further invitations to visit Suzanne's home.

When the girls were sixteen, Suzanne suddenly left the school and Katherine was surprised and a little hurt that she had not said anything to her about leaving. A few months later, Katherine received a letter from Suzanne that had been posted in Kimberley, a town many miles away in the centre of South Africa where there was a very big, open-cast diamond mine. Suzanne explained that she was with child and that her parents had sent her there to stay in a convent with the nuns and that her baby would be taken away and given up for adoption. Suzanne said that it was a very serious secret – that she was afraid and that her parents would disown her if they knew she had written to Katherine explaining her sudden disappearance and plight.

Katherine wrote back to the convent in Kimberley and replied to Suzanne that she hoped that they would always be friends and to please make contact if she ever came back to Cape Town, but she never did.

Katherine was an exceptional student and worked extremely hard, particularly after Suzanne left as she missed her friendship and was not as close to any of the other girls.

Elsie kept reminding Katherine of her opportunities and encouraged her to do her very best in all her school activities. She took up piano lessons and sang in the school choir, and acted in many of the school plays.

Disaster hit Cape Town during the summer of 1918, with the arrival of two ships from Sierra Leone. The *Jaroslav* and *Veronej* docked in Cape Town harbour with sailors infected with Spanish Influenza, which caused a national epidemic amongst the citizens. Half a million people died in South

Africa and most of them were from the Cape area. The railway line from Cape Town to Johannesburg simply served to spread the epidemic at an alarming rate, and the return of soldiers by ship from the Great War in Europe further exacerbated the crisis. Cape Town became a city of mourning and nothing else was talked of or thought about other than the influenza; 1918 became known as 'the year that God was angry'.

Before the outbreak took hold, Katherine's convent boarding school was immediately put into isolation in the hope that the nuns and the girls would not get infected. No day pupils could come to the school and deliveries were left at the front entrance. All the boarders at the convent had to wear garlic cloves threaded through with string around their necks, which was thought to prevent the spread of infection.

Sadly, Alfie, who was often down at the docks, was soon infected and died within days of getting the flu. Somehow, Marie did not get ill, even though she had nursed him. Funerals were forbidden so as not to spread the epidemic any further.

One of the most immediate consequences of this epidemic was the creation of many 'flu orphans' who were put up for adoption or placed in orphanages. Those who fell through both the familial and institutional nets were left to care for themselves as 'street children'. After Sister Brigid and Elsie had finished their teaching duties in the mornings, they started to make up large pots of soup to try to feed as many of these street children as possible. Sister Brigid even took to knocking on doors in the wealthier suburbs of Cape Town to get money, clothes and food to feed the street children who were badly affected, both emotionally and psychologically, by the death of one or both of their parents. For others, the decimation caused by the pandemic showed that their existing religion was not defence enough against evil, thus promoting a flurry of conversions to Christianity or Islam by traditional believers, or of reversions from Christianity and Islam back to traditional beliefs. Elsie quietly debated with herself why God would have brought such misery in the form of this flu she was again witnessing. She was beside herself worrying about Katherine in the boarding school and had to console herself that no news was good news. The memories of how both her parents had succumbed to a flu virus constantly haunted her during this time. She gave thanks that Marie and Katherine and most of the nuns seemed to be in good health. Bargaining with God for their survival, she spent many exhausting hours trying to feed and comfort the orphaned children, of which there were far too many to make much of a difference.

Another ugly result of the flu was the blame element that drove the apartheid divide. The Black people accused the Whites of bringing the flu to the country and the Whites argued that many of the Black and Coloured people lived in squalor and poorly sanitised conditions that caused the flu to rapidly spread. The epidemic eventually passed, but Cape Town continued to lick its wounds for many years to come, as most families had lost members and close friends.

Later that year, Elsie received a letter from Jane, who informed her that this time the flu had thankfully not come St Helena.

Chapter 9
1920

Two years later, Katherine had written her final matric exams at school and achieved excellent results. She had dreamt of studying to be a doctor, but she never mentioned this to Elsie as the university fees would have been way beyond her earning capacity. When Mother Superior asked Katherine what she planned to do with her life, she mentioned her dream of becoming a doctor, but that she also realised that tuition fees would be more than her mother could afford. They discussed the matter at length and decided that Katherine could train as a nurse and see where that led, and whether the medical world really was her calling. Mother Superior did point out that it was almost unheard of for a woman to become a medical doctor, but that she would make enquiries about availability for training to be a nurse at a hospital in Cape Town, or even the possibility of some voluntary work to gain nursing experience.

Katherine and Elsie went back to District Six to spend that Christmas and New Year with Marie, who was still desperately saddened at the sudden death of her beloved Alfie. They all missed his generous nature and gentle presence.

True to her word, early in the new year of 1921, Mother Superior sent a letter asking Katherine and Elsie to visit her at the convent so that they could discuss Katherine's future.

What both Elsie and Katherine were still unaware of was

that Luke Viljoen stayed in contact with Mother Superior on a regular basis and had insisted that copies of Katherine's school reports be sent to him. This was the condition he had set down for the anonymous financial support towards Katherine's welfare and education.

Luke had advised Mother Superior that he would like to continue to support Katherine anonymously with the costs of her tuition fees and he had arranged for a bursary fund to be set up at University of Cape Town in the form of a scholarship for talented and deserving women students. The condition was that Katherine would be the first recipient of the scholarship. Again, he made Mother Superior promise not to reveal the source of this funding, but to make the arrangements for Katherine to start her studies and attend the necessary interviews prior to acceptance at the medical school at Somerset Hospital, which served to train doctors studying medical practice at the University of Cape Town. The new Somerset Hospital was the first centre for teaching of clinical medicine in South Africa.

On arriving at the convent to meet Mother Superior and waiting in the entrance hall for their appointment, Elsie was reminded of how nervous she was on her first interview at the convent when she got her cleaning job. How things had moved on with her relationship with the nuns, who had been continuously supportive towards both her and Katherine! How proud she was of her beautiful, blonde and confident daughter sitting beside her! The statue of the Virgin Mary still stood in the same spot, flanked by doors either side. This time the vase had a beautiful arrangement of protea flowers standing at its base.

Katherine appeared to be a little anxious and Elsie took her hand saying, "I am so very proud of you, my child. You could not be more loved."

Both Elsie and Katherine believed that Mother Superior may have been able to organise some nursing experience for Katherine and were looking forward to hearing the details, but what she had to tell them was beyond their dreams and expectations.

Mother Superior was obviously pleased to see them and enquired after Marie and how she was managing her grieving for Alfie. She said how everyone at the convent also missed him and his kindness.

Pausing and taking time to choose her words carefully, Mother Superior said, "I have made some enquiries at the hospital and the university regarding your future training and studies, Katherine." Taking a deep breath, she continued, "There appears to be a new bursary set up for promising female medical students and there is a possibility that you may qualify for this."

Elsie and Katherine were amazed and a little shocked. Katherine was grinning from ear to ear and eagerly asked, "What do I need to do to secure this bursary, Mother?"

Elsie felt the need to touch her arm, saying, "Let's hear more about it, my child. This seems almost too good to be true."

Mother Superior advised that Katherine was to attend an interview with the Clinical Professor of Medicine at Somerset Hospital in Cape Town. The hospital had, in the past few years, served to train doctors studying medical practice and, in fact, had only very recently started accepting women.

"Who is the donor of the bursary?" asked Katherine and Mother Superior looked down at her hands.

She quietly replied, "I am not at liberty to reveal that, but sometimes people like to do good deeds anonymously, which one should graciously accept."

Katherine was too excited to question her about the bursary any further and continued to ask numerous other questions.

"Would there be accommodation available for me during my studies? What am I to wear? How will I be able to afford the books?"

Mother Superior assured her that it was a full bursary that would take care of all her needs. This really was a marvellous opportunity, but she would first need to meet with the clinical professor the following week in order to be accepted on his recommendation. Elsie was as shocked and thrilled as Katherine was with this news, as she knew she could never have afforded the fees and living expenses for Katherine boarding away from home. She still loved teaching and working at the little school in District Six and knew how important her role was to the children. The soup kitchen was still very much in demand and was often the only meal some of the children got each day. She and Sister Brigid had managed to secure some regular donations of vegetables from some of the local farmers and sometimes they even put in crates of fruit for the children.

It was still school holiday time and Elsie was glad of some time off as she needed to take Katherine shopping for something smart to wear for her interview. She had some money saved for a rainy day but never thought she would be spending her savings on getting her daughter ready for an interview which would allow her to study to become a doctor. Her heart swelled with pride, and she could not stop smiling. Katherine felt confident but reminded her mother that she did not have an acceptance… yet.

The very next day, Elsie and Katherine went into the city,

ambling along a few paces apart as it was not done to be seen walking together: a Coloured person and a White person. They walked down Adderley Street and came to a very nice shop with the mannequins in the window displaying the latest fashion straight from London. Katherine and Elsie admired the elegant designs of drop-waist dresses, loosely fitted trousers for women and flowing silk blouses. Of particular fancy were the fine knitted fabrics that looked wonderful in skirts and cardigans. Elsie and Katherine admired a light grey knitted suit and thought that would look perfect for the interview. Katherine entered the shop alone to try on the suit, whilst Elsie waited outside. The shop assistant suggested Katherine try on a light grey cloche hat and some two-toned Oxford pumps. On a whim, Katherine decided to take the complete outfit. She also made up her mind that the next step would be to cut her hair into short blonde bob like the mannequins' wigs in the shop window. Elsie was horrified at the idea of Katherine cutting off her long blonde hair but was aware that she was now eighteen and wanting to enter the grown-up world with her own personal image and style.

The following week, Katherine made her way by tram into the city and changed trams towards the hospital for her interview. She was sporting her new outfit and had her blonde hair cut into a short bob. She had grown tall and slim and looked very elegant, certainly much older than her mere eighteen years. Her school certificates and a notebook were tucked safely in her bag. On arriving at Somerset Hospital on Beach Road in Green Point, she thought her legs may collapse with sheer nerves as she walked towards the entrance of the hospital and announced to the receptionist that she was here for an interview with the professor. Katherine became aware of some of the admiring looks she was getting. She suddenly thought that she had overdressed for the interview and maybe she should have come in her old school uniform, but it was too late as she was called to follow the professor's secretary to his office. Katherine was shown into a very large room that smelled of furniture polish and disinfectant. It had a lovely view looking towards the beach and she thought how sensible it was to position a hospital next to the seaside, where convalescing patients could take in some sea air.

Soon the door opened and the professor entered. He was a kindly looking man in a white coat with frameless spectacles and a shock of steel grey hair that almost matched the suit Katherine was wearing. Around his neck hung a stethoscope. Katherine jumped to her feet and extended her hand to greet the professor.

"Good morning, Professor, sir. I am Katherine Georgina Viljoen."

"Good morning, Miss Viljoen. I am Professor Barker." He smiled at this confident young lady, who he knew was more than likely quaking inside and desperate to make a good impression. He continued, "Mother Superior tells me that you were one of the best and most hard-working pupils at the convent and that you are interested in studying to be a medical doctor." Looking out of the window, he took a very long pause and Katherine wondered if he had forgotten she was there.

"You are no doubt aware," he said very slowly, "that this is a somewhat unusual career choice for a young lady. You may be better suited to becoming a nurse?"

Katherine's heart sank, but she quickly composed herself and replied, "Professor, sir, I know I can achieve more than being a nurse which is, of course, a most noble career. Here, please look at my final matric schooling results," and with that she handed the certificates across to the frowning professor.

He took a while to study them very carefully and replied, "Miss Viljoen, I cannot fault these results, as you certainly seem intelligent enough, but becoming a medical doctor takes passion and dedication. Tell me why you think you deserve a place to study here?"

Katherine took a moment and then, from her heart answered in a clear and determined voice, "Professor, sir, I believe that there can be no greater personal joy and satisfaction than to use one's knowledge to nurse a very sick person back to health. And…" she smiled, and sheepishly said, "to wear a stethoscope around one's neck." The last comment made the professor laugh heartily and reply that he had not heard that answer before. He did, however, admire her ability to be lighthearted in a rather serious situation, which she may well need if she was going to train in the medical world.

The professor continued to explain to Katherine that this would be a path of many years of sacrifice and a career that imposed marriage bars on women, as it needed total dedication. He cleared his throat and said, "Miss Viljoen, what I am trying to say is that celibacy is recommended."

Katherine was a little shocked at his bluntness and thought that was an unnecessary price to have to pay for her chosen profession. She replied, "I have no intention of marrying, Professor, sir." What she did not say was that the reason she had no intention of marrying was that she did not want to take the risk of her children inheriting her mixed-blood and the price that such innocent children would have to pay for all of their lives. Katherine knew that she had somehow escaped her mother's darker skin colour and always assumed that she must look more like her late father and grandfather. She still debated whether this was a blessing or not as, in her heart, she was neither one nor the other. It pained her that she could not be

117

openly proud of her mother and St Helenian heritage.

The professor said that, in that case he would give her a trial for six months or so and see how she managed with the tough schedule and studies. They agreed that Katherine would study general medicine, minor surgery, obstetrics and gynaecology. There was a women's residence in the form of a boarding house near the hospital and arrangements would be made for her to stay there. The landlady would inform her of the very strict rules she would need to adhere to, such as no social visitors. She would have access to the medical library and a pass would be arranged for her entry. The professor said that classes would commence in the middle of January and that she should be in residence two days before to settle and be ready to start her studies immediately. He opened his drawer and gave her a list of the medical books she would need and the stationery requirements.

Katherine began to realise that he was giving her a chance to prove herself. At the end of the interview, she said that she would work as hard as she possibly could. The professor replied that she really did need to prove her worth and dedication. He rang a bell on his desk to call in his secretary and asked her to take care of Katherine's registration and brief her fully on what she was required to do in the next few weeks in order to prepare herself to start her studies.

The professor's secretary looked very stern, but she turned out to be very motherly. She informed Katherine that she was one of the first women to start medical studies at Somerset Hospital and mentioned how envious she was as she too would have loved to have had such an opportunity. She told Katherine that she had been informed that, due to the bursary she had been awarded, all accounts for books, residential fees and equipment should come to her for processing and payment. She opened her desk drawer and handed Katherine an envelope, saying, "This is your pocket money for incidental expenses, which you can collect from me at the beginning of every month."

Katherine stammered saying, "How…?"

The secretary merely smiled and said, "I believe you to be a blessed young lady."

Katherine left the hospital with her lists of things to do and to buy. She peeped in the envelope whilst on the tram going back to Elsie and Marie and there were five one-pound Bank of England notes inside. Who was this most generous and anonymous sponsor?

Chapter 10
Starting at University

At the top of Katherine's list of textbooks to collect from the bookshop was '*Gray's Anatomy – 21st Edition.*' This thrilled her to her core and she decided that she would try to read it from cover to cover prior to starting her studies, as that would surely give her a head start.

The next few days were a whirlwind with Marie and Elsie barely able to contain their pride and delight at Katherine's having the opportunity to study, and hopefully one day becoming a medical doctor. Katherine wrote a long letter to Mother Superior thanking her for all her support and for believing in her ability. She promised to visit between semesters and to keep her posted on the progress of her studies and experiences.

There was another visit to the city to pick up more stationery, books and clothes. Katherine could not resist a pair of the loose-fitting long trousers in navy gabardine and a blue silk blouse to match her eyes. Purchasing the books on her list was **the** most exciting moment. Both Marie and Elsie had come along, although purposefully lagging behind and waiting outside the shops for Katherine and carrying her parcels. They laughed at the ridiculous situation that they were having to act out, but secretly quite enjoyed the conspiratorial nature of this shopping spree for Katherine. No one would have guessed that they were a unit of mother, godmother and Katherine, as they gave the outward impression that they were not together. An outsider would have assumed that Katherine was shopping and had brought along her maids to carry her parcels. How they would have loved to have gone into one of the cafes or hotels for a nice cup of tea and a slice of cake, but that would never have been acceptable in the Cape Town City that was becoming ever more segregated by the day. They were even forced to use separate public conveniences for White and Black people and, when they rested their weary feet in the park, it had to be on separate benches. This did not dampen their spirits one bit and in fact made them enjoy the moment even more because, in a way, they were defying the system and unfounded prejudices held by many white Capetonians.

Katherine went alone to meet the lady who ran the boarding house to which she had been allocated and to view her room and facilities. It was so difficult to leave Elsie out of this, but they agreed it was for the best. The boarding house was only about a ten-minute walk from the hospital and looked a very neat building with a well-maintained garden. There were steps leading up to the front door, with a veranda either side where a few tables and chairs with checked, red and white cushions were neatly arranged. The house was on a quiet street, which seemed ideal to Katherine. She knocked on the front door and a very stern-looking lady immediately answered.

"Ah, you must be Katherine Viljoen. Ja?" said the lady in a very strong, Dutch accent.

"Good day, ma'am. Yes, I am Katherine."

"Come in, come in. Please take off your shoes as this is a spotlessly clean house and I don't want my highly polished wooden floors getting dirty or damaged."

Katherine quickly removed her shoes before entering the

house, which truly was quite spotless. The landlady introduced herself as the widow Smit and said Katherine was to call her 'Ma Smit'. She led Katherine down the passage to her room, which faced the back garden of the house. Looking out of the window, Katherine saw a neat vegetable garden and a shed in the far corner. The room was airy and had a single brass bedstead covered with a pretty patchwork quilt. There was a washbasin in the corner with a tap for cold water. In the opposite corner, next to the window, was a narrow oak desk and chair with a matching bookcase. Neatly folded over the back of the chair was a multi-coloured, crocheted knee-blanket that would be helpful when studying on chilly days. There was also a chest of drawers with a freestanding mirror atop and an oak wardrobe beside. On the wooden floor lay an aged Persian rug that had been woven with the most beautiful colours and still displayed its exquisite design under a layer of faded pile. Katherine was delighted as she could not have imagined anywhere more perfect to study and rest. There was a wonderful calm atmosphere and she immediately felt at home.

Ma Smit showed her the bathroom and informed her that there were three other young ladies also accommodated at the boarding house and they would need to work out a roster between them for bathroom usage. She told Katherine that no more than three inches of water was allowed when she took a bath. There was a dining room where breakfast and dinner would be served. A packed lunch would be left on the table at the front door each weekday morning, and dinner would be served at six o'clock and not a minute after. There were no visitors allowed, other than immediate family, and they could be entertained on the veranda but not too often. On the weekends, they would need to make their own arrangements for lunch as most girls visited their families.

Katherine hoped the other girls would be good company as she would be taking most of her meals with them and sharing a bathroom. She had never had her own bedroom before as she had always shared with her mother at home and had been in a dormitory with other girls whilst at the convent.

A few days later, when Katherine returned in a taxicab with her books and clothes, she met the other residents who seemed friendly and nice. One of the girls was a medical secretary at the hospital and the other two were second year medical students which pleased Katherine as she hoped they may be able to give her some advice. They took Katherine under their wings, walking to the hospital together most mornings and making suggestions about how to take notes and what they believed was the correct way to do so.

On the first morning of lectures, Katherine was very excited but soon began to realise that, although she had been one of the brightest and cleverest students at school, here at medical school, everyone seemed considerably more intelligent. The other students all seemed quicker at understanding the subject matter than she was. Some days the lectures were so long and complicated that she doubted her brain would be able to absorb anymore medical knowledge or challenges. There was endless theory to read and learn about, but what Katherine enjoyed most of all was when they accompanied a qualified doctor or surgeon on the ward rounds. This was when she got to meet the patients and discuss specific medical cases, rather than learning out of books and in lectures. Katherine found in herself a morbid fascination for all things that would turn most people's stomachs, whether it be skin diseases or assisting with an amputation.

Women were certainly in the minority as trainee doctors and some patients were adamant in declining to have a trainee woman doctor attend to them. Katherine refused to get upset by this and simply pitied them in their silly prejudices, as she had observed this frequently over the years, albeit skin-colour related.

Ma Smit had had a telephone installed in the boarding house for the girls to use, but not too often and they had to speak quietly so that no one else could hear their conversations. The telephone was a central battery type and stood proudly in the entrance hall of the boarding house with the ear and mouthpiece elegantly cradled above the black and white dial. Next to the phone was a little box for the girls to deposit coins into for every call to pay for the telephone bill. Katherine had used some of her pocket money to have similar phones installed in both Elsie's cottage in the school grounds, as well as Marie's home in District Six. She knew that neither Elsie nor Marie could ever visit her at the boarding house and so justified the expense of the telephones as her way of staying in touch with her mother and godmother. She made a point of phoning them on the weekends as she only went home to visit during the holidays. The work and the hours of study were long and tiring and, even on the weekends, she needed to study and prepare assignments for her lecturers to mark.

As the six months' probation period drew closer, Katherine began to wonder when the professor would call her in and tell her to leave or continue her studies. The subjects were all so fascinating and she could not have been more interested and keener. However, her results from her submitted work continued to be below the average requirements.

One day when she went to hand in her monthly boarding house bill and collect her pocket money from the professor's secretary, she was told to wait as the professor wanted a word with her. Katherine waited in the secretary's office feeling quite ill as she mentally played through her anticipated conversation with him.

What if she had not made the grade?

How would she explain this to Elsie and Marie?

What would she do with her life if she failed as a medical student?

Could she bear the shame?

After about half an hour of pure torment, Katherine was eventually summoned into the professor's office. He greeted her in a friendly manner and asked her to please sit. Katherine remembered how confident and invincible she had felt the last time she was in this office, compared to this time where, had she not been asked to sit by the professor, she may well have fainted.

The professor made some small talk about the strong winds Cape Town was experiencing. He also asked if the boarding house was suitable. Katherine replied with little thought to her answers as all she could focus on was whether she was to remain as a medical student and continue her studies under the tutorship of the professor and his fellow professors at the hospital or not. At last, he moved on to the subject of Katherine's results to date and the quality of her work. He said that he felt she was very enthusiastic and reasonably responsible in the hands-on situations, and went on to explain that he thought her patient care and empathy to be very good. It had come to his notice that the quality of the written work that she had submitted to her tutors for marking was not quite what he was expecting from her. Katherine's heart sank and she felt her throat constricting so tightly that she was unable to breath.

The professor took a long pause as he looked out the window in contemplation. He continued to speak slowly, saying that he was not sure that Katherine would be able to cope with the syllabus, as it would only get more involved and difficult with time. The studies would become even more intense and detailed the further into the course she would get. For the very first time, Katherine began to question if she was not clever enough, as she certainly felt that she had given her all in the past six months.

Katherine was about to apologise and leave the room and her studies behind her. But then she envisaged the disappointment on her beloved mother's face if she left medical school, and this made her resolve **not** to give up. And so, she replied to the professor,

"Professor, sir... I have worked extremely hard these past six months and I know I am meant to be a doctor. I really am fascinated by and do so love my studies. Therefore, I beseech you to give me until the end of the year to prove myself. I feel I must do this, as I have such a passion and a calling to help heal sick and poorly folk. Please, Professor, sir?"

The professor's brow furrowed, and he slowly paged through a file lying on his desk with Katherine's name written on the outside.

"I cannot fault your enthusiasm, Miss Viljoen, but your attention to detail needs to be improved. May I suggest that you speak to some of the students further advanced in their studies for some pointers? You have until the end of this year," he advised. "Good luck and good day to you."

Katherine quickly rose and left the office, not sure whether to be relieved or terrified at the prospect of even longer hours of study and research. She would ask some of the older medical students for their advice when she got the opportunity. She had no lectures for the rest of the day and so headed for the medical library to do some studying. Perhaps she could find a book on how to study more efficiently?

The library was almost deserted, other than two male medical students sitting at the far end under the windows. They were obviously working on a project together and quietly whispering to each other whilst making notes.

Katherine asked the librarian to assist her with books on efficient studying techniques and note making, and the librarian brought her a couple of related books. She stared at the volumes before her and willed the knowledge to enter her brain. The professor's words that her attention to detail needed to be improved kept replaying in her subconscious mind. She truly had no idea how to start to train her brain to store the details more efficiently. She was feeling so frustrated and overwhelmed that tears started to roll down her cheeks and she quietly began to cry. Whilst mopping her eyes with her hanky, she had not noticed that one of the male students had walked across to her and, when she glanced up, he was standing opposite her desk.

"You are obviously not happy? Hello, I am Michael, Michael Clavering, and you are, I believe, a first-year med student?"

Katherine felt so embarrassed that she had been caught crying in public that she felt herself blush uncontrollably. She tried to smile and introduced herself saying, "Yes, I am a very frustrated first-year student, and my name is Katherine Viljoen." With that she laughed at her silly behaviour and took a closer look at the pleasant-looking young man standing opposite her.

"What's upsetting you, Miss Viljoen? If I may ask?"

"I have just had a review with Professor Barker, and he has given me until the end of this year to improve the quality of the work I am submitting. He says my attention to detail is lacking. I am rather angry with myself, Mr Clavering, as I was a top student at school and now it seems I am unable to submit work up to the required standard," she explained in an exasperated voice.

"Oh, I see," replied the young Michael Clavering. "My friend and I are currently working to a tight deadline, so I don't have sufficient time to assist you right now. But if you like, I can meet you here on Saturday afternoon and give you some suggestions on how to study more efficiently and offer you a few pointers on how to submit your projects, encompassing more detail as required by the professors here. I too needed a little assistance a few years ago and was helped at the time by a more advanced med student and his advice has proved invaluable."

"Why, thank you, Mr Clavering," she quietly replied, blushing and embarrassed, as this young man seemed to immediately grasp her problem, plus the fact that he was also rather good looking.

"Great. See you here on Saturday afternoon then? Good day, Miss Viljoen," and with that he returned to his friend at the far end of the library to continue working.

Katherine felt rather foolish for letting herself become overwhelmed in public but, as a consequence, she had somehow managed, sooner than she thought, to secure the help she so badly needed and without even asking. She continued to try to study, making notes from the textbooks before her, but at the same time could not resist the odd sly glance across to where Mr Clavering was sitting. He was a handsome young man, she thought, with thick, dark curly hair, rather high cheekbones and a pronounced Roman nose. She guessed that he was probably about the same height as herself, which was tall for a girl.

Saturday afternoon soon arrived, and she thought carefully about what she would wear. She chose her navy-blue gabardine trousers, the blue silk blouse that matched her eyes perfectly, and draped her navy cardigan across her shoulders. The wind was blowing a gale, so she popped her grey cloche hat on top of her very blonde bobbed haircut and set off for the library.

She was due to hand in work on the forthcoming Monday and had almost finished her current assignment on tonsillectomy procedures and possible complications. She took along this project for Mr Clavering to get a measure of the quality of her work, although feeling uneasy that she was undoubtedly exposing the level of her competence to a virtual stranger, which again made her quite anxious. What if he thought she was totally stupid? Whilst waiting in the library for him she continued to make amendments in the margins of her written work.

When Mr Clavering arrived, he was dressed in cricket sportswear and apologised to her for being later than he planned and explained that the practice went on a little longer than he had thought it might. He looked most distinguished in his cream, loose fitting trousers and cream cable-patterned, sleeveless pullover. He removed a sporting cap when he entered the library and laid it on the desk next to Katherine's cloche hat.

Katherine explained the details of the work she was to submit to the professor on Monday and showed Mr Clavering her attempt. He started reading it through and said, "Ah, I see some areas where I believe you could improve on the presentation. May I make some suggestions, Miss Viljoen?"

"Oh, yes please, if you would be so kind. I really would welcome your suggestions."

Mr Clavering spent about an hour or so going through her prepared work and making suggestions like: a diagram would be helpful here, more detail in this section, and indicating elsewhere that perhaps Katherine should not assume that the professor knows what she thinks is obvious. Katherine found the session extremely helpful, and it was a revelation to be shown alternative ways to present her work. She planned to rework the project the next morning in time to submit it on Monday before her lectures.

She was so grateful to Mr Clavering that she impulsively offered to buy him a cup of tea at the beachfront tearoom. He seemed a little surprised at Katherine's suggestion, but readily accepted. As they left the library, he asked that Katherine call him Michael, to which she eagerly replied, "If you call me Katherine." They both laughed nervously and headed towards the tearoom. Their conversation was soon very relaxed and comfortable, and they spoke at length about their respective school days. He mentioned that his family had vineyards in the Cape Town area that yielded some delicious wine. Katherine avoided talking of her family, which he appeared not to notice or was too polite to question. They laughed easily together, even at the expense of some of the professors. On parting, Michael suggested that they meet again the following Saturday afternoon to help her with her next project. He also insisted on paying for their afternoon tea.

Michael's guidance and pointers on how best to study and present her work were immeasurably helpful and she found herself immediately more comfortable and confident in her studies. At school, where the volume of work and study had been so much less, she was able to manage with little or no advice or training on how to study. This transition to medical school was a huge step up and an undertaking that she had not been prepared. She was so grateful for Michael's help and really looked forward to their next meeting.

The next Saturday, Katherine again took great care with her appearance and went as far as applying a little lipstick that she had bought at the local pharmacy with her precious pocket money.

Michael commented that he was impressed with the improvement in the presentation of her work and made fewer suggestions this time. They continued to meet every week in the library on a Saturday afternoon, but Michael now mostly did his own studying and only assisted Katherine when she asked for his advice. Their regular Saturday afternoon tea became something of a tradition and they both looked forward to sharing the news of their respective past weeks. Sometimes they saw each other at the hospital and always stopped for a quick chat. They did receive some curious glances from their fellow students though, as Michael was some three years ahead of Katherine in his training and she was by far the prettiest female student out of all the undergraduates.

By the end of the year, Katherine was feeling more comfortable with her studies and her surroundings. The professor called her in again for a further assessment of her progress and reported that there certainly had been a marked improvement in her work and its presentation. He happily confirmed that she could continue her studies into the second year. Katherine could have jumped for joy and, on leaving his office, she could not help dancing a happy little jig in the corridor outside.

It was the end of the semester and, with Christmas fast approaching, Elsie and Katherine joined Marie at her neat little home for the festive season. Marie was less saddened by this year's festivities, but they all still missed Alfie, particularly around the table during meal times.

Katherine had taken a walk up on to the slopes of Table Mountain and returned with a small spruce tree that they decorated with red ribbons bought from the haberdasher in the high street. She had seen decorated Christmas trees in the windows of the shops in Adderley Street and thought what a lovely idea it would be to brighten their Christmas with Marie. With her pocket money, she had bought Elsie two beautiful tortoiseshell combs for her hair and a silk headscarf for Marie.

During the Christmas holiday, Katherine raised the question with Elsie and Marie about whether they had any idea of the identity of the anonymous bursary donor who was supporting her medical studies. Neither of them was able to shed any light on whom it could be. Elsie suggested that Katherine should respect the anonymity of this person or institution, as they clearly had reasons for discretion. This set Katherine thinking that she may try to investigate further about whom her benefactor could be. She felt that the least she could do would be to write a letter of appreciation.

It was a happy and relaxed festive season and the three of them sat most evenings on the balcony of the little house, enjoying the cool breeze and watching the activities in the street below them. There were so many different nationalities living in District Six: the orthodox Jewish folk who would always greet them with 'Shalom' when passing on their way to and from their synagogue, the local street children who often called in for a slice of bread from Marie, and the Indian neighbours who regularly sent in some delicious samosas as a gift. One could often hear someone singing or the strumming of a banjo. District Six was a happy and vibrant place in which to live, and Katherine loved the fact she was accepted there, despite the pale colour of her skin. Most of the neighbours had already started calling her Doctor Katherine and sometimes came to Katherine for advice about their various ailments.

Elsie continued to teach the Coloured children and reside in her tiny cottage in the school grounds. She visited Marie for Sunday lunch on most weekends after they had attended Sunday mass together. They were almost like mother and daughter, Elsie being the daughter Marie never had and Marie a motherly figure to Elsie. Often, they would reminisce about the day Alfie had brought Elsie and baby Katherine home with him and how lucky they were to have become a family.

Elsie recalled her days as a young girl on St Helena and wondered if much had changed there. Mostly, her thoughts were of the little school that she had managed to get rebuilt and she wondered how some of her pupils had fared in life. She fondly remembered the times when she and Luke had secretly met, and the thrill they had found in each other when they were both so young. She did so miss walking along the scenic paths of St Helena, although she also loved Cape Town and the looming Table Mountain that seemed to rule the city and define its mood. However, she sometimes longed for fewer people around her. Living on St Helena had come with hardly any class distinction and certainly the colour of one's skin bore no relevance to their everyday lives. As much as she loved Cape Town, she also missed the friendly and non-judgemental attitude of the locals of St Helena: her 'Saints'.

Elsie was immensely proud of Katherine and loved their weekly phone calls when Katherine would tell her some of what she had learnt about during the previous week. Elsie would sometimes ask one of the nuns to get a medical book out of the library for her so that she could also learn and understand what Katherine was studying. Due to the colour of Elsie's skin, she was forbidden to borrow books from the city's library, and that was the reason the nuns very kindly borrowed books in their names for her. This colour divide was, at times, still a little painful for Elsie but she counted herself fortunate that she was at least able to overcome some of the obstacles because of her close association and friendship with the nuns.

Katherine continued to thrive and enjoy her studies and, although she was never again the top student amongst her peers as she was during her school days, she got by well enough and believed she would be a good doctor one day, perhaps specialising in obstetrics and minor surgery.

She and Michael continued their tradition of meeting for Saturday afternoon tea after their studies and, one Easter holiday, he invited her to come and meet his family. Katherine immediately said she was unable to join him as she had commitments. Her fear was that once she had met Michael's family, he would expect to meet her family. How could she ever explain that her mother was of mixed-race? Michael had seemed disappointed but respected her reply without question.

The time eventually came for Michael to graduate, and he invited both Katherine and his parents along to the ceremony, forcing them to meet each other for the first time. Michael's parents were delighted to meet Katherine as clearly, they had heard a lot about her. They surreptitiously asked about Katherine's family, and she managed to refrain from going into much detail, telling them briefly that her mother was a school teacher and that her father had died before she was born. This seemed to make them a little uncomfortable and they quickly changed the subject, which suited Katherine. She always found it strange that, whilst death is what happens to all of us, most people found it incredibly difficult to discuss the subject until the event was upon them.

Michael had been fortunate enough to secure a position to

further his studies at Oxford University and would be heading to England the next year. He had been accepted to specialise in orthopaedics. He made Katherine promise to write to him regularly as he would be away for some three years, which would coincide with the time when she would hopefully be graduating as a medical doctor herself.

Katherine was terribly sad to see him go but, in a way, his departure made it easier for her as she had not got around to explaining to him why she was unable to ever get romantically involved with him. She believed that she could never tell him about the complicated reasons for her chosen celibacy and, because of this, almost felt thankful to the medical fraternity for preferring woman doctors not to get married.

The day Michael left, they arranged to meet down at the harbour to say farewell. Katherine looked particularly lovely that day in her pale lilac, floral, drop waist dress and a matching lilac hat that she had bought especially for the occasion. On her way to the harbour, she had passed a heather bush and picked a sprig which she tucked into the band of her hat. Before Michael made his way up the gangplank, he took her aside and gave her a little box, which Katherine immediately opened to find a beautiful gold watch, the likes of which she had never seen before. It had a small delicate face set into a solid gold bracelet and looked extremely modern and elegant. Katherine was somewhat overwhelmed by the generosity of the gift and slightly embarrassed at the realisation that she had nothing for Michael, other than her promise to write. She took the sprig of heather from her hatband and threaded it into the lapel buttonhole of his jacket. He hugged her at length before he finally made his way quickly up the gangplank. At the top, he turned to wave and looked dapper in his perfectly tailored suit and fedora hat. She realised how much she was going to miss him, more than she should be allowing herself. Suddenly, she was so overcome with emotion that she began to cry. She dabbed her eyes with her hanky and waved it in the air so that Michael would see her and hoped he had not noticed her tears. When the Union-Castle boat left its mooring and set sail out of Cape Town harbour, Katherine felt a huge vacuum tugging inside her. She was already missing his friendship more than she had anticipated.

Whenever she looked at the time on the elegant watch, he had given her, she felt a little pang of sadness that she may well never see him again. Oh yes, there was the promise of writing letters, but three years was an awful long time, and he was sure to meet someone else far more sophisticated in England.

Her Saturdays now seemed so empty, and the only way Katherine could fill them was to study even harder and spend more time at the hospital, volunteering in the children's ward which was always welcomed by the nurses. She mostly enjoyed reading to the children as her own mother had done for her.

Michael's first letter arrived about six weeks later. He must have posted it when the boat docked as the postage stamp was from Southampton.

PART III

Chapter 11
September 1902 – Luke

Luke walked down the road towards the wharf, escorted by the POW guards, after he had given Elsie the box containing the letter.

What *had* he done?

He should be a man and turn around and acknowledge his wife and child.

Should he have applied to stay on the island and live as a family with them?

What about his family back home?

Little Katherine was a beautiful blonde-haired and blue-eyed baby girl, who certainly had Luke's colouring and likeness already. He sighed to himself, knowing that it would be impossible to take a Coloured woman home as his wife, and he forced himself to keep walking, feeling like a yellow-bellied coward. At the time, he had decided that it was best that Katherine be told he had died before she was born, but he knew deep down that this would one day come back to haunt him. He would always wonder what she looked like and how she imagined her father to be. Would she ever think of him and wished he had lived?

Only when he was on board *The Tagues* did he look back. He caught sight of Elsie standing there with his child in her arms and had never hated himself more. At that moment, he made a promise to himself that he would continue to send them money whenever he could.

The voyage back to Cape Town was cramped and everyone was anxious because no one aboard knew for sure whether their families had survived the war or the camps. There had been reports of terrible incidents and conditions in the camps in South Africa where many women, elderly men and children had perished. Lord Kitchener's tactics were not so much through *direct* operations against the fighting Boer commandos, but rather *indirect*, by bringing the pressure of war against defenceless women and children. The British soldiers poisoned the wells, looted and burnt the Boer homes, livestock and crops, so that they were unable to support the Boer commandos. It was called the *'Scorched Earth Campaign'* and Luke hoped that somehow his mother and sisters had survived this.

He had spent many hours over the past couple of years remembering the Boer war, and how he and his late father had joined General Piet Cronje of the South African Military Forces in 1899. For many days, they had drunk only water and eaten 'biltong' (dried strips of meat). The guerrilla war had ended for Luke when General Cronje's men were defeated at Paardeberg on 27 February 1900, by Lord Roberts' British Forces. General Cronje, along with his wife Hester, Luke, and many others, had been captured and eventually sent to St Helena as prisoners of war. The city of Bloemfontein in the Orange Free State Republic had been taken at about the same time without a shot having been fired.

General Cronje had stayed under guard in the very comfortable Kent Cottage with his wife on St Helena, but he regularly visited his men in the POW camps. He was later seen as a sell-out by many and excluded from all peace negotiations by the other South African generals after the war.

There had been an illustration in the famous Punch

magazine circulating among the POWs which depicted a Boer general saluting the ghost of Napoleon and saying, 'Same enemy, Sire! Same result!'

When arriving back in Cape Town, most of the men were pleased to be back in their country, but also anxious as the political situation was still extremely complicated.

Luke spent the first few days at the war offices trying to find out what had happened to his family. Eventually, they were traced to a POW camp near Bloemfontein, where they had all died of various illnesses following severe malnutrition. A devastated Luke took himself to a local drinking spot and consumed more local brandy than he should have. He awoke outside the building the next morning, unaware of how he got there, but the reason he was in this state thundered in his head as he sat on the side of the street aching for everyone he had lost. He had failed to protect all the women in his life: his mother, his sisters and now his wife and baby daughter. All gone... forever!

He was constantly haunted by the memory and horror of hurriedly having to bury his father in a shallow grave during the Boer War. The statistics were emerging that nearly 28,000 Boer elderly men, women and children had perished in the camps. This number was four times as large as the number of Boer fighting men who died during the Anglo-Boer war. It appeared that more children under the age of sixteen had perished in the British camps than men were killed in action on both sides. One in five children did not survive these concentration camps. This news was shocking and devastating to the men returning from St Helena where they had been reasonably well treated, whilst their families had suffered the worst possible treatment. They felt guilt that their families had suffered so badly, and some wanted accountability and revenge.

Luke wondered what had happened to his family's farm, which he could hardly run on his own. He had no papers to even prove it was his, he thought, although the farmhouse had probably been burnt down like most others. There was no work in Cape Town and so he took the next train he could get a place on, towards Bloemfontein. He hoped to find out for himself what, if anything, was left of the family farm.

The train carriages moved the mostly depressed men back inland to see what they could retrieve of their lives prior to the war. There were no facilities to wash on the journey and the carriages were crammed full of sweating, unwashed and miserable ex-prisoners of war. Their mental pain was almost tangible. The few years they had been away at war and then prisoners on St Helena had left them feeling like strangers back in their own country. The train passed burned down farmhouses and a few, very thin, unhappy survivors along the track, with some even begging from the returning soldiers when they stopped along the way at the various sidings.

When Luke got to Bloemfontein, he went to see the authorities at the property deeds office to establish if he was able to claim back the farmlands that his family had owned prior to the Anglo-Boer War. One of the officials in the office vouched for Luke as they had attended Grey College School in Bloemfontein together and he knew the Viljoen family. Luke was advised that they would search for a copy of the deeds of the farm in the land records, to prove that the farm had belonged to the Viljoen family. Then it was time for Luke to ride out to visit the farm, or what remained of it. He borrowed a horse from another of his friends with whom he had also attended school, and set out on the three-hour ride to the family farm.

After a couple of hours in the saddle, he stopped next to the stream that ran towards the farmlands which belonged to his family. He sat quietly under a tree anticipating what he would find, whilst the horse grazed and drank from the stream.

He continued his journey and, on approaching the brow of the hill where he knew he would get the first glimpse of what remained of the farm, some small local Black children came running from their huts towards Luke.

"Young Master, welcome home," they shouted to him. Their little faces lit up to see him and their perfectly white teeth shone even brighter in the sunlight, contrasting with their deep chocolate brown skin.

Luke stopped to talk to them and asked how they were and how their families were. The delight on the children's faces at seeing Luke faded with his questions and all tried telling him at once how those 'other' men in uniforms had come and taken all the cattle and had burnt down the farmhouse. "Everything dead. Everything gone, baas. Also, the madams. Sorry, baas, so sorry. We happy you here now. Please help us?"

Luke now knew what was facing him when he went over the brow of the hill, and his first glance at the burnt-out shell of the farm house and cattle ranch made him cry out an involuntary, "No! No!"

He rode down the hill and on approaching the charred home saw that there really was nothing left, and that most of the furniture had been dragged outside and placed in a pile that had been set fire to as well.

On raising his eyes from the deliberate destruction before him, he noticed that there was a large herd of springbok grazing on what had once been their cattle pastures. They looked so graceful in their sleek coats of light brown with darker stripes along their flanks, snow white bellies and neat little horns. Their presence made him feel that somehow, he still belonged to this land. There was also a flock of blue cranes elegantly parading and pecking at the ground looking for seeds, roots and insects. The flat and endless lands had been scorched but, despite the deliberate and devastating destruction, it was still home. Luke felt a deep-seated connection and loyalty to this place. The green shoots had encouraged the birds and wild animals to return, as he had too.

He found some water in one of the troughs and let the horse drink while he examined the devastation of the homestead. There were the odd things left behind and he thought that one of the rooms that had not been too badly damaged would be habitable for a while, at least until he was able to start repairing and rebuilding. He felt the need to stay a while and think about what to do next. He was mourning deeply for all his family.

With the help of some of the children who had followed him, they cleaned up one room and found some pieces of furniture that were not too badly burnt and that he would be able to use. He had brought along some dried biltong that he shared with the expectant helpers. He walked down to the stream where he and his sisters used to swim and collected a couple of pails of water.

Luke took a long walk across the ranch and succumbed to his catharsis as he paced the family property, trying to come to terms with his losses.

Much later that night, he lit a fire to stave off the chill of the veld. Watching the flames lick at the wood always seemed to calm him down and he was able to think a little more clearly. He came to the conclusion that he would not allow his recent painful experiences and losses to be a liability to him, but rather a gift of strength to pick himself up and live life as his family would have expected of him.

Whilst sitting there he remembered that his mother used to have some old tobacco tins carefully hidden, in which she kept money from the sale of milk and cattle. He thought that she may well have taken these with her when they were forced to leave the farm. Luke went to check the places he remembered.

He looked behind the loose bricks under the steps at the back door. Using his belt buckle, he prised some of the bricks away and probed with his fingers until he found something hard buried in the sand. There was one of the tins he remembered with a considerable number of bank notes. His mother had gone to great lengths to ensure that the tin was not easily discovered.

Luke dug around at the front doorsteps searching for more tins, but to no avail. Then he remembered that, when he was a very young boy, his mother also used to keep a stash behind the old, outside bread oven, and discovered there were a further two smaller tins containing more bank notes. The last place he looked was at the back of the outhouse where, many years before, he had helped his mother bury a larger metal box containing documents that she said she was keeping safe from any fire. With the absence of any tools, he eagerly dug with his hands and rocks until he uncovered some kind of container. There it was… the box they had buried containing the original deeds of the farm: his parents' marriage licence, the birth certificates for him and his siblings and additionally, his father's death certificate which must have been delivered to his family whilst he was on St Helena. The metal box also contained an old cigar box wrapped in muslin, and this too contained some newer bank notes and a letter from his mother addressed to him.

Luke returned to the fire with his findings to read the letter from his late mother by the light of the flickering flames.

To my only son, Luke,

I write this as I believe the time is coming when we will be forced to leave our farm. I can only pray that you will have survived the perils of war and come to find this letter someday. Hopefully, you have found other things I left for you in the two places we both know.

The British have set up a concentration camp near Bloemfontein which they say is to keep us safe and feed us after they burn our farms. Your sisters and I will probably be taken there. I pray to our Lord that we will survive, as I believe the conditions are dire.

I heard you went to St Helena Island with General Cronje, who is now seen as a sell-out to the British. I hope that when you return to our homeland, you will not be tarred with the same brush!

Your father would have seen opportunities out of all this adversity, and I believe myself to be a conduit from him in heaven. I suggest that you use the money I am leaving you to buy some of the surrounding farms if you can... Try to buy as much land as you can and become the biggest cattle farmer in the Free State. Show them what you are made of, my son. Breed the herds up again and transport the cattle by train to the markets in Johannesburg. I believe they sell for a higher price there.

I pray that your sisters and I will return to our home one day and that we may be reunited to live as a family again.

I know you are a good man and will be a success. God Bless and keep you, my son.

With my love,
Ma

It was more than Luke could cope with as he thought about his strong and wise mother, who always put her children first. Even in the most dangerous and difficult times, she had been making plans to continue to support her beloved son. There was a deep need in him to hug his dear ma once more, but this was not to be.

With these words, his beloved mother had empowered him to believe in himself and also given him the means to move on to become a successful entrepreneur. He owed so much to her. She had given him perspective and meaning, and an opportunity to find his inner strength and purpose. He knew from reading his mother's letter that he had no option but to prove himself a success.

Luke looked up to the starry sky and felt uplifted by her strong presence.

"Thank you, Ma. I love and miss you… always," he said aloud.

The next few days, Luke continued to try to tidy the ruin of the farmhouse and make a list of what he would need to start again and to rebuild the farming business. Later he set off back to Bloemfontein to see if he could buy some of the surrounding farms from widows or despondent neighbours. He knew he could not run all the farms himself. However, should he be able to negotiate the purchases, he planned to lease them, either back to the original owners or to tenant farmers, thereby cashing in on a good percentage of the profits. He believed that he would be in a stronger position in the market when he and his tenant farmers had built up the cattle herds again, so he would have to find some good strong bulls and cows. His family had always bred the Nguni African breed as they were more suitable to the area, relatively long-lived and with a long calf-bearing life. He knew that they would thrive on low quality grazing and were mostly resistant to diseases and drought conditions. Luke loved their colourful patterns and mild manner. He had so many wonderful memories of times spent on the family farm managing the cattle with his father when he was alive.

When Luke returned to Bloemfontein, he met his friend in the deeds office who was able to give him details of where to contact some of his neighbours or their widows. News soon spread in the town that Luke was buying property and some landowners approached him as they had decided to try their luck working at the mines or wanted to move to bigger towns, where they hoped to get employment.

Luke's available cash had put him in a strong position, and he was even able to get a loan from the bank to purchase a couple of farms he had not even thought of. It was a very large gamble, but he had no family to consider, and the risk was entirely his. There was some gossip and questioning about how Luke had suddenly come into money. Others speculated that the family had left him something, although the Viljoens never appeared to have much money when they were all alive working on the family cattle farm. Local people were looking for hard cash so both land and cattle came his way easily and soon Luke was moving a small herd of cattle and a couple of bulls back to his farmlands.

Before he left Bloemfontein, Luke sent a letter to the reverend on St Helena enclosing some money for Elsie and Katherine and asking for some news of them by return to a postal box, where he would collect his mail upon returning to Bloemfontein for supplies from time to time.

A reply from the reverend did eventually arrive about a year later, informing him that Elsie and Katherine had moved to Cape Town and that Elsie was working at the Catholic Springfield Convent School. The reverend informed Luke that

148

he had given the money he had sent to Elsie before they had left the island. He also gave Luke the convent's address and details, and there was an air of expectation therein that Luke would honour his marriage and commitments to his wife and child. In the interim, the mother superior of the convent would, on receipt, manage any financial assistance Luke could provide towards their keep and Katherine's future education.

Although Luke's expenses and outlay on the farms had been great, he sent money whenever he could, requesting always that he remain anonymous.

Luke threw himself into working the lands and managing the herds. He kept to himself and saw very little of his neighbours other than for work reasons. He tried not to get involved in the local gossip and politics as he felt the scars from the Boer war and his losses remained just beneath the surface.

Within a few years, the cattle herds had grown at a tremendous rate and soon the farms were well established and profitable again. The tenant farmers were loyal and grateful to him for their homes and jobs.

Luke was not required to participate in the First World War, as farming was regarded as one of the essential services that had to continue to support the population and troops. Part of him was secretly grateful as many a night he had sat watching the flames around the fire, thinking what a dreadful waste of life war brought, where nobody seemed to ever be the winner. The cost was too great for any family to bear. He still experienced regular nightmares as a result of having had to shoot British soldiers and, whilst he had believed in the fight for independence from Britain, he sometimes found himself carrying overwhelming guilt for killing and injuring those men who may not have cared too much for the cause one way or the other. Luke had got to know some of these Englishmen as his English was very good, having attended a dual-medium school that had taught its pupils in both English and Afrikaans. He enjoyed the British sense of humour. It was only just over a decade since the Boer War where the British and Boers had been enemies and, bizarrely, now they were fighting as comrades in arms. How fickle the reasons for war – with the common citizen paying the biggest personal price for freedom.

He wondered, if he had not been exempted from the conscription during the First World War, whether he would have been able to cope emotionally with watching death and destruction surround him again. He doubted that he would have maintained his sanity but kept his thoughts to himself as he knew some people believed that he deserved a white feather, regardless of the fact that he was really playing his part in the conflict by supplying beef to the allies.

It was during 1918 that troops returned to South Africa from the First World War, bringing with them and spreading the deadly flu epidemic. Some 300,000 South Africans died within six weeks. Luke again wrote to Mother Superior at Springfield Convent to see if Elsie and Katherine had survived. It took many months to receive a reply to his letter as he stayed away from Bloemfontein to avoid infection. Finally, a letter arrived informing him that, through God's grace, they had both survived.

These were tough times indeed for the entire population that had already had so much to cope with following the Boer War, World War I and then the 1918 flu epidemic. One of Luke's immediate neighbouring tenant farmers died from the flu whilst on a visit into town and he left behind a wife and two teenage boys. Luke did his best to help them out as they had nowhere to go and no one else to turn to for help. The widow, Sophie, asked Luke if she could continue to try and run the farm and slaughterhouse with the help of her two sons after her husband's death, as otherwise they had no other form of income or anywhere to live. Luke agreed to give them a chance and quite regularly visited the farm to advise them regarding various farming issues. Sophie's two young sons were already quite skilled in farming habits and butchering, as they had been observing and learning from their late father. They were always pleased to see Luke when he visited and followed him about asking many questions, keen for him to share his cattle ranching knowledge with them.

Luke was as lonely as Sophie and found himself spending more and more time across at their farm, helping them and seeking out their company. They began to depend on him more and more whilst inviting him to join them for meals, and even Christmas dinner. Sophie often expressed her gratitude to Luke as she knew that most landlords would have sent her away and found another tenant farmer to step-in and manage the farm. However, she was a very capable and clever woman, who soon learnt the ropes of how to successfully run the cattle ranch. Luke enjoyed her company and the fact that they could talk about the management of the ranches and discuss ideas. Sophie was a very good cook, which Luke enjoyed and appreciated. He often brought extra supplies back for them on return from his town visits. They would sometimes read aloud to each other, alternating chapters of some of the classics they both enjoyed.

One could not say that Luke fell in love with Sophie, or she with him, but having been thrown together through circumstances, they became good friends and grew very fond of each other. They laughed and enjoyed picnics together and outings back into town with Sophie's sons.

Luke was now in his forties and, other than Elsie, had not had another meaningful relationship. His life since the Boer War had been difficult, and he carried the secret guilt of still being married to Elsie, plus having a daughter that he had only seen once as a baby.

One evening as they were sitting around the fire, Luke asked Sophie if she would ever think of marrying again and she replied, "Only to you, Luke."

Luke was astonished at this revelation and found himself embarrassed and in a somewhat awkward position. He continued to stare at the fire.

Sophie took a deep breath and solemnly said, "People are talking, Luke. I think we should get married. My boys are also so very fond of you."

Luke did not have the heart to tell this kind widow and good friend that he was already married, but who would ever know this fact? Besides, he had told Elsie to tell their daughter he was dead.

"Okay. Next time we go to town we can get married? No fuss though."

That was it, Luke was about to commit bigamy. He knew that entering into a marriage with one person while still legally married to another was a crime. He had never told anyone that he had been married to Elsie on St Helena or that he had a child. He had given this some thought before he and Sophie decided to get married, and reckoned that no one would find out. Who would ever think of looking at the marriage records on St Helena Island?

And so, they were quietly married in Bloemfontein. Luke was almost physically ill when, during the service, the minister asked,

"If any of you have reasons why these two should not be

married, speak now or forever hold your peace."

Only Sophie's two sons and some of Sophie's family were present. Luke invited no one to attend as he was concerned that someone may, by some chance, know that he had been married on St Helena, although he doubted it. When the Minister paused to await a possible response, Luke could only visualise Elsie, the beautiful Elsie with red roses in her hair on the day they were married, looking up at him with her large expressive eyes. He almost wished someone had been able to call him out as it would have released him from what he suddenly realised would be a lifetime of guilt towards Sophie **and** Elsie.

After their marriage, they moved into the farmhouse where Sophie lived with her two sons. Luke arranged for improvements to the property and some new furniture to be made. Although Sophie and Luke were now husband and wife, not much changed in respect of their relationship. They felt little need to move from a situation of very good friends to being lovers, and their intimate moments were few and far between.

On these occasions, Luke would leave their bedroom immediately afterwards and sit on the veranda, when thoughts of Elsie always came back to haunt him. She had been so natural, clever and fun to be with. He endlessly questioned his own integrity and how he had been able to walk away from that relationship when she needed him the most. The only night of their love making still tormented him. He knew that making love to a Coloured person was not acceptable in most societies. That was why he could not look her in the eyes when he entered her that night. But, on reflection, he realised that it had probably made Elsie feel unacceptable to him. He felt cruel and wished so many times that he had acted differently. If only they had had more time together, to express their love

153

completely, with no barriers and judgements.

Luke thought about the somewhat cruel letter he had handed to Elsie in the wooden box he had made when he had been on St Helena. He could not recall his exact words, but he felt like a coward to have fobbed her off with money, a letter, and that box which seemed to endlessly haunt him. He recalled that he had spent many hours working on the box, mostly thinking of Elsie and her lively spirit, sparkling eyes and beautiful smile. She would never know how she was totally responsible for his sanity when he was a POW. She had been the only true and carefree happiness he had ever known. The only other person who had given him such unconditional love had been his late mother. He knew Sophie loved him, but he felt this love was more like a sisterly love with an element of gratefulness for caring for her and her sons.

He had now committed a double crime in the eyes the law: bigamy and marriage to a Coloured person. He questioned how he could be so decisive and strong in business, and yet make a complete muddle of his personal life.

Even in his forties he knew so little about women. The talk of them sometimes got dirty when he was a POW on St Helena. A colleague once said that if you did not bring a woman to orgasm she could not get pregnant, so he advised the others to do it quickly if they did not want babies. Another colleague said women were like cows and they could not have orgasms. Luke wondered if any of that was true and if Elsie had or had not had an orgasm that night of their lovemaking next to the waterfall. His lack of knowledge about women at his age was hardly likely to be resolved, as it would not be appropriate for him to ask anyone's advice. He was concerned that he would look the fool.

Since his marriage to Sophie, he seemed to think more and

more about Elsie. Without consciously realising it, he would often catch himself rubbing the scar from his stabbing and thinking of her. He wondered how Katherine was managing at university. He was still secretly kept up to date from time to time by the convent's mother superior, but she obviously saw less of Katherine since she had started university.

Luke knew that now he would never be able to acknowledge Katherine as his child as this would expose his crime of bigamy.

What had he done?

Chapter 12
Michael's first letter to Katherine.

December 1924
   On board the ship to Southampton from Cape Town.

My dearest Katherine,
   I did not want to leave you behind. The memory of you looking so elegant and beautiful in your lilac outfit, dabbing your eyes with your handkerchief, will remain with me forever. I have kept the sprig of heather you gave me, now pressed in the front of my diary.
   Continue with your studies as I recognise your passion for medicine. You will be a great doctor and one never knows, perhaps you will join me in England one day, even if it is just for a visit.
   I miss our Saturday afternoon tea and chats. I have grown very fond of you, dear Katherine. Please, think of me each time you look at your watch and remember that the time could be nearer when we can hopefully see each other again.
   The voyage is proving to be fun, and I have met some interesting people. There is another doctor on board from Johannesburg who has also recently qualified, but he is heading to London to specialise in surgery. We plan to stay in touch and visit if we have time.
   We have called at a number of ports to refuel and get supplies. These ports are certainly not as sophisticated as

Cape Town, but very interesting all the same.

I believe I will be getting a train from Southampton to London, and another to Oxford.

I shall write again once settled in.

Your faithful and best friend,

Michael

Katherine was delighted to receive the letter as, although Michael referred to them as possibly seeing each other again, he seemed not to suggest that their relationship was a committed one. She decided she would reply after all, just as a friend. She was sure he would meet someone else in Oxford then she would never need to have the conversation with him about why she could never risk having children, beside the fact that, as a doctor, she was almost expected to devote her entire life to her calling and sacrifice ever having a family of her own. She knew that the chance of her giving birth to a child of mixed-race like her beloved mother was very high, and she would hate to put that burden on a child in a racist society.

Katherine had decided to accept that her bursary sponsor wanted to be anonymous, but wished she could thank whoever this person or institution was for such generosity. She was able to save almost half of her pocket money every month, which she deposited in a savings account at the bank to earn some interest. Katherine longed to have her own home one day so that she could take care of Elsie.

The further she got into her university studies and experience at the hospital, the more she realised that she could never have done anything else as fulfilling in her life. Obstetrics still gave her the most enjoyment and she hoped to be able to continue her studies further in this area. Minor surgeries like tonsillectomies and appendectomies were of great interest and she was sometimes called to assist during other small operations. She enjoyed visiting the little children after a tonsillectomy, as they delighted in being given jelly to soothe their throats after the operation. She loved their innocence and honesty.

Michael and Katherine continued to write to each other on a regular basis. Mostly they exchanged stories about their studies and accounts of what happened in their respective hospitals. Michael often suggested in his letters that she may like to visit him in Oxford once she had qualified as a doctor herself. Katherine never declined his offer, but continually remained vague in her replies and mentioned that she would need to work first in order to pay for her fare to travel. She had little intention of travelling to England, not because she did not want to do so, but because she planned to buy her own home as soon as possible and take care of Elsie.

Elsie continued to live at the cottage in the school grounds and teach the Coloured children in District Six. She lived for visits from her beloved daughter and particularly the time they spent together at Easter and Christmas – that was, if and when Katherine was not on duty at the hospital.

Marie still stayed in District Six where she had recently opened a little store on the ground floor of her home. There, she sold homemade chutneys, jams, biscuits, dried fruit and many other traditional South African delicacies. She had been approached to supply some of her goods to one of the fancy grocery stores in Cape Town, which enabled her to employ a young lady to assist her with the making of her produce. Her brand name was 'Tannie Marie'.

Katherine was so pleased for Marie and proud of how she had managed to create her own business. Elsie still visited after Mass on Sundays as they mostly attended together. They were so like a mother and daughter that most people thought they really were family.

Katherine did not always manage to visit Elsie and Marie as often as she would have liked, as many a time she was asked to work in the hospital as they were always short-staffed. This did, however, mean that she was paid for her extra hours, which boosted her savings account for her own home.

And so, the years passed.

Part IV

Chapter 13
Graduation

Katherine had finished her studies, written her final exams, passed her practical assessments in the hospital, and it was at last time for her to officially graduate as a medical doctor. She was advised that she could invite two guests. Katherine bought her cap and gown to be worn on the day. Whatever she wore, she always looked elegant and stylish. For the ceremony, she had chosen a black dress with a wide scarlet satin belt. The scarlet colour exactly matched the gown she would be donning.

Somehow, it all seemed a little pointless with her being unable to invite the one person who should be there to see her graduate. Katherine was terribly upset when she spoke to Elsie on the phone, who calmly suggested that she invite Mother Superior instead, as she had been so involved and apparently responsible for her education. Mother Superior truly was delighted to be asked but insisted that Elsie attend too. She came up with a brilliant idea. They arranged for a taxicab to collect them from the convent and take them to the ceremony on the day of the graduation. Mother Superior had organised for Elsie to push her in a wheelchair and pose as her helper. That way, no one could stop Elsie attending and it also meant that they were in the front row for the graduation ceremony for ease of access. Even though people would notice that Elsie was not European, Mother Superior emanated a pious authority which no one had the audacity to question. They smiled conspiratorially at each other, and Katherine was thrilled. Once again, they had thought of a way to overcome stupid and unnecessary racial prejudices.

What Mother Superior had not told either Elsie or Katherine, was that she had informed Luke that his daughter was graduating in Cape Town and given him the date of the ceremony. She had kept the secret of his anonymous contributions towards Katherine's education, but she felt he should be given the choice of attending.

Luke could not resist the opportunity of seeing Katherine and Elsie again, even from a distance. He was so proud and thrilled that his daughter was graduating as a medical doctor. He had told Sophie that he needed to go to Cape Town to meet with some cattle breeders and to look at possibly supplying the Cape Town beef markets as well. He took the train south and thought it would be an opportunity to browse in some bookshops, as he still loved reading and collecting for his personal library. The journey took a couple of days and the delays at the junctions and sidings to refuel and top up with water and supplies seemed to take ages. Luke was glad he was able to travel first class and at least have a compartment to himself.

On the day of the graduation, Luke was there at the very back of the hall. He had made sure that Elsie did not see him arrive and planned to leave as soon as Katherine had been capped.

When Katherine was called up to the stage as 'Dr Katherine Georgina Viljoen', Luke had so many conflicting emotions running through his mind that he felt he might faint. It was the first time he had seen Katherine since she was a baby in Elsie's arms on St Helena when he left them there all those years ago. He was astounded at how elegant and beautiful she had become; how much she looked like one of his late sisters. The pain of not being able to acknowledge her as his daughter was quite overwhelming. He had never met Mother Superior, with whom he had corresponded for many years, but realised it was her in the front row in a wheelchair as he also recognised Elsie sitting on a chair next to her, beaming with pride at her daughter graduating. He could not help but admire their ingenious plan of getting Elsie in to attend the 'Whites Only' graduation ceremony. He noticed that Elsie's hair had turned grey, as had his, but was neatly plaited and wrapped in a chignon at the base of her neck. She was still slim and was dressed simply in a stylish navy-blue suit with a cream blouse. A quarter of a century had passed since they had spent time together on St Helena. He wondered what she would think or say to him if she knew he was in the same room, watching their beautiful daughter graduate. How Luke would have loved to have shared that moment with Elsie, but he had made his decision a long time ago. He also had to remind himself that Katherine believed he was dead.

Luke assumed that Elsie and Katherine were now both practicing Catholics as they were so closely associated with the nuns. He was suddenly overcome with emotion and was forced to blow his nose and dab his eyes. How anchorless and meaningless his life had become just making money building up his cattle ranch to what was now an extremely profitable business. He stared at Elsie and saw a serene expression that he well remembered. She had had the joy of raising their daughter, their beautiful and intelligent daughter. Luke thought that by having secretly financed her education and living expenses, his guilt at deserting them both would somehow be quelled, but staring down at Elsie and Katherine, he realised that all he had done was deprive himself of familial love. The emptiness felt like an expanding sinkhole in his chest, and he was finding it difficult to breathe.

Luke had the overwhelming realisation that his life had so little depth and no inner resources to turn to. He suddenly felt the need to believe in something greater: Perhaps God? Or maybe to come clean with Sophie and tell her that he had been married on St Helena to Elsie and had never filed for a divorce? He was living a lie and Sophie deserved better. He had deceived her by offering her so-called security, after she was widowed. They had both been lonely and it seemed like a mutually good solution at the time but now, watching his daughter, he felt like a deserter and a cheat. The hollowness of being an empty soul pervaded his whole body.

He was forced to leave the graduation ceremony to get some fresh air and to try to think logically, with fewer overwhelming emotions.

He hurried away hoping to calm himself down, but his guilt and self-loathing followed him down the street like a haunting shadow that one is unable to escape in the bright sunlight. He glanced up at Table Mountain glaring back at him like a giant conscience, aware of his weakness and deceit.

He wandered aimlessly through the streets and thought of finding a bar to throw some strong alcohol into his aching soul. On passing the Catholic Church, he felt an urge to enter the peace and tranquillity therein. Perhaps if he sat for a few minutes, he would be able to think more clearly or even say a prayer for some much-needed guidance.

On entering through the tall, solid aged oak doors, his nostrils were filled with the calming smell of incense and beeswax furniture polish. There was a chill rising from the cold floor that he found quite welcoming. He looked up at the altar and the large crucifix of the bleeding and suffering Christ greeted him. For the first time in his life, he identified with a little of that pain too. Next to the altar there was a candle flickering behind a red-glass lamp that Luke remembered was an indication that the Eucharist was present in the tabernacle. He felt a sacred presence that moved him in a way he did not understand, and this feeling forced him to drop to his knees onto one of the church benches. He found himself silently praying to a God he had never really felt a need for previously. He begged for forgiveness and guidance and began to question what his reason for living was when his father, mother and sisters had all perished so tragically and all too soon. He alone had been spared to live a dishonest life, where only money and reputation had become his gods. How shallow he felt… how insignificant!

Looking up at the coloured shafts of light streaming into the church through the stained-glass windows, he felt smaller and more worthless than the minute dust mites drifting past. There was a large arrangement of white arum lilies next to the pulpit and they reminded him of those growing wild on St Helena, the very same ones that he and Elsie used to admire on their walks there, many years ago. He recalled how they laughed together and shared stories of their respective childhoods. She had taught him to appreciate and notice the birds, trees and plants. He rubbed the scar on his arm and smiled, remembering fondly again how nervous and yet caring Elsie had been that night when he had knocked on her cottage door asking for help. It always gave him a strange kind of comfort when he rubbed the scar on his arm, almost like a badge from when someone truly once cared for him.

Luke lost all track of time, but slowly felt calmer even though he knew he was no more in control of his very shallow and flailing life than he had been prior to entering the church.

Luke spent the next few days in Cape Town visiting bookshops and adding to his extensive library back home. He also attended a few business meetings.

A couple of days later, he was walking in the city and a man started shouting after him and calling his name. Initially he did not recognise the chap with grey hair and a very large unkempt beard.

"Hey, Viljoen. How are you?" the man called.

Luke vaguely recognised his voice but battled to place his face. Then, suddenly, the penny dropped, and he remembered this was the man who had stabbed him in the arm on St Helena, when there had been the dispute between the Boer prisoners of war: those who wanted to return to South Africa (of which Luke was one) and those who wanted to continue the war of independence. Luke remembered the man as Dan Venter. He came up and grabbed Luke's hand, shaking it with vigour.

"Hey, how you been, Luke? How is that arm I redesigned for you some, what is it, twenty-five years ago?"

"I am very well, thanks, and the scar…? Well, it's just a memory of our youth," replied Luke, who was trying to think of a good reason to excuse himself from further discussion.

Before he could do so, Dan said, "Hey, and so what happened to that Coloured teacher-girl you got up the spout on St Helena and married? You were crazy, man! There were other bastards left on the island by some of us, and we never married the bitches."

Luke winced at his words. He swallowed hard and forced himself to snigger without a reply, hoping he would drop the subject, but Dan continued, "So, what happened to them?"

"I lost contact," replied Luke and thought it best that he asks how Dan had done since they last met, to at least change the subject. Luke asked about his career and family. It seemed that Dan had not done very well in either area and was currently estranged from his family and out of work.

Dan commented on the expensive shoes and suit Luke was wearing and asked if he had a job for him.

Luke lied and said that he was visiting friends in Cape Town and had no job connections. Hopeful to escape, he asked Dan where he could contact him if he heard of an employment opportunity. Dan wrote down the address of a residential boarding house in Sea Point, which was an area Luke would now determinedly avoid so as not to run into him again, and so excused himself, saying he had an appointment to attend.

The meeting-up with this character from his past disturbed Luke even further, as did the realisation that some POWs had not forgotten about his marriage to Elsie. There was still the potential risk to being exposed as a bigamist which was a huge cause for concern.

So much seemed to be happening to open old wounds that Luke began to feel slightly panicked. He thought he had been in control of his emotions and had only come to Cape Town to witness his daughter's graduation from a distance, but instead a can of worms had been opened and it felt like they were beginning to consume him.

He headed back along Government Avenue towards the gracious Mount Nelson Hotel, where he was staying. He was deeply lost in thought and continually replayed the overwhelming events of the past few days. He walked up the avenue of palms that led to the entrance of the hotel. These palms had been planted earlier that year in honour of the visit by the Prince of Wales. On closing the door of his room, he immediately called room service and ordered a large whisky. He sipped the golden liquid and quietly tried to rationalise the events of the day.

He had been so lost in his thoughts whilst walking back to the hotel that he had not noticed that Dan had followed him at a distance to see where he was staying.

The following morning, there was an envelope pushed under the door of his hotel room when he awoke. Luke picked it up on his way to breakfast and put it in his pocket, planning to read it when he was in the dining room. He ordered his morning breakfast and coffee and removed the envelope from his pocket to read it. The paper the letter was written on was of poor quality and the writing looked like that of a child.

Morning Luke, old chap,

I have reason to believe that you have remarried and are doing very well in the Free State, with large cattle farms. People talk, you know!

As I told you, I have fallen on hard times, and it is time for you to help me out for my silence. Bigamy is a serious crime even if you have friends in high places.

I am suggesting you may like to pay for my silence every month...?

You have my address and £20 a month will be expected from you.

Should the first payment not be delivered by the end of today, I may need to pay a visit to the police and The Cape Times newspaper. Small price to pay for me to keep my mouth shut.

Dan

Luke felt his anger rising. He immediately started rubbing at the scar on his arm that Dan had been responsible for all those years ago. He had a good mind to go to the residential hotel and physically threaten Dan. The waiter serving his breakfast enquired about his wellbeing as Luke was sweating and had become red in the face. The thought of Dan blackmailing him made him more furious, and more afraid of the consequences than he had ever felt before. The impudence of that waste of life!

Luke tried to calm down and think clearly about what his next step should be. Part of him wanted to get on the next train back north and pretend it had not happened. However, Luke knew he could not defend himself against bigamy as marriage records could be checked. While the debate raged in his head, he took himself off for a walk in the beautiful, lush gardens of the hotel, planted with many exotic and endemic plants, and back down the drive of palm trees towards the city. He thought he would return to the church he had sat in after the graduation, where he had felt a little more at peace with himself. May be some divine intervention would come his way whilst he was in the presence of God?

On arriving at the church, he removed his hat and sat on one of benches at the back. The arum lilies were still there, as was the red light next to the altar. He felt wretched and angry with himself for his poor handling of his personal life. He questioned why it was so much easier to make good business decisions than it was to make good life decisions.

He knew he had to head back to his cattle farms and possibly tell Sophie that he had been married before on St Helena when he was a POW. He was sure she would be neither forgiving nor understanding of the situation he found himself in, as she had such high principles.

Breathing in the calmness of the church and the sacred presence, Luke came to the realisation that he probably had no option but to pay Dan the monthly blackmailing money. There was also the fact that he was allowing himself to be controlled by this low life. While he sat there debating his dilemma, he had not noticed that the priest had sat down near him on the same bench.

Luke eventually looked up, made eye contact, and greeted the priest awkwardly,

"Er... ah... Good morning, Father."

The kindly looking priest smiled and replied, "Good morning, my son. You appear to have much on your mind again today, as you did when I last saw you sitting here... looking for some answers?"

Luke smiled and replied, "Yes, Father, you presume correctly, but I am not a Catholic."

The priest explained that he felt everyone to be a child of God and if Luke had been drawn into the church it may well have been through God's guidance.

And so, Luke and the priest ended up taking a walk along the waterfront. Without much encouragement or persuasion, Luke poured out his life story, starting from the guilt he carried at killing British soldiers in ambushes during the Boer War and how some of their young innocent faces, along with their cries of anguish as the bullets from his gun ripped into their pale flesh, still haunted him.

Of how his father had been shot and killed during the Boer War and Luke had had to hurriedly bury him in a shallow grave. His perceived desertion of his mother and sisters, whom he never saw again after the war, as they had all perished in the horrific concentration camps. He explained the unselfish gesture of his mother leaving him money to start again, with or without her and his sisters. He was haunted at how they must have suffered in the camps in such shocking conditions with so little food and their basic needs ignored. He informed the priest that, post the Boer War, he had discovered that the more senior one was in the Boer ranks, the less food your family received in the camps. As his father had led a commando unit of Boer guerrilla militia, he feared that his mother and sisters may well have starved to death.

Luke explained how his time as a POW on St Helena had probably been a picnic by comparison to what his family must have faced. He confessed that he had made a beautiful young, local Coloured woman pregnant whilst on the island and then abandoned her, even though he had married her before God. He spoke of the guilt of leaving a woman with a small daughter on her own, but he could not justify bringing a Coloured woman home as his wife. Guiltily he admitted that he had asked Elsie to tell his daughter that he was dead, but explained that he had paid for his daughter's education as an anonymous donor and that she had just graduated as a doctor from the University of Cape Town. Luke told the priest how he had travelled down by train from Bloemfontein to watch her graduate. He confessed that he was a bigamist by marrying Sophie, with whom he now lived on one of his cattle farms in the Free State. He confessed that it was a comfortable and respectful arrangement, but not a particularly loving marriage.

He explained to the priest that he had bumped into a wretched man in Cape Town that he knew from the POW camp, and told him about the blackmail letter he had received that morning. This man was one of the POWs with whom he had had a disagreement on St Helena which had resulted at the time in Luke being stabbed in the arm. This man had remembered that Luke had married Elsie whilst on St Helena. Luke explained that he knew he had little option but to pay him and was obviously concerned that he may get greedier in the future, and he may well still inform the press or the authorities about his state of bigamy.

The priest hardly seemed surprised or shocked by Luke's confession. After walking in silence for a while, listening to their matching footsteps and the rhythm of the rolling waves against the shore, they both stopped and stared out to sea, caught in their own thoughts, or a prayer asking for divine guidance in the case of the priest, who said to Luke, "Our painful experiences can feel overwhelming at times, but try to step back and view them from a higher platform. This distance can sometimes give one perspective, meaning and even a sense of our purpose here on Earth."

Hearing this sage advice, it all suddenly seemed quite clear to Luke. He replied that he would plan to divorce Sophie and leave her and her sons with a large section of his cattle farms so that they could continue working there and have a comfortable living. He would probably get a manager to run his remaining farmlands. He knew he would keep the original family farm that had belonged to his parents. There were too many childhood memories there and those brought him comfort.

Perhaps it was time to start afresh and invest in one of the mines in the Johannesburg area. The recent strikes and labour disputes seemed to be mostly over, and Luke thought that it seemed a good time to invest in that sector.

The idea of contacting Elsie to see if she could ever forgive him crossed his mind. Of course, getting to know his daughter and gaining her acceptance would be the ultimate prize.

Chapter 14
A Big Decision

In the meantime, Katherine was delighted to see both Elsie and Mother Superior in the front row when she graduated, and was thrilled at their ingenious plan to get Elsie to attend.

There was a short drinks reception for the graduates and professors, held in the foyer of the Great Hall after the ceremony. The chancellor of the University spoke briefly, wishing them all luck for the future. The guests waited outside and enjoyed the lovely view and the university gardens. Whilst Katherine was sipping a glass of wine with some of her fellow graduates, there was a tap on her shoulder. There, boldly, stood Suzanne's father, the awful professor. She stepped away from her colleagues and turned to face the dreaded man.

"Congratulations, Dr Katherine Viljoen. My, but you have grown up and done well, despite yourself."

Katherine swallowed hard as she remembered how this man had abused her as a little girl. Through a very false smile she replied, "And how is Suzanne?"

The professor coughed and mumbled that she had moved north. Suddenly he reached for Katherine's hand, and she felt a shudder of revulsion at his touch. "Let's meet for dinner one evening to discuss your future?" He smiled at Katherine with a meaningful look.

Katherine decided that the opportunity was now or never. Keeping eye contact with the professor, she gently removed her hand from his and placed it slightly provocatively on his trouser belt. The professor looked surprised as she pulled his belt away from his stomach and swiftly poured the contents of her almost full wine glass down the front of his trousers and into his crotch. The fabric of his light grey trousers turned darker as it absorbed the red wine and made him look as though he had wet himself.

"May you rot in hell," said Katherine in a loud voice and turned back to her astonished colleagues. She smiled at them saying, "A long overdue score that needed to be settled."

With his very damp crotch, the humiliated professor left the foyer as quickly as he could, with many students laughing at his demise and guessing at the reason for Katherine's entertaining performance.

Katherine had visualised this scenario so many times in her head. She was delighted it had played out so smoothly. She chose not to explain to anyone the reason for her actions, but certainly felt satisfied that she had taken her revenge in a small way.

With her head held high and a big smile on her face, she left the reception to meet up with Mother Superior and Elsie. They walked back to the convent, taking turns to push Mother Superior's wheelchair. They laughed and giggled like schoolgirls all the way back. The other nuns had cooked a delicious luncheon to celebrate Katherine's success. She was the first pupil from the convent to become a medical doctor. Katherine felt so loved by them all and, in her little speech of thanks, said that she was the luckiest graduate that day, as she felt she had more mothers supporting her than anyone could ever dream of.

Mother Superior asked Katherine and Elsie to stop by her office for a chat before leaving that afternoon to return to

District Six for a further celebration with her godmother and some neighbours. On entering the office, both Elsie and Katherine reflected on their respective first visits to the convent and how their lives had changed since then. The nuns had truly become family and given them both so many opportunities. Elsie was a little overwhelmed and again expressed her eternal gratitude. Mother Superior smiled at them and steepled her fingers as though in prayer.

"Elsie, Katherine," she said, then paused. "There is an opportunity for work as a doctor at a couple of our Catholic hospitals in Johannesburg that may interest you. Both hospitals are within close proximity to each other, with one being a sanatorium mostly for smaller procedures and the other a maternity hospital. I know that these are areas where you have specialised, Katherine. I don't want to interfere too much, but it has come to my attention that they are looking for a newly qualified doctor. I have the details here and wondered if you would consider the positions...? Should you agree, then I will write to them advising of your acceptance, Dr Viljoen."

Mother Superior smiled indulgently at Katherine and then, taking a deep breath, focused on Elsie.

"There is also a school for blind children in Johannesburg which is looking for a part-time teacher and someone who can sometimes be available to read to blind adults. This may work for you, Elsie, and you could continue your teaching which you do so well, although in a slightly different role, as you will have to learn braille.

"I know you are both thinking that you cannot live together due to skin colour differences, but there too I may have a solution. One of the doctors at the sanatorium has a house for rent that is within walking distance of the hospitals for Katherine. However, Elsie, you would need to catch a couple of trams to the school a few days a week. My thought about how to overcome living together is to do so as a young, qualified doctor and her live-in housekeeper, maid, char or whatever the terminology used in Johannesburg is."

Katherine burst out laughing in delight at the cunning plan. "You are a genius at thinking around the colour-bar, Mother Superior."

Katherine and Elsie said they would need to think about moving so far away from all they knew and loved. It seemed a wonderful opportunity and they thanked Mother Superior for all her planning on their behalf. Katherine had given very little thought to her next move, having been concentrating on her recent exams. What she had not addressed or faced up to, was the letter recently received from Michael, offering her the opportunity of joining him in England. He had advised her that there were many job opportunities for newly qualified doctors. He had offered to pay for her passage on the boat to travel to England to join him.

Katherine had not replied to his letter, which he had followed up with a telegram congratulating her on graduating and advising her that he was sending her a first-class passenger fare. Although he had not mentioned it, she now felt he was wanting to take their relationship to the next level. She feared that she may break his heart by not joining him in England. There was no easy way other than to be completely honest with him and tell him that her mother was Coloured. She worried that such a reply may be presumptuous; what if he just wanted to continue to be friends?

Katherine and Elsie returned to District Six to celebrate the graduation and they decided to postpone any thoughts about their future until the following day, wanting instead to continue to enjoy Katherine's achievement. On arrival at the entrance to District Six, there was a large banner strung between two buildings near Marie's home that read,

'Congratulations, Doctor Katherine.'

Elsie beamed with pride and Katherine felt a little embarrassed, although delighted to spend this time at home with her mother and godmother, Marie, both so very proud of her achievements. She knew she was forever indebted to them and fondly remembered her godfather, Alfie. How she wished he was there to witness her graduation too. Katherine also gave a brief thought to her anonymous sponsor and again wondered why this person or institution had never wanted to meet her.

The day was one of celebration and much handshaking. Katherine felt exhausted as she fell into her old childhood bed that night. There were so many questions running though her head that she found herself unable to sleep. She walked out onto the small balcony and looked up to her beloved Table Mountain, and across the bay to where the sea glistened, and she could just about make out Robben Island in the distance. The night was balmy and the gentle breeze outside the house was cooling. Comforting sounds of someone strumming on a banjo and a donkey braying in one of the yards met her ears.

Should she accept Michael's offer of the passage to England? To work there and possibly continue their relationship? No... she could not deprive him of becoming a father. She would have to decline his offer, but was not quite sure she was strong enough or brave enough to tell him her true reasons for ending their relationship. By only now telling him that her mother was Coloured, she would almost be admitting that she had avoided the truth of her real heritage, and was that not as bad as lying? When they had become friends, it did not seem to matter, but she should have been honest when they started having feelings for each other.

Katherine feared that if she told Michael the truth now, he might begin to wonder what other truths she may be hiding from him. He had become by far the best friend Katherine had ever had and she had truly missed their time spent together. He wrote to her regularly about his work in the hospitals in England and the wonderful places he visited in his spare time. Katherine found it hard to visualise exactly how life would be for her there. Besides, she could not leave her mother alone in South Africa.

Now, of course, there was also the possible offer of the position at the Catholic Marymount Maternity Hospital and the Kensington Sanatorium in Johannesburg, together with Mother Superior's cunning plan of how she and Elsie could live under the same roof. In her heart, Katherine knew this would be her only option. There was the added attraction of being able to work in obstetrics, which was still her first passion.

Katherine had never really given her father much thought as Elsie would shut down the conversation about him and avoid answering her questions relating to Luke. She would reply, "Leave him be..." and that would end the discussion. However, standing outside in the pleasant night air, Katherine wondered what he would look like today, had he lived. She had never even seen a photograph of him, though Elsie had told her that she had her father's colouring. She hoped that he too would have been proud of her becoming a doctor.

Tomorrow she would have to write a letter to Michael declining his offer and telling him that she was accepting the offer of work and the house to rent in Johannesburg near the hospital and sanatorium. She decided, after all, to refrain from telling him her other reason for not wanting to join him in England.

Chapter 15
Move to Johannesburg

December 1925

My dearest Michael,

Yesterday was the day of my graduation, thus the realisation of one of my dreams.

Thank you for your kind telegram of congratulations.

Mother Superior and my mother attended the ceremony and then, afterwards, we celebrated with the nuns who have always been so supportive to both Mother and me. At the convent they cooked a delicious roast chicken luncheon, and it was rather an emotional occasion.

Thank you for your regular letters. I apologise for not having replied as often as I should have in recent times, but the final examinations were extremely time consuming, as you will well remember.

I also thank you for your generous offer of sending me the fare for a passage to England to come and work there. However, I have been offered a position in Johannesburg with the opportunity to rent a house nearby. As you know, obstetrics is my first passion and minor surgery of great interest too. This position will allow me to work in both areas and so I feel I cannot decline. My mother will accompany me to Johannesburg and will hopefully be teaching a few days a week at a local Catholic school for the blind – she will also have some time for reading to blind adults. Mother is delighted at the prospect, as she will be living with me again.

It is for these reasons, Michael, that I am declining your offer. I truly am so very sorry.

I wish you the very best for the future.

Yours, most sincerely,

Katherine.

Mother Superior was delighted that Katherine and Elsie had decided to accept their respective positions in Johannesburg and immediately wrote to the heads of both the hospitals and the school to make the final arrangements. The school wanted Elsie to begin in January, which was the start of the academic year. Both the sanatorium and the maternity hospital were eager to get Katherine settled in as soon as possible.

Arrangements were made to pack up their belongings early in January and take the long train journey from Cape Town to Johannesburg. Their boxes and some furniture would accompany them on the train.

Although they were both excited about this new chapter they were beginning together, it also meant that they were leaving Marie behind in District Six. Katherine was going to miss her godmother's unconditional love and care. There was little chance of them visiting each other again and this fact made them all very sad.

The day arrived, and the consequence of their different colour skins again raised its ridiculous head – Katherine travelled first class in a sleeping berth and could use the very nice dining carriage whereas Elsie was forced to travel third class, where there were no sleeping facilities and no dining carriage. Fortunately, Marie had packed a substantial tin of food for her journey. The situation was hateful as they parted company at Cape Town train station. Elsie had to go to the back of the train and Katherine the front. The journey was slow and the carriages very hot. When opening the window even slightly, the black soot from the coal-burning engine soon covered everything in fine black dust. Katherine was feeling guilty about her relatively luxurious accommodation and was concerned about her mother in a far worse situation at the back of the train, but Elsie had grown used to being treated as a second-class citizen over the years in Cape Town and was not overly perturbed. She soon found some interesting people to talk to and had packed a couple of books to read and study during the journey.

The train stopped at many stations, heading north-east. After leaving the green hills and beautiful scenery outside Cape Town, they started to travel through the arid Karoo area. There was little sign of life other than around the small towns that they stopped at to refuel the train and refill the water tanks. There were always vendors selling food and trinkets at the stations, and Katherine and Elsie would take the opportunity to stretch their legs and meet back on the station platforms to check up on each other. They were travelling under the guise of a young doctor with her maid. No one seemed to question this, and they both realised that this was the image they would have to continue to portray in the future if they were to continue to live as mother and daughter in an increasingly racist society.

Arriving at Johannesburg station a few days later, they both felt drained and dusty. Katherine spoke to the platform manager who organised for a delivery van to transport their boxes to their rented house and for Katherine and Elsie to follow in a taxi. The taxi driver was very concerned about accepting Elsie as a passenger, but Katherine explained that she was her maid and she needed her assistance. The taxi driver told Katherine to tell her 'Coloured girl' to keep her head down in the car in case anyone saw her in a White taxi. This was how Elsie would be referred to in the future – the girl. Not the lady, housekeeper, char or maid, but the 'girl'. Katherine found this terminology so offensive for a grown woman – especially one who was her mother – but Elsie appeared outwardly not to notice or care. This was the only way to disguise their mother and daughter relationship and so they had to accept it. Rather than getting her down, it always made Elsie smile to think that White people believed themselves to be superior to her by virtue of their skin colour. Quite bizarre!

The streets of Johannesburg seemed wider and busier than those in Cape Town. There appeared to be many more Black people and hardly any Coloured people walking about. The White ladies in the city were all dressed up wearing gloves and hats and the White men were in smart suits and fedora-type hats.

The taxi followed the van east, towards the residential suburb of Kensington. They finally arrived at the given address on top of the hill. The house had a dark brown, painted, corrugated roof with a front veranda next to the stained-glass, wooden-framed front door. There was a flowering jacaranda tree in the garden and the entrance path covered in the blossoms that had dropped to make a lilac carpet. A low wall was topped with an intricate iron railing and a metal filigree gate. The garden looked a little dry, but someone had clearly planted many roses that were now blooming, filling the air with a welcoming, gentle perfume. Flowering blue agapanthus plants with their long green, strap-like leaves nestled in the far corner. An envelope was tucked under the doormat addressed to Dr K. Viljoen. Inside was a note from the doctor who was renting the house to Katherine, advising her to collect the keys from the lady next door and indicating that he would be around later in the week to meet Katherine in person and collect the first month's rent in advance.

Katherine immediately went to the neighbouring house and knocked on the door where a kind and polite lady with her two children answered. The very small blonde boy with bright blue eyes was holding on to his mother's skirt and peeping up at Katherine, whilst the other little boy, carried in her arms, appeared to be handicapped – possibly as a result of polio, Katherine thought.

Katherine introduced herself as the new neighbour and requested the keys. The lady said she was called Marjorie and that she was a dressmaker, should Katherine need any outfits made or alterations done. She welcomed Katherine and said she had seen her arrive with her Coloured 'girl'. Marjorie suggested Katherine send her 'girl' around to the back of the house to collect some tea when they had settled in. Katherine thanked her and said she would do so. This discrimination towards her mother was already becoming a very bitter pill to swallow.

Her angry feelings were soon set aside when Katherine turned the key in the front door and entered the house. It was sparsely furnished and a little dark inside, but spotlessly clean. The driver of the van and his Black assistant, 'the boy', carried in the boxes and chests that had come from St Helena with them some twenty-five years ago, plus a few side tables that Alfie had made for Elsie's little cottage in the school grounds in Cape Town. Katherine paid and thanked the men, before she and Elsie explored the rest of the house.

From the front door, one entered a small entrance hall. On the right side, there was a lounge with a fireplace surrounded by glazed green tiles with yellow tulips hand painted on them. On the opposite wall, there was a window that looked over the veranda and the front garden; two threadbare sofas, an occasional chair and a bookshelf furnished the room. There was another door that led outside to a private, sunny little courtyard with a few wilting pot plants looking like they badly needed watering but, on closer inspection, were thankfully not dead. Elsie suggested it would be a delightful spot to enjoy eating outside and drinking a cup of tea whilst affording them a good degree of privacy.

Next to the lounge was a fairly large kitchen with a gas stove, a wooden table with two chairs and a wooden bench against one wall. Elsie was delighted to see the small pantry with many shelves and a cool box. There was also a covered veranda that led to a backyard, where they discovered a large water tank that collected water that ran off the corrugated iron roof. There was even space for a vegetable garden.

Back inside, to the left of the house, were two bedrooms with two beds in each, a small chest of drawers, a wooden wardrobe, and an upholstered chair. There was even an inside bathroom and toilet that included a linen cupboard. At the far end of the property was another building that housed a garden shed, an outside toilet and another small room which appeared to be the servant's room.

The house seemed perfect for the two of them and they soon got themselves unpacked. Katherine completely forgot about the offer of tea from her neighbour and only remembered when there was a knock at the front door. Elsie went to answer the door and their neighbour handed her a tray of tea with one cup.

"Here is tea for your madam," she said.

Elsie thanked Marjorie and, when she had left, they both

burst out laughing and immediately set about enjoying the tea and purposely sharing the single cup. Elsie giggled, saying how she would need to get used to calling Katherine 'madam' when other people were around. Mother and daughter soon felt at home in their new surroundings. Katherine settled into the slightly larger bedroom and Elsie took the other.

Katherine said she would walk to the shops that they had passed on their drive to the house to collect some provisions whilst Elsie continued to settle in. Elsie unpacked her belongings and clothes into her bedroom. On the bedside table that Alfie had made her, she carefully placed the wooden box that Luke had given her all that time ago when he left St Helena. The key still hung around her neck and her fingers strayed to touch it as they always did when she remembered Luke and the island with bittersweet memories. Katherine had asked her a few times over the years what was inside the wooden box and Elsie had simply responded that they were her own private memories. She had confessed to Katherine only recently that the box had been made by her father. Katherine was delighted that her initials were carved on the lid, KGV for Katherine Georgina Viljoen. When in Elsie's room, Katherine would often run her fingers over those carved letters and wonder about her father. Elsie did not have the heart to tell her that the initials stood for POW in Dutch. That would all be for another day in the very, very distant future! Right now, they were starting a new chapter together as mother and daughter, or 'girl' and 'madam' to the outside world.

The street where their new home was situated was a cul-de-sac and very quiet indeed. There was a spring in Katherine's step as she set off to get supplies. On the way to the shops, she passed the sanatorium where she would be working. It was a lovely stone building with a sweeping drive shaded by large trees and a lovely little stone-clad chapel in the grounds.

It all seemed so perfect and exciting, although Katherine was a little concerned about Elsie having given up her teaching role in Cape Town and now having to travel so far to her new job to work with the blind. Elsie would need to catch two trams there and two trams back every working day. The tram terminus was in Johannesburg City, where one connected to the suburbs. Of course, there was a Black Terminus and a White Terminus!

The little row of shops within walking distance from their new home seemed to have all they would need. There was a clean-looking butcher's shop, bakery, pharmacy and a large store called Gray Smith Grocer on the corner. Katherine introduced herself as being a doctor who had just moved into the area to work at the sanatorium and maternity hospital. Mr Smith, the grocer, immediately said that she should open an account, which she could settle at the end of every month. He took her shopping list and popped it in a basket that he lowered down into the basement of the shop on a pulley system through a hole in the floor. This was then filled by the staff downstairs with the items on the list. A bell rang to advise Mr Smith that the order had been fulfilled and the basket was raised up behind the large wooden counter for the customer. Mr Smith asked Katherine for her home address and said that his 'boy' would deliver her purchases later that day on his bicycle. He also suggested that, in the future, she should simply telephone through her shopping list or send her 'girl' in with her list and they would take care of the delivery of the goods. This arrangement pleased Katherine and she immediately ordered more groceries to stock the pantry. She was glad that neither she nor Elsie would need to carry heavy groceries home in the future. On the way home, she stopped in at the butcher's and bought a few lamb chops, some vegetables from the greengrocer's and a loaf of bread from the bakery, plus two small chocolate eclairs for dessert that evening. This felt so right and, in her excitement, she almost skipped back home wanting to tell Elsie her news.

Elsie had already unpacked most of their belongings and had made up their beds. She was rinsing the crockery in the scullery on the back veranda. She had even placed an arrangement of roses that she had cut from the front garden on a narrow table against the wall in the entrance hall, and their perfume filled the home with a delicate fragrance. Roses always reminded Elsie of those growing next to the front door of her cottage on St Helena. She paused and reflected fondly of her time there and the coincidence of roses growing in the front garden of this new home.

Katherine was bubbling with excitement after her little adventure to the shops and, shortly after she arrived home, there was a knock at the front door for the delivery of the groceries. Elsie cooked them a delicious dinner and they both slept like logs after each having a lovely hot bath. As Katherine was drifting off to sleep, she thought of dear Michael and wondered if he had received her letter yet. Part of her wanted to write to him to keep up the contact and share the news of her new home, but at the same time she felt she needed to cut contact. Her decision was made: She and Elsie would share a wonderful life here in Kensington. What could go wrong?

PART V

Chapter 16
Life in Johannesburg

For the next two years Katherine continued to work at the Marymount Maternity Hospital and also performed minor surgeries like tonsillectomies and appendectomies at the Kensington Sanatorium. Her first love was obstetrics, and the nuns were wonderful midwives to work with. Their care and empathy towards the patients and doctors were a true calling. By some strange social osmosis, Katherine knew she was learning so much from them, including their bedside manners, and she was never shy about calling on their years of experience in midwifery. The joy of assisting with the safe delivery of the babies into this world always felt like a small miracle. It was a thrill to hear the babies' first cries, and the delight and love on the faces of most of the mothers when their babies were gently placed in their arms.

There was a slightly unhappy side in the maternity home also, and that was the delivery of babies to unmarried mothers who were mostly extremely traumatised at having to give up their babies for adoption, which the Catholic nuns managed very discretely. These babies were normally homed with suitable Catholic families who would be able to give their adopted child a better life than the single birth mothers could ever hope to do themselves.

There were some women who were most unhappy with having a lady doctor attend to them and wanted a 'proper doctor': A man! One of the nuns would normally step in to reassure the objecting patient that Katherine was indeed a very experienced doctor and that they should count their blessings that she was attending to them. Katherine assumed that it would still take many years for women to be accepted in the medical world, but obstetrics seemed a good place to start. She accepted the odd prejudice as the way things were, but could not help questioning why most people seemed unable to accept gender and racial equalities.

Elsie travelled twice a week to the school for the blind and soon finely honed her skills in braille. She spent many hours reading to both blind children and adults. There was never any race discrimination from her pupils, probably as they did not know the colour of her skin and her English accent, learnt from her father, did not betray her identity.

The biggest racist problem that Elsie experienced was from a most unexpected source. This came from the Black maids, nannies and housekeepers in their neighbourhood. Elsie was accused by these women of being 'the fancy Coloured woman' who worked for the lady doctor. This title amused rather than concerned Elsie and Katherine. However, they had to be vigilant about keeping their curtains closed at night so that the neighbours did not suspect that Elsie lived in the house without any segregation. The other maids generally lived in a small room in the backyard of these houses and used the outside toilet, or a commode which they cleaned out when the boss and madam were not around. Mostly these maids' rooms had neither washing facilities nor heating, and the maids had to wash themselves in a basin of water and cook their food on a small primus stove. Most of the maids were not allowed to use the toilets, baths or stoves belonging to their employers for their personal use, although they were good enough to clean them.

These maids were normally referred to as 'the girl' and the gardeners as 'the boy', even though they were adults and sometimes older than those who employed them. Possibly referring to them in diminutive terms stemmed from laziness and poor vocabulary as many of the early settlers may not have been well-educated and came from multi-cultural backgrounds and language origins. Or perhaps, it was easier and somewhat of a put-down to call someone 'a boy' or 'a girl' rather than to use the correct titles of a maid, gardener, bricklayer or farm labourer. This terminology sadly became the norm and few Europeans stopped to think about it or listen to themselves. There was very little or no respect across the colour bar for age. This way of addressing staff was the norm amongst the middle-class White community, and to have referred to 'the girl' as even a housekeeper or a maid would have been seen as not conforming and having some fancy highfalutin ideas. Moreover, they would likely be regarded as a 'Kaffir Boetie', which was a very derogatory term for a White person sympathising with the Black people and roughly translates as being 'a brother of the Kaffirs'. Notwithstanding that, most White people would likely have given the terminology very little thought, as it was accepted as the norm by everyone, even the children. Whilst employers expected to be called Madam or Sir, most men were usually addressed as 'Baas', meaning boss.

The maid living and working next door to Elsie and Katherine would often call across the fence to Elsie to have a chat; mostly gossip and complaining about her 'madam' and her kids. This seemed to happen only when the 'madam' next door had gone out to take the little boy, who suffered with the results of polio, to the hospital. After work, the maids would sometimes cook their dinner together. This put Elsie in an extremely difficult position, and she was always having to find excuses for the neighbouring maids not to visit. Firstly, Elsie did not live in the outside maid's room, and secondly, it was used as their storeroom. Elsie could imagine the gossip if it was discovered that Katherine was really her daughter and that they shared the house as equals. It was unacceptable for Black, Asian, Coloured and White people to live together and the neighbours could potentially report them to the police.

Afrikaner intellectuals and government officials started to use the word 'apartheid' in the 1930s – the word meaning apartness.

So Elsie continued to draw the curtains before the sun set and always wore a maid's uniform when indoors, just in case someone, like the postman, a neighbour or a salesman, came to the front door.

One day, there was a knock at the front door, and, on answering, there was a well-dressed, Black gentleman standing and asking if the boss or madam were home. Elsie replied that she was the only one there at the moment, but enquired about what this man wanted. He introduced himself as Norman in very well-spoken English and said he was a gardener, painter and general handyman looking for work. Elsie thought that was exactly the sort of person that she and Katherine needed around the house for all the odd jobs and to help in the garden. Elsie said she would speak to her madam that evening and that he should return the next day for a decision. Elsie got the feeling that he was a real gentleman. He wore a silver star pinned to his chest, which suggested that he was a member of the Zion Christian Church (ZCC). To her, this was an immediate indication of a man to be trusted.

When Katherine got home that evening, after a long day

at the maternity hospital and a few complicated deliveries, Elsie mentioned that a handyman had called during the day and was looking for some gardening, odd jobs and painting work. Both Katherine and Elsie agreed that it would be good to have someone to initially redecorate some of the duller rooms in the house and then, perhaps, even come back once a week or so to help in the garden and do a few other odd jobs. He would obviously have to come on a day that Elsie was not working at the school for the blind, so that she could tell him what to do, having supposedly been previously instructed by her madam.

And so, Norman became their handyman, gardener and, eventually, a good friend. The incident that made Elsie, Katherine and Norman true friends occurred from a rather nasty, but not unusual event for the times.

Elsie had set off early one morning to get to the school where she taught and read to the blind, on the northern side of Johannesburg. There was very little public transport, and she was rushing to catch her tram. As she came around the corner, she saw that her tram was already at the stop. She started running and must have slipped or tripped on something in the road and twisted her ankle and went sprawling across the road. She tried to get up, but was unable to do so as her ankle was extremely painful and gave way under her each time, she tried to stand on it. She hobbled to the pavement and watched as the Non-European tram she was planning to catch disappeared up the road. There was a bench nearby that Elsie sat down on and gathered herself for a while as she was extremely shaken and in pain from her fall. She had grazed her knee and realised that she was unable to bear weight on the injured foot. She thought it best to sit a while where she was and wait for Katherine, who would be following after her about fifteen minutes later. In her shock, Elsie had not realised that she had come to rest on a bench that was marked 'For Whites Only' and 'No Blacks'. Without warning a rough-looking man came up to her and started shouting insults and throwing accusations at Elsie that struck her dumb, as she had never personally encountered such a racist rant before. She tried to explain that she had fallen and was waiting for help, but the man hit Elsie across the face and shouted that she should sit in the gutter where all Blacks and Coloureds belonged. The force of his blow knocked Elsie off the bench and on to all fours. She tried to reach for her handbag, which he maliciously kicked into the road before kicking Elsie in the ribs a few times. Tears were streaming down her face, and she looked around to see if anyone would defend her but the group of White people that had gathered simply watched, with some looking a little shocked whilst others sniggered at her.

A woman started shouting at Elsie, saying she was going to call the police as Elsie had sat on a White bench making it filthy. The insult and fury made Elsie sob even more, and she had no idea how to get out of this hurtful and terrifying situation. Quite suddenly, Katherine arrived on her way to work at the hospital. She had not witnessed Elsie being attacked by the man, but nevertheless heard the woman's verbal abuse. She immediately ran to Elsie's aid and all she wanted to do was hug her beloved mother and protect her from the White supremacists surrounding her.

"Leave her alone. Can't you see she is injured," screamed Katherine at the crowd. "I am a doctor, get out of my way." She knelt down in the gutter next to Elsie. Katherine whispered to Elsie to stay calm and asked her what happened.

Hearing that Elsie had been kicked in the ribs by a man objecting to an injured Coloured woman sitting on a White bench enraged Katherine to a red-mist state. Her training as a doctor thankfully kicked in and she realised that this was not a war that could be won in a gutter surrounded by racists.

As luck would have it, Norman happened to be walking past on the other side of the road and spotted the commotion. He realised that Elsie and Katherine were in some kind of trouble, so he immediately came to them to see if he could assist. Katherine asked him if he could carry Elsie back to her house which, with Elsie being slim and used as he was to physical labour, he managed effortlessly.

On arriving at the house and with Elsie in his arms, Norman kicked open the side gate and started heading to the back garden and the maid's room. Katherine told him to bring Elsie through the front door and into the main house. The front door entrance was never used by a maid, other than to clean the windows and polish the veranda floor with red wax polish. A few of the neighbours were standing, watching this very unusual sight of a Black man carrying a Coloured woman and being escorted by a White woman. Well, this sort of thing never happened in the White suburbs of Johannesburg! Katherine could hear the gossip and speculation as they walked by, and she whispered to Norman and Elsie to please ignore what they heard.

On entering the house, Katherine slammed shut the front door and fiercely drew the curtains of the rooms facing the road in the hope that the curious neighbours and maids would go back to their respective houses. She directed Norman to put Elsie in her bedroom. Norman was looking extremely uncomfortable, particularly when Katherine asked him to go to the kitchen and make them a pot of tea whilst she examined Elsie.

It looked as though Elsie had sprained her ankle badly and

seemed to have a couple of cracked ribs from the kicking she had received from the vicious man. Katherine bandaged her ankle and washed her grazed knees. She explained to Elsie that the ribs would take time to heal and could be extremely painful if she laughed, sneezed or coughed.

Katherine found herself crying in frustration and sadness over how her mother had been treated by people who thought they were better than Elsie. The frustrating thing was that Katherine knew there was nothing that she could do about it.

There was a gentle knock on the door, and there stood Norman with a tray of tea asking where he should put it down. Norman seemed somewhat embarrassed to be in the bedroom and said he was leaving.

Katherine, with some minor surgeries booked for the morning, realised that she was by now very late for work. She asked Norman if he could stay for the day to look after Elsie, saying she would get back from the hospital as soon as she could. Norman said that he would have to leave by four o'clock to get back to Soweto to the room he shared with three other men. Katherine immediately decided that he should move into the maid's room at the back of the house and suggested he use the day to sort the room out and said that Elsie would tell him where to find linen and what he needed. Katherine told him to move the spare bed in Elsie's room to the outside room for his use. Again, Norman looked embarrassed and nervous at Katherine's suggestion, but he respected her as his employer and a doctor. He felt he had no option but to oblige her and take care of Elsie that day. He also seemed rather confused by the very unusual relationship that Elsie and Katherine seemed to have.

As she rushed out to work, Katherine felt a little guilty that she had put a huge burden on Norman's shoulders and realised that they would have to trust him sooner or later with their secret of being mother and daughter. She resolved to explain this to him on her return home from work later that afternoon.

By the time Katherine eventually got home that evening, Elsie and Norman seemed very organised and Norman had even been instructed by Elsie on how to cook their evening meal, which they all shared together around the kitchen table. Norman proved to be good company and had wonderful tales of his childhood to share with them. He had not attended school for very long as he had had to tend the cattle for his family, but he was a deeply religious man and read the Bible every night.

Katherine decided that this was as good a time as any to take Norman into their confidence. She explained the situation at length and on hearing that Elsie and Katherine were mother and daughter, Norman began to cry. When he was calmer, he told them that he too was the result of a mixed racial situation with his father being Indian and his mother Black. He had never known his father and he had been sent to live with cousins when he was born to his mother who was, at the time, the maid to the Indian family. He had received love from his maternal grandmother but hardly ever saw his birth mother, who found him a huge embarrassment.

Norman went on to tell them an interesting story about the first time he had ever seen Coloured people. They had moved into the village near Norman's family. He would walk past their house on the way home from school and, not wanting to stare, he would try to look at them out of the 'side of his eye'. One day, he plucked up enough courage to ask his older cousin where the "funny Mlungu people" came from (Mlungu meaning White people). His cousin sharply whacked him across the ear and told Norman, in no uncertain terms, that these were mixed-blood people like himself, but they were Coloured - which was half White and half Black. His cousin went on to say that their blood was the same colour as all God's people and, therefore, Norman had better respect them.

Norman chuckled at his own story and finished his tale by saying that wisdom is more important than knowledge.

And so, Norman came to live on the property in the servant's room in the back yard, a far more comfortable and private arrangement than a shared room in Soweto. A pact was made between the three occupants to fiercely guard their respective secrets.

Chapter 17
Local News

Michael continued to write to Katherine on a regular basis, telling her about the medical world in England and the seminars he had attended where he was learning new methods to use in orthopaedic surgery. He explained how huge advancements had been made in this field, post the serious lessons learnt during World War I. He had also travelled to Paris to visit one of the teaching hospitals there. He did say that she would love Paris and suggested that one day they could meet there. Katherine doubted that would ever happen but did ask Elsie to pick up a book for her about Paris from the local library.

Elsie was not allowed into the library, which was for White people only, so she would stand at the window where the librarians stamped the books and hand them a note from Katherine along with the library membership cards, asking them to please give her 'maid' the books she wanted to borrow. Yet another slight on Elsie's olive skin!

Michael never referred to the letter that Katherine had sent declining his offer to join him in England. She knew that he had received it as he asked her how she was getting on at the sanatorium and the maternity hospital; he also enquired about her settling into the house with her mother. She initially ignored his letters, but thought it childish and silly as they had been such great friends. She still missed him but knew in her heart that she had to stick to her decision of total celibacy, for the sake of her chosen career. She simply couldn't risk the chance of having an unplanned child and the upheaval that would bring. She felt that it would be unbearable to worry for nine months of pregnancy about the skin colour of an unborn child.

Thankfully, Michael clearly respected her decision to remain in South Africa, but he had no idea about her concerns or fears of having children. He seemed to be very settled in England and Katherine felt sure that, soon enough, he would meet and marry someone there and that would be it. However, little did she know that Michael most certainly was **not** over her. He missed her intelligent conversation, her enquiring mind and her natural, elegant style. Even on the windiest and wettest days in Cape Town, he recalled fondly how she would arrive to meet him, looking as though she had just stepped out of a glossy magazine. None of the young ladies in England seemed to come close to Katherine. He decided that he would finish his current course and head back to Cape Town to visit his family. Thereafter, he would travel by train to Johannesburg and pay Katherine and her mother a surprise visit. His instincts told him not to announce his intentions, as he felt sure Katherine would make an excuse, and he knew he had to get to the bottom of her reasons for wanting to stay in South Africa when there was an opportunity for her to travel and explore the world, as well as for both of them to further their medical experiences in other countries.

Katherine continued to enjoy delivering beautiful babies at the Marymount Maternity Hospital and to perform, what were for her by now, simple surgical procedures at the Kensington Sanatorium. The home ran like clockwork with Elsie and Norman taking care of all the domestic duties.

Katherine was able to support them all financially and get on with her career without distractions. She counted her blessings that things were working out so well for all of them.

The neighbours assumed that Elsie and Norman were husband and wife, so there was nothing to gossip about. As Norman was living there, the other maids did not want to come and visit Elsie as they did not want to be in the way. This arrangement suited both Norman and Elsie perfectly. Every afternoon, Norman would walk to the local shops to buy the newspaper and any daily shopping that was required. They would have tea together whilst they read the newspaper, seated at the kitchen table. Elsie always liked to complete the crossword and she enjoyed including Norman in the task, whilst teaching him new English words too. Afterwards, the newspaper was carefully folded and left next to Katherine's chair in the lounge for her to look through after dinner.

Elsie had become a fine cook and baker. She had even started writing a cookery book which included household tips. Many of them included the wonders of white vinegar for cleaning. She did smile at herself, remembering how her mother on St Helena feared she would never be able to run a house or keep a husband. The latter had proved true enough, although she was still Mrs Luke Viljoen. Elsie dreamed of one day having the book published, which would include some wonderful Cape Malay dishes that Marie had taught her to make, along with dishes and baking recipes that she had learnt from the nuns at the convent.

One day, Norman brought in the newspaper, and there, on the front page, was a picture of Luke Viljoen. The article below his picture reported that he had recently purchased a gold mine in the area. He was obviously looking much older these days but, almost annoyingly to Elsie, he looked extremely distinguished. In the picture he was shaking hands with President Jan Smuts at the Rand Club in Johannesburg, and it was purported that he was intending to be an equal opportunity employer. Elsie scoffed at the article, but the next day she carefully cut it out of the newspaper and locked it in her little wooden box. This was the first time she had had any news of him since she locked away his original letter. It came as a shock to her to know that he was probably living in Johannesburg. Elsie still always wore the little key to the box around her neck on a chain. The surprise of seeing Luke's picture in the newspaper had disturbed feelings she thought she had long since buried. It also raised the guilt that she felt for withholding the truth from her beloved Katherine, that her father was not dead, but in fact alive and well and on the front page of the local newspaper. What good would it do if she did know anyway? He had made his decision when he handed her that letter, and life had been difficult, but probably simpler without him. A little part of her wished that he knew that, despite his chosen desertion, she had got on with her life and Katherine had made a huge success of hers. Anyway, Elsie assumed he was probably married to a White woman and had a string of overindulged, privileged children. She felt slightly smug at the thought. Little did she know…

Chapter 18
Chance Meeting

Luke had returned from Katherine's graduation in Cape Town depressed and very shaken at having been blackmailed. He continued reluctantly to pay Dan but had decided to divorce Sophie anyway. As part of the divorce settlement, he gave her some money and the cattle farm that she and her sons managed. He kept his family's homestead and farm but sold the rest of the properties.

Sophie had not been entirely surprised when he had returned and said that he was moving to Johannesburg, to make a new start and to invest in a gold mine. She knew in her heart that he did not love her as her first husband had. Luke always seemed distracted, and although they were good friends, he seemed to be growing more and more distant. It was a very amicable separation and even her sons seemed to understand that Luke needed to move on without their mother. She doubted that she would have enjoyed living in the busy city of Johannesburg anyway, as she was a country girl. Luke chose not to mention that he was still married to Elsie, as the situation was complicated enough.

Thus, he moved alone to Johannesburg. He bought a very nice home in the estate of Houghton that was just starting to develop. His office was in the financial district of Johannesburg and the mine was on the eastern side of the city. He was not involved in the day-to-day running of the mine and

207

had a very strong team doing that for him. From his office in the city centre, he oversaw the management and finances, and frequently met other potential investors. Luke loved the challenge of big business and was learning so much about life in the city. No matter what the business, the bottom line on the financial statements still mattered above all else. He had been studying business management himself from the many books he purchased and from his own personal library at home, which was by now quite substantial. Living alone, he had more time to research, read and browse the book and antiquarian stores in the city seeking out first editions and rare signed copies.

In 1930, Luke became a member of the Rand Club in Loveday Street, which was a grand gentlemen's club emulating those on Pall Mall in London. As an investor in a small gold mine, it was a good meeting place for mining magnates, businessmen and celebrities of the time.

The Rand Club had been built in the 1880s at considerable cost, with the importation of carved mantelpieces from England. A grand staircase led upwards from the main reception area, and the walls of the rooms were panelled and decorated with hunting trophies and valuable paintings.

One evening, Luke was in the members' bar after a long day meeting with the management of his gold mine when he noticed a dapper man with steel-blue eyes sitting quietly in one of the leather club chairs, sipping a brandy and smoking a cigarette. He looked a little like Prime Minister General Jan Smuts with his goatee style, well-trimmed beard. Luke felt like some company, so he walked across and asked to join him. It turned out that this man was Frank Wild, who had accompanied Shackleton to the Antarctic three times, as well as Scott and Mawson on two other occasions. Luke had followed their adventures in the press with great interest at the time and, although he was aware that Shackleton had died of a heart attack on his last adventure, he had no idea what had happened to the rest of the team. Luke and Frank Wild spent the rest of the evening chatting about some of these adventures in the Antarctic.

Frank recalled the time he and twenty-one men had been left on Elephant Island in the Antarctic, after the Endurance had sunk in the Weddell Sea, having been beset in the ice for over fifteen months. After some five months on the drifting ice, which eventually started breaking up, and six days at sea with three lifeboats, they managed to reach Elephant Island. Unbelievably, all the men survived, although some were virtually in a comatose state on arrival. Shackleton and a few men left Elephant Island after a few days, with the hope of reaching South Georgia to get help. Frank Wild and the remaining men waited for Shackleton to return with a rescue ship, which took another three and a half months. These men had miraculously all survived on the few remaining rations and by eating seals and penguins. Frank recalled that one of their greatest hardships was not having any tobacco and that they had even attempted drying and smoking seaweed. To keep their spirits up and remain positive, the motto on Elephant Island had been 'The less said the better'.

Luke smiled to himself, as he too believed that to be an excellent life motto.

Frank explained how they had upturned the two remaining lifeboats, placing them on four-foot walls made from stones found on the beach, and used these 'huts' as their living quarters.

It had taken Shackleton four attempts to reach them and, when he finally arrived, he immediately handed out tobacco to his men, whom he clearly knew and understood very well. They all quickly retreated from Elephant Island in case the ice closed in around them again.

Frank recalled being invited to have dinner with Prime Minister Jan Smuts on their return to Cape Town, following Shackleton's death.

He explained that he had later been invited to come and farm in South Africa by Smuts, but had unfortunately not been able to grow cotton successfully north of Durban due to very difficult climatic conditions, including wildlife and malaria threats. Frank had named his farm 'Quest' after the Quest Expedition from 1921 to 1922.

Frank mentioned that on their way back from Cape Town to the United Kingdom, the Quest had called in at St Helena Island. This comment jerked Luke's conscience and brought many happy and sad memories flooding back to him at once. They ordered another brandy and Luke shared some of his stories of being a POW on St Helena during the Boer War. They both fondly remembered the island and its people and the uniqueness of its setting, with Jamestown sitting snugly between the two steep cliffs and clearly visible on approaching the harbour.

Frank watched Luke drift into deep thought and commented that maybe Luke had left his heart on St Helena, to which Luke replied, "I may well have done but I am sure you will agree, Frank, that hindsight is a prism that alters everything."

"Yes, very profound! …And as misery loves company, let's have another brandy, shall we?"

Frank told Luke that he and Smuts had become close friends and that he and his wife and her boys from a previous marriage were often invited to stay at Smuts' home,

Doornkloof, near Johannesburg. Smuts was a much-admired statesman, philosopher and military man, and he and Frank enjoyed many hours of discussion around a fire. Frank suggested that his immigration to South Africa in 1923 was partly due to the sad fact that he was unable to come to terms with Shackleton's death and there also appeared to be more opportunity, prospects and perhaps adventure in the colonies. Shackleton had clearly been Frank's hero, his best friend, his leader, and ultimately had been like a brother to him.

Frank was then only fifty-seven years old, and it appeared that he may have fallen on hard times, which Luke was really surprised about as clearly, he was well connected, respected and admired in South African society, as well as amongst the Freemasons.

Luke left Frank Wild with his calling card, saying he was exactly the sort of man he would like to employ in his gold mine management and suggested Frank think about coming to work for him. They said good night and Luke never heard from Frank Wild again. Luke respected Frank's decision not to contact him and chose not to pursue the matter. However, he never quite understood why. Luke was a little surprised that Frank never got in touch with him as he believed that they could have had a mutually beneficial relationship and perhaps even become good friends. He did reflect that Frank was obviously an intensely proud and principled man and possibly he felt that Luke was offering him charity.

A chance meeting indeed, and Luke counted himself honoured to have met such a hero and a gentleman.

Chapter 19
Spying

Luke had been following Katherine's progress and, in fact, had even found out where she and Elsie lived in Kensington. He thought it unwise to drive past but, one evening, he was unable to stop himself from driving across town and up the road to where they lived. He was pleased that they appeared to live in a very nice, quiet road. He stopped the car opposite their quaint little home and sat there for a few minutes staring at the light shining through the drawn curtain. There lived his wife and daughter, so near and yet so very, very far from him. He felt overwhelmingly sad sitting in the car and drove back to his home with the window open as the tears dried on his cheeks in the breeze.

Elsie too was haunted by the fact that Luke was living in Johannesburg and a morbid curiosity overcame her. She felt the need to see where he lived. After mulling this over for a few weeks, she one day thought to look up his name in the Johannesburg telephone directory. His address and phone number were there, printed out for all to see. Elsie made a note of the details on a piece of card and locked the information in the little wooden box, although they were imprinted in her mind. She thought that one day she may walk past Luke's home, for curiosity's sake.

A few months later, she found herself purposefully looking for Luke's home in the street that it was listed under in the directory. On arriving at the address, she was somewhat shocked to see the size of the double storey house and the beautiful surrounding garden. There was a gardener trimming the lawn on the pavement who greeted her in passing. Elsie stopped to chat to him and asked if the madam in the house needed a maid as she was looking for work. The gardener advised her that there was no madam and the boss lived alone there. He said that the boss was home if she wanted to go and ask him if he needed another maid. Elsie quickly back-pedalled and said that it was not necessary if there was already a maid employed there. She continued to chat to the gardener about the flowers on the pavement and the weather and, whilst they chatted, a large shiny black car drove down the driveway. Elsie immediately recognised Luke from his picture in the paper. She turned her face away and Luke stopped to talk to the gardener, giving him some further duties and suggesting he stop chatting to the lady and get on with his work. Elsie wanted the ground to open up and swallow her and was thankful Luke had not recognised her. She said goodbye to the gardener and hurried back to the tram stop. Her heart was still pounding when she got home and her emotions were scrambled as she tried to calm down to analyse how she felt about seeing Luke again today, albeit very briefly.

Did she still care for him in some strange way?

Had Luke never married again?

What if he had recognised her?

How would he have reacted?

Did he ever think of her and Katherine?

Did he even care?

There were further articles about Luke and his company in the newspaper from time to time, and Elsie always cut them out for safekeeping in the little wooden box. She wondered what she would ultimately do with the contents, as all it would do was prove to Katherine that she had lied to her all her life about her father. She even questioned whether she should write to Luke and tell him about his wonderful daughter, but what would be the point? She decided to let sleeping dogs lie.

Chapter 20
An unexpected visitor

It was Christmas Eve, 1931. Norman, Elsie and Katherine had planned to walk to midnight mass together at the local Catholic Church. It was a lovely evening and the one time of the year when a few of the households would set aside their racist prejudices and attend church together. Elsie and Katherine felt quite safe walking in the night with Norman escorting them. The priest invited those who knew the words to Silent Night in the Zulu language to sing it. The result was a moving and beautiful service.

However, Christmas did not last forever and, after leaving the church, life reverted back to segregation as usual. Elsie, Norman and Katherine privately thought of how they needed each other and were thankful.

The next morning, they opened the gifts that they gave each other. Katherine had bought Norman a new white shirt and tie and her mother, a lovely red cardigan from a department store in the city of Johannesburg. Elsie had bought Norman a box of handkerchiefs and for Katherine, her favourite 'Lanvin' perfume. Norman had potted them each a hydrangea plant he had grown from cuttings.

The three of them started preparing Christmas lunch together and were all in high spirits anticipating their meal of roast chicken to be followed by the Christmas pudding that Elsie had made earlier in the year. The kitchen table was covered in a snow-white damask tablecloth and Katherine was busy decorating the table with stems of ivy she had cut from their garden when there was a knock at the front door. "I'll get it," she called out. "It's probably one of the neighbours."

On opening the front door, Katherine almost fainted at the sight of Michael standing before her with a very large smile on his face. He was even more handsome and distinguished-looking than she remembered. Katherine still had her hair trimmed into a neat fashionable bob and was wearing a pretty blue floral cotton dress. Michael too was not disappointed as he took in her beautiful image, still as elegant and poised as ever.

"Happy Christmas, Dr Viljoen," said Michael with a deep admiration in his voice at saying that for the first time to Katherine's face.

"And happy Christmas to you too, Dr Clavering," said Katherine with a tinkling giggle.

There was a taxi waiting in the street outside. They were both at a loss for words and stood staring at each other for a long while until, eventually, Michael asked if he could come in, or suggested that he could leave in the waiting taxi if that was what Katherine wanted? Katherine apologised and asked him to 'please come in.' Michael quickly nipped out to tell the driver of the taxi to return in a couple of hours.

He was beaming from ear to ear as he came through the front door, commenting on the lovely little house. He could immediately smell the luncheon being prepared in the kitchen and had not really given a thought to the fact that Katherine and her mother may well have been having their Christmas lunch at the time of his calling upon them.

"I am so sorry about my timing, as you and your mother are probably about to eat," said Michael feeling rather awkward.

"No problem," replied Katherine lying, "please join us for lunch. I will go and set another place. Would you like a sherry before lunch?"

She led Michael through to the sitting room and into the courtyard, thinking that if he was out of earshot, she could quickly brief her mother and Norman of his arrival and decide how they should handle it. Michael was about to meet her mother and she was not going to be able to hide the truth a moment longer.

Katherine dashed back to the kitchen in a panic and hastily explained to Elsie and Norman that Michael had arrived unexpectedly from England. They had not ever thought of this scenario and realised their secret was about to be revealed. Michael would now have to know the truth of her heritage.

Elsie said she would bring the sherry and glasses through, and Katherine had best go and explain the situation. The normally confident Katherine had no idea how to start explaining her family history to Michael, and felt a sense of panic rising in her.

Katherine joined Michael sitting in the courtyard, enjoying the sun, and immediately started babbling on about how much warmer it must be than in England. She knew she had little time to get to the point.

"Michael, my mother will be bringing through the sherry shortly."

"How kind. I look forward to meeting her."

"The… the… the… thing is, Michael, she is…" Katherine stuttered.

"She is what?"

With that, Elsie joined them in the courtyard and finished Katherine's sentence.

"She is Coloured."

Handing Michael and Katherine a glass of sherry, Elsie took a glass herself and raising it said, "And a happy Christmas."

"Michael, please meet my mother, Elsie."

"Pleased to meet you, Mrs Viljoen," replied Michael calmly.

Katherine sat down on one of the chairs, not taking her eyes off Michael's face, as she knew she could not miss even a trace of his reaction.

She was so impressed with her mother's confidence in announcing herself to Michael like that.

There was not even the slightest sign of shock or surprise on Michael's face that Katherine or Elsie could read. They sat and casually chatted about England and his voyage back to South Africa.

Norman came through shortly afterwards, to announce that lunch was ready, and Michael looked quizzically at him.

"Ah," said Katherine, "this is our friend Norman, who lives here and works for us. He will also be joining us for lunch."

Michael immediately stood to shake Norman's hand in the traditional African manner, which is to shake hands Western style, then each folds the fingers around the other's thumb before reverting back to the initial handshake.

"Pleased to meet you, baas," said Norman quite shyly.

Michael replied, "And I you, sir."

Norman looked slightly embarrassed at being called 'sir' by a White man.

They all went through to the kitchen and sat together, enjoying the most delicious meal. Everyone was telling stories about their childhood Christmas memories.

Norman made them laugh when he said they were so poor that the chicken jumped into their porridge for flavouring on Christmas day. Elsie recalled her mother making spicy chicken stew in their little cottage on St Helena. Michael was delighted to hear that Elsie came from St Helena as his ship had recently stopped there for supplies on the way from England to Cape Town. Elsie eagerly questioned him about Jamestown and what may have changed.

Katherine remembered the wonderful Cape Malayan meals shared with her godparents in District Six. Michael, on the other hand, remembered lavish meals at the family vineyard. None of them were judging each other and all enjoyed the stories that involved time with loved ones.

The homemade Christmas pudding was delicious and was served with a creamy custard that Elsie had made. There was one sixpence hidden in the pudding, pushed in for luck, and the one who got it was said to have their wish come true. Michael was the lucky recipient and, smiling conspiratorially, said that he hoped that would be the case.

He remembered that he had gifts in his bag for Elsie and her mother and after apologising that he had not expected anyone else to be at home with them, he pressed a very well received pound note into Norman's palm. Michael had brought some lightly scented Yardley English soaps and talcum powder from London for Elsie; for Katherine, a long string of pearls presented in a beautifully wrapped, leather covered box from a renowned London jeweller. Katherine was astounded and quite lost for words as Michael hung them around her neck. They were truly beautiful, but she could not help wondering when she would have the occasion to wear them. She impulsively hugged Michael and they both blushed at her unexpected show of affection, particularly in front of Elsie and

Norman.

The couple of hours that Michael spent with them passed too quickly and, before he knew it, the taxi had returned. He advised them that he would be staying with friends in Johannesburg for a few more days and that he would like to visit again the next day, to take Katherine for a walk in the local park. They settled on him returning the next morning.

Katherine stood in the garden and waved goodbye, wondering if Michael would really return. Now he would understand why she had kept her mother a secret and even why she tried to discourage his friendship and affections. She wondered whether, on reflection, he would think better of their friendship. What she knew for certain was that her heritage would not bring them acceptance from his family and some of his friends. She did not like hiding her mother and not being able to acknowledge her, but there had been, and really was, no other option. Well, Michael now knew the truth and it was possibly best that he had not announced his arrival, as Katherine would surely have had no idea of how to handle the situation. She did reflect on how delightfully bold Elsie had been in announcing to Michael that she was Coloured.

Katherine went inside and put her arms around Elsie, saying how proud she was of her, and they both had a silent little weep in a moment of some strange kind of relief. Norman continued with his task of washing the dishes and whistling the tune of a Christmas carol.

Norman always believed that his current situation, living with Elsie and Katherine, would not last forever, but he had seen something in Michael's eyes that made him think that he would not be put off, even if Katherine's mother was Coloured. Norman saw the longing and the way he hung on Katherine's every word. He too had felt like that once, about a young lady, but she never knew and went on to marry someone else. Norman had such polarised emotions of wanting Katherine to find a husband but at the same time selfishly not wanting things to change for himself. He would chat to Elsie about it when they were alone again, but he suspected she may have similar feelings. He declined their offer to help tidy up the kitchen and sent them to the lounge to relax, making them a tray of tea accompanied by two fruit mince pies that he and Elsie had made before Christmas.

Had Michael's visit been a Christmas gift or not?

The truth was now out and only time would tell what the consequences would be.

Chapter 21
A Walk in the Park

Despite Katherine's mixed feelings and anxieties of wanting Michael to return and then not return, he arrived as promised the next morning, driving a smart car that belonged to the friend he was staying with. It was not a common sight to see a very shiny open-top car arrive in their quiet street and the little boys from next door came out to admire the vehicle and ask lots of questions. Michael kindly offered to take them for a ride. He picked up the handicapped little boy, who was very short with his torso leaning to one side from polio, and gently placed him on the front seat next to him, propping him up with the cushion offered by the little boy's mother. His little face lit up with joy and excitement and his older brother bounced up and down enjoying the back seat to himself.

Katherine looked on with their mother and admired Michael for taking the boys for a short joyride, as he too clearly had a lot on his mind. Maybe he was delaying the inevitable.

After returning the very thrilled boys to their mother, Michael held open the passenger door for Katherine to take a seat alongside him, which she did, feeling her heart pounding so hard that she was sure Michael was able to hear it.

Katherine had made a greater effort than normal to get dressed that morning and was wearing navy wide-legged linen trousers and a silk cream blouse. On her feet, she wore a flat pair of fashionable two-tone brogues in navy and cream leather. She had draped the pearls around her neck and made the decision that morning that they were to be worn as often as possible. There really would be no point leaving them to lie in a drawer at home. She placed a large straw hat on her head when she went outside, which she secured with a pale blue chiffon scarf when they started to drive. What a handsome couple they made. As it was Boxing Day, many people were out walking with their families and, seeing Katherine and Michael, admired the two of them driving past in the shiny open-top car.

They spoke about this and that and Michael told her about the nice evening he had shared with his friends after he had left her. Katherine realised that he was staying in a very grand part of Johannesburg in a suburb called Houghton and that clearly her little cottage must have been a real comedown for Michael to visit, although he certainly did not imply as much.

When Michael had parked the car near the entrance gate to Rhodes Park, he turned in his seat and looked long and hard at Katherine. She braced herself for what was coming and, although she had told herself long before seeing Michael again that she wanted to call the whole thing off, she realised this may not be the case anymore. Sharing Christmas lunch with him had stirred feelings that she thought she had buried and now brought to the fore a longing to hold him that she had never felt quite so strongly before.

Michael smiled at her and said, "Katherine, darling, you look as elegant and beautiful as ever. No other girl even comes close to you."

Katherine had not been expecting a compliment, but rather an explanation about why he could not see her again. He took her hand and gently kissed the back of it and then jumped out of the driving seat to come around the car to open the passenger door for her. She remembered the deportment lessons she had received at school, slowly swivelled in her seat and, like a ballet dancer, alighted from the car. Michael took her arm and linked it through his as they started walking through the park gates. It was a beautiful sunny day, and the flowerbeds were all in bloom. They walked toward the rose garden and the perfume welcomed them to linger longer and admire the different varieties. There was a brass band playing in the bandstand and families were sitting around listening to the music, seated on their blankets, enjoying picnics boxed up for Boxing Day from their leftover Christmas dinners. There were only White people allowed in this park and Katherine wondered where the Black and Coloured people were allowed to have a picnic, if anywhere? They continued walking around the lake and at the far end found an empty, secluded bench in the shade, where they could look across the lake and still hear the band playing. A few ducks and swans swam towards them, but soon left when they realised no treats were coming their way.

Katherine knew the conversation about her mother had to be opened, as although they had been walking arm in arm, she felt as though a huge crevasse was forming between them.

"Have your recovered from your shock at meeting my mother yesterday? I didn't think you would come back today, although I am still sure it is to say goodbye. If that is the case then please, get it over with… as I know there is no future for us."

"Shhhhh," Michael replied, quietening her, and continued in a very measured tone, as though he had practiced at length what he was going to say to her.

"Yes, I cannot deny that yesterday was initially a shock,

but also a happy Christmas Day; in fact, one of my happiest. As doctors, we both know that colour and race certainly count for nothing. Working in England has highlighted that even more for me, but the racial segregation and divide is growing here in South Africa." He paused and took a deep contemplative breath, "Katherine, I could walk away from you and break my own heart, but I came back from England to see you and to get to the bottom of what was really holding you back from travelling and not wanting to visit me there. Now I know, and it is a lot to digest, which I cannot deny. I slept very little last night, thinking of all the ways around our dilemma, and there are not many options, I have to admit."

At this point Katherine would have got up and run away, but she was feeling so weak and physically ill that she knew her legs would not carry her. Then, annoyingly, the tears ran down her cheeks and she dabbed them with her scarf. Michael produced his hanky and put his arm around her shoulders.

"Yes, this is a crying matter and don't be surprised if I weep with you," he said quietly. "There are a few things we need to consider and the first being, do we want to be together and live together as husband and wife ….although I have not yet even proposed to you, my darling Katherine. Secondly, we could be married quietly, and later announce it to the world thereafter. Your mother could continue to live with us under the guise of being the housekeeper; or we could move to England and take her with us as skin colour does seem to matter less over there."

This made Katherine sob even more and she felt so silly at not being able to think clearly enough to give him an answer or even comment on his suggestions.

Michael took both her hands in his and cautiously said, "There would be the issue of children too. In this current world, there is no place for children of mixed-race and we both know the possibility would be very high for a child of ours to carry Coloured genes. We could, of course, adopt a couple of kids?" he smiled broadly. "I have got way ahead of myself here, my darling Katherine, but no doubt you have thought of all of this already?"

Katherine nodded her head replying, "Yes, these issues have crossed my mind too," giving Michael a very wary and teary smile. "I should have been honest with you a long time ago, but it would have seemed presumptuous saying that our having children may be a problem. Also, as you know, there was the unwritten agreement that woman doctors should not marry and have children, but be totally committed to their careers. When you left for England, I assumed you would meet a nice lady there and marry her — a pure White lady with no baggage. So, your unannounced arrival yesterday has caught me off-guard. You know I would have certainly made an excuse not to see you, but now I am glad you know the truth. You are now free to move on, Michael. Go and find yourself a girl with a mother she does not need to hide from the world."

Michael gently held both her hands between his and looked deeply into her blue eyes. She was so beautiful, even with tears again streaming down her cheeks. He wiped them away with his thumbs and kissed her on the lips. "Katherine, you are the girl I love and want... no other. This will be difficult, but we will work it out by loving each other. Believe me."

"How, Michael, how? This will only create hurt and pain to both my mother and your family. There is no way around it. The truth is I have Coloured blood in me and that is unacceptable in White society."

"I feel that would be concentrating on the negative, albeit

226

the truth. Going forward with our relationship would take a huge commitment beyond what most marriages would call for... But, Katherine, darling, we have so much in common with our medical backgrounds, we have endless empathy, even for those who may choose to judge us. Please, think about our future together... just about us, then we can work out what to do from there. If you reconsider and believe, as I do, that there is an excellent chance we can make it, I will propose to you. I will either marry you or walk away, but I am not sure that I could bear your declining my proposal."

They sat together for a long while, both lost in their own thoughts, feelings and intensely deep love for each other.

"Michael, I need some time to think about the consequences... for my job, my mother... and if we left for England, what would happen to dear Norman?"

"I agree we both need time to think, not too much time though as I plan to travel to Cape Town to visit my family in the next few days, and I will be returning here in a fortnight or so for your answer. I think you should know also that I have agreed to take up a new position at a hospital in England called The Haslar Royal Naval Hospital near Portsmouth, in a couple of months. They are looking for more doctors to support the local community and the Royal Navy. It's possible we could both practice at the hospital and find a home in the area. It is on the sea and there are some lovely homes overlooking the Solent towards the Isle of Wight. Please think about this, Katherine, as I know we could be so good together. Maybe your mother will even agree to come along and keep house for us?"

Katherine nodded as she felt the infuriating lump that was almost choking her with her overwhelming emotions come back into her throat. Of course, she wanted to say yes to

Michael and to hell with the rest of the world, but she was responsible for her mother, for Norman too and her work as a doctor. There were so many people counting on her, and Michael could be the best prize or the greatest regret for the rest of her life.

They drove back to Katherine's home and Michael stayed for a cup of tea in the lovely courtyard that Norman had filled with many exotic potted plants and creepers. Norman was out visiting friends for the day, so the three of them enjoyed slices of the delicious Christmas cake Elsie had made.

Elsie shared with Michael that she was hoping to one day publish a cookery book, after he had complimented her on her cooking and baking. Michael thought that would be a wonderful idea and mentioned that he knew a publisher in England who may be interested when she had a draft ready to show. Elsie was delighted, as to get any book published would be such a personal achievement. She immediately thought back to her father, who would have been so proud of her, and to her mother who would have been astonished at her having been a single mother and now a reasonably accomplished homemaker, cook and baker. She smiled to herself and said to Michael that she may well take him up on his offer.

When Michael left, he kissed Katherine gently on the lips as though she was the most precious person in the world, and to him, she was. He wrote down his parents' address and said that, should she *not* want to go ahead, she should send a telegram and then he would not return in a fortnight. He promised Katherine that he would honour her decision, whichever way she decided. With that, he drove away, dragging her heartstrings in his wake.

Katherine knew that the next few days would entail a constant debate in her mind and soul. She knew that when the time was right, she would sit down with Elsie and explain her position, although she felt none of this would be a surprise to her mother.

Katherine had an early start the next day and so retired to her bedroom straight after supper that evening, knowing there would be little sleep but much consideration of the pros and cons of her and Michael marrying.

At about midnight, still unable to settle, she tiptoed to the kitchen to make herself a drink of warm milk and honey hoping that would encourage some sleep. Elsie, knowing that there was much troubling her daughter since Michael's departure, went to join her in the kitchen, asking if she wanted to talk.

"Oh Mother, I have come to such a crossroad in my life with Michael's unexpected visit and well, his sort of... proposal," sobbed Katherine.

Elsie sank down in the chair opposite her daughter and gently took her hand. She listened as Katherine relayed how they had met in Cape Town and how she had purposefully tried to keep him at a distance and just as a friend. Part of her had hoped that he would meet an English lady and fall in love, making him unavailable to even think about, but now he had returned and rekindled her love for him. Even with him learning that Elsie was of Coloured descent, he still wanted to marry Katherine. He had even suggested that they think about adopting children. He was hopeful that if they married and settled in England, the race issue would be less of a problem and that Elsie would think of joining them. At this stage, Elsie also had tears streaming down her cheeks on learning of Michael's kindness. This may mean that she could continue to live with Katherine as mother and daughter without the stigma they experienced in Johannesburg. She felt she could not bear to have her daughter move overseas and never see her again.

Katherine began asking Elsie how she knew Luke had been the right man to marry and how it had felt for her to be in love with him. Elsie had always previously shut down such questions with an explanation that it hurt her too much to talk about those times, but she knew she could not take away this moment from Katherine, so replied vaguely saying that it was different as Luke had been a POW and they certainly had not had the freedom that Katherine and Michael enjoyed. She did, however, manage to share that Luke had made her heart smile when she used to see him walking towards her.

Katherine laughed as she said she knew that exact feeling.

Elsie said no more, as whenever Katherine raised any questions about Luke, she felt a vice like grip on her heart, remembering that he had chosen to desert them and make a life without his wife and daughter. Elsie had carried out his request, but this also meant that she had lied to Katherine all these years. She had carried the heavy burden of the untruth and Luke was scot-free from guilt, or so she thought. Katherine was her daughter and, even though he was now living not too far from them, she felt he had no right to know anything regarding her. Elsie wondered what he would think if he knew how successful Katherine had become. Besides being beautiful and elegant, she was about to marry a wonderful man. She was hopeful that they could move to England and put a greater distance between Luke and themselves before he accidentally came tumbling back into their lives. Johannesburg was not very big and although they were in different suburbs of the city, there was always the possibility that their paths could cross.

One day, if the time was right, she could tell Katherine the truth and let her see the contents of the box. She fingered the key around her neck and shuddered at the thought of the secrets it could unlock and the resulting consequences.

Elsie said she would certainly follow them to England if they invited her to do so, but she expressed concern about what would happen to Norman. Katherine had already given that some thought and planned to speak to the maintenance manager at the hospital to see if he could employ Norman, with Katherine providing him with an excellent reference. She too was concerned about losing Norman as he had become part of this strange little family, each loyally guarding the others' secrets.

Katherine told Elsie that she had made up her mind to accept Michael's proposal and would send him a telegram saying, "Yes".

They would have many things to iron out and overcome. She planned to speak to the local priest about marrying them quietly, in the little chapel attached to the sanatorium where she worked. She was unsure how Michael's family would react to the news and doubted that they would approve of him marrying a lady of mixed-race; she therefore assumed that the wedding ceremony would be extremely small. Elsie said that she would stay away if it made things easier, but Katherine refused to hide her mother any longer and particularly now that Michael was prepared to accept the situation. Elsie squeezed her daughter's hand in thankfulness, but also knew that they were entering a quagmire of racial problems and prejudices. She jokingly suggested to Katherine that they should all move back to St Helena Island, where the Saints all got on together with no racial issues.

Chapter 22
Michael's family

Michael had sent a telegram to his family announcing his arrival at their wine estate and they were thrilled about his visit. From his letters to them, they were aware that he was planning to return to England to take up a new position at a hospital in the south of the country. The family were saddened when Michael told them he was planning to leave again so soon. His father tried on several occasions to get him to change his mind and come back home to the Cape. He said he had doctor friends who could arrange for him to have an interview to work at a hospital in the Cape Town area. His mother and sister cautiously asked if there was a young lady he was returning to. Michael replied rather nonchalantly that there could be…

When Katherine's telegram arrived the next day, Michael feared the worst as he had left her saying that she should send him a telegram if she decided to *decline* his proposal, such as it was. When the telegram was handed to Michael by one of the members of the household staff, he could not bear to open it. He stuffed it into his pocket before taking himself off for a long walk through the vineyards and up a large hill overlooking the Franschhoek Valley.

The vines were all neatly laid out on the side of the slopes with blooming roses planted at the end of each row. Since both vines and roses are susceptible to some of the same diseases, roses acted as an early warning of mildew and fungal problems.

There was a storm brewing in the hills on the other side of the valley, and the threatening dark clouds seemed to match his mood. He sat there, almost oblivious to the beautiful view, with a million scenarios running through his head, until he eventually ripped the envelope open to read just one word, "Yes!"

He leapt for joy and shouted the word again and again into the wind, realising that he was crying and laughing at the same time. He stood for a moment, hugging the telegram against his heart, and only then did he really notice and appreciate the view around him. He knew he would cherish this moment for the rest of his life. The shafts of sunlight shining through the clouds on the other side of the valley suggested an image of the fingers of God reaching out to touch him. No man could be happier. But now, to tell his family.

When he made his way down the hill back towards the picturesque gabled family homestead with the thatched roof, he realised that by marrying Katherine he could possibly be walking away from his family. He planned to tell them all after dinner that he would be marrying Katherine and they would hopefully both be able to work together in the same hospital in England. He realised that his parents would obviously want to host the wedding at the wine estate, but Michael doubted that would be an option when he told them that Katherine's mother was a Coloured lady from St Helena.

He was hardly able to swallow his dinner that evening with the flood of emotions running through his head as well as the anticipation of possibly being disowned by his family because of his choice of wife. After dinner, they moved through to the library where the open doors perfectly framed the views of the valley at sunset and then outside on to the patio to enjoy the uninterrupted vista across the large estate. After the snifters of local brandy had been enjoyed, Michael decided that the time had come to announce his decision to his family.

"Ma, Pa and Sissie... I have something to tell you. You remember Katherine? Well, I am in love with her. She is the most wonderful and beautiful lady and has now also qualified as a doctor. I am planning to marry her very soon."

The family were all delighted and asked many questions about Katherine, whom they had indeed met a few years before at Michael's graduation. They immediately started planning the wedding, as of course it was taken for granted that it would be held at the family estate.

"I think we all need to go inside and sit down to discuss this further, as the situation is somewhat complicated," said Michael hesitantly.

Once they had all moved inside and were seated, looking very solemn and concerned, Michael began his explanation.

"I first met Katherine whilst we were both studying at university, as you know. She was a few years behind me with her studies and, after she qualified, she moved to Johannesburg with her mother to work at a maternity hospital and at the local sanatorium. We have continued to correspond whilst I have been in England and I have tried on a number of occasions to get her to come and visit me there, and possibly look at working in England too. She seemed reluctant, without an explanation, when I suggested this initially and so I decided to make an unannounced visit to her home in Johannesburg for Christmas."

"I arrived at her front door on Christmas Day and was invited to stay for a delicious luncheon. This was the first time

I had met her mother and therein lies the complication which I feel I must explain: Katherine's mother is a Coloured lady from St Helena Island!"

The family gasped in unison and started objecting to the forthcoming nuptials and voicing their strong opinions at the same time. They were suddenly all unshakeably against the marriage and their obvious concerns were raised. The grandchildren could be Coloured! What would people say? Miscegenation cannot happen in this racially pure Clavering family. The Immorality Act of 1927 under the Hertzog government made intermarriage between Europeans and Africans illegal; besides, it was a positively revolting thought to them. How could Michael possibly disregard all the family morals? These Coloured people carry disease. Why did Michael not realise this? Had he forgotten his roots and family values?

Michael's mother and sister began to weep and asked him how he could even think of bringing a Coloured woman into their family. "Surely you realise that all the household servants and workers in the vineyard are Coloured? If this union were to go ahead, this would make the Clavering family the laughing stock of Cape Town!"

They vowed never to accept her and declared that he would therefore have to make a choice: Katherine or his family.

His father finally intercepted the ruckus and asked the family to remain calm and to discuss the matter again in the morning.

By morning, they were no more accepting or at ease with the situation. In fact, they were furious that, no matter what their arguments and points were, Michael was steadfast and determined to marry Katherine. He simply would not be swayed by their racial rants and objections.

"Ultimately," Michael tried to explain, "…it is Katherine… and that is my choice, and by moving to England we are hopeful that we will be able to live a more 'normal' life with fewer racial prejudices. By the way, Katherine's late father was a White South African POW on St Helena and at least he had the decency to marry her mother."

Sadly, this made no difference to the family who, like most White families, chose to ignore the ever-increasing Coloured population in the Cape and how they came to be; obviously from some 'indiscretions' on the part of the White males. The family's Calvinist morality and their deep-seated colour prejudice was totally incompatible with Michael's attitude. It was clear that there was an irrational horror of interracial relations. His father went as far as to say that sex with a person of dark skin colour was linked with sin and damnation.

Michael realised that this may well be the first of many battles that he would face by marrying Katherine, but not for one moment would he be swayed by his family's pleas and arguments. With the threat of the family disowning him becoming more apparent, he decided to make his excuses and, much relieved, departed for Cape Town the next day where he booked himself onto the next train to Johannesburg.

The journey through the Karoo and on into the Free State was long and dusty. Even travelling first class, it was a tiresome trip and he felt sorry for those people at the back of the train in the second and third-class carriages. He had lots of time to think through his family's reactions and it saddened him deeply that they could be so racially prejudiced. When they had met Katherine previously, they had been very friendly and nice to her but now that they knew her heritage, it was a very different story. Now she was suddenly not good enough for them. The stark reality of his decision kept him from sleeping on the journey, but not from knowing in his heart that he did not want to live his life without her.

A part of him was deeply embarrassed that he would have to explain his family's reaction to Katherine and Elsie, but he also knew that this would come as no surprise to them, as they had long been living with these stark racial judgements.

On arriving in Johannesburg, he took a taxi straight to Katherine and Elsie's home in Kensington. Neither were back from work, but Norman was at home and let him in with the offer of a cup of tea, which Michael gratefully accepted.

While the kettle boiled, Norman proudly showed Michael his very successful vegetable patch in the back garden and the exotic plants thriving in the enclosed courtyard, which were his pride and joy.

They sat down together at the kitchen table. Norman went straight to the point and asked Michael if he had come back to marry Katherine? Michael was somewhat taken aback at the bluntness of the question, but realised that the truth would be out soon enough.

"Yes, Norman. I am planning to ask her to marry me."

"I know her father is dead, so I am willing to give you permission to marry her, but you had better always treat her like a real lady. She is a wonderful woman and like no other White woman I have ever known. Other people always judge you by the colour of your skin or the way you speak, but not Katherine; she sees the real person inside and I really respect her for this. I suppose you will be taking them both back to England with you?"

"Yes, Norman, that is my plan, as there are far fewer racial issues in England than here and hopefully Elsie can live with us as Katherine's mother, and not have to hide from the neighbours and pretend to be the maid as she does now."

"So… I had better start looking for a new job and a place to stay. Life will never be the same here for me. Nobody will treat me like an equal again and make me feel as welcome as I have been here. Did you know that I am half Indian? So, my own family don't really want me around. You see, I remind them that my father was Indian, and probably forced my mother to have sex. Not good! No place in this country for us mixed-race people. You must take them to a better place, where they at least don't have to hide and pretend. Good luck to you, and you had better look after them!"

Norman wiped his eyes as the tears started to sting and walked out into the back garden, blowing his nose in a large hankie, leaving Michael to drink his tea and digest the fact that Norman's life was inevitably going to change for the worse when he took Elsie and Katherine away. Hopefully, Katherine could find him some work with a good employer and a decent place to stay. The conversation had certainly taken the edge off his euphoria and excitement at seeing Katherine again. With that, he heard the front door being unlocked and he stood to walk down the passage to find Katherine standing in the entrance hall. She dropped her bag and flew into his arms as he picked her up and held her tightly. They were both soon laughing with the delight of not having any inhibitions, with their love having finally been declared to each other. Michael stood back and held her at arm's length, looking deep into her eyes. He slowly dropped on to one knee, saying, "Katherine, please marry me?"

To which she replied, "Michael, please marry me?"

The moment could not have been better planned or more romantic as he stood and kissed her long and passionately.

They tenderly embraced for a long while and Michael gently whispered, "We will overcome with our love for each other."

"Yes, we will, Michael, but I am under no illusions that we have chosen a difficult road."

Elsie arrived not long after that and they immediately told her their news. She was obviously thrilled and tried not to think about the negative implications that this marriage was sure to bring.

They all prepared dinner together and, although there were many concerns, they still managed to have a wonderful evening, only focusing on the positive.

Katherine mentioned that she had spoken to the local Catholic priest, who had agreed to marry them but would need to meet Michael to ensure that he agreed that any children from their union would be raised as Roman Catholics. They smiled conspiratorially at this. The question of Michael's family attending the wedding was raised. He chose not go into the hurtful details of the arguments and discussions he had had with his family, but just informed Katherine that they would not be attending their wedding. Katherine realised that there was more to it.

It was already late, so Elsie and Katherine shared a bedroom and Michael stayed over in Elsie's room that night. Katherine had to work at the hospital the next day and Michael made his way to his friends in Houghton, where he had stayed before. An appointment was made for them to meet the Catholic priest that week, who agreed to marry them when Katherine was not on duty.

There was no time to get a wedding dress made, but Katherine had a beautiful, very pale blue, fitted, fine silk dress that she had bought on a whim and not yet had the occasion to wear. Margery, the dressmaker next door, made a beautiful cream silk sash to tie in a large bow at the back of the dress with a matching cream headband to which she attached a delicate cream lace veil, the same length as the dress. Katherine, of course, wore the long string of lovely pearls that Michael had given her for Christmas. The nun who did flower arrangements for the chapel offered to tie a bouquet of lilies and ferns for Katherine to hold.

Michael had taken a room at the Rand Club whilst they made plans for their wedding and move to England. He visited when Katherine was not on duty, to discuss the progress of their forthcoming arrangements. After a fortnight, the very small wedding reception dinner at the grand Carlton Hotel was booked and their passages on the ship to England confirmed.

Elsie had been extremely anxious about attending the wedding as she did not want anything to be spoilt for her beloved daughter and future son-in-law. She could not help but recall her wedding day on St Helena when she walked to the church alone to marry Luke, before he was returned by the guard to the POW camp. She also wondered more often than she would have liked to admit, how Luke was and even thought that perhaps she should drop him a note saying that Katherine was getting married. Then, as she fingered the key hanging around her neck, she recalled his words that it was best to tell their daughter that he was dead.

Katherine was determined that her mother would be attending both the wedding ceremony and the reception dinner. Her plan was to buy her mother a very large grey hat with a large low brim hiding her face and long cream gloves to cover her hands. The outfit she had picked out for Elsie to wear was a grey suit with a calf-length skirt and a cardigan-style jacket, trimmed and decorated with black embroidery and black buttons, which she wore with a high-collared, cream blouse all in the new Coco Chanel style. Elsie had kept her slim figure and although her hair had greyed, she still looked younger than her years. Katherine had visited a beautician at one of the cosmetic houses to get a light foundation that she planned to apply to Elsie's face. They would proceed with confidence as if all was normal, hoping that no one would have the audacity to question the race of the bride's mother on the day.

The wedding party would be very small with just Elsie and a very good, old school friend of Michael's and his widowed father in attendance. Michael had explained the 'awkward' situation regarding his own family to them and, being like-minded folk, they happily accepted his decision.

The day of the wedding arrived, and Michael came to collect Elsie and Katherine in a car loaned from his friend. Norman was reluctant to attend the ceremony, although he was smartly dressed. Michael convinced him to at least come along to see them married in the little chapel. There was an unspoken agreement that Norman would not be attending the wedding dinner at the Carlton Hotel, as that was a complication too far. In fact, the doorman would not have allowed him to enter the hotel anyway. Only Black people who worked at the hotel were allowed inside.

They drove the short distance to the chapel next to the sanatorium and Michael went in with Norman to join his friend and his friend's father, being the only other people to attend beside the priest and the nun who had arranged the flowers in the chapel and Katherine's bouquet.

Elsie was to walk Katherine down the short little aisle. Michael stood at the front of the chapel and, although he had already seen his bride that morning, he was astounded at her beauty and elegant grace as she walked towards him holding her mother's hand. He knew he was doing the right thing marrying Katherine and felt even more determined to protect her and her mother from any possible future racially motivated situations. He felt optimistic about their future together, although he knew it would be an ongoing difficult balancing act.

The ceremony was short and deeply meaningful with their vows sincerely taken and looking deep into each other's eyes. Michael's friend had brought along a camera as he was a keen photographer. They were an exceptionally handsome couple, and Elsie was quite overwhelmed at times to see her beautiful daughter so happily married.

They made their way to the Carlton Hotel and enjoyed a delicious meal with no one giving a second glance at the bride's mother. Well, if they did, nothing was said. Michael and Katherine stayed on at the hotel for their honeymoon night and Elsie was driven home by Michael's friend.

Elsie had brought back the remainder of the wedding cake that the hotel had provided, and she and Norman enjoyed a slice each whilst chatting about the day. Norman reported that the neighbours had been cross-questioning him about the wedding, but he felt sure they still believed that Elsie was the lady doctor's maid, who had just attended the wedding. Elsie knew there would have been questions about how she had managed to mix with the Whites and was slightly relieved at the thought that soon they would be heading to England, where hopefully her living with Michael and Katherine would not be such an issue and certainly not a criminal offence.

There was a band playing American-style jazz in the hotel's ballroom and Katherine and Michael went to have a glass of champagne and gently swayed in each other's arms to the music. They headed to their suite and their lovemaking was gentle and magical. They were both virgins and so their experience was beyond anything they could ever have believed possible. Their honeymoon night was what a first night of making love should be, although so few get to experience the wonderful magic of true and unselfish love.

They woke in the morning to the delight of being able to do it all again and felt quite decadent when ordering breakfast to be delivered to their suite.

Chapter 23
Luke's regrets

The following week, Luke was browsing through the newspaper and was flabbergasted to read the wedding announcement of Dr Katherine Georgina Viljoen to Dr Michael James Clavering in the 'hatches, matches and dispatches' columns. There was no mention of parents on either side. Luke felt a physical pain in his heart realising that he would never walk his daughter, his only child, down the aisle or attend her wedding. The last time he had seen her from a distance was at her graduation, and he knew she would have been the most elegant and beautiful of all brides. The memory of him marrying Elsie when he was a POW and never making love to her again after their coupling at the waterfall on St Helena, filled him with deep sadness. He felt sure that Elsie would have attended the wedding somehow and wished he had known about it so that he could have observed some of the marriage in secret.

With each passing year, he became lonelier and less likely to ever know Katherine. He assumed Elsie had stuck to his request to tell Katherine that he was dead and so there was no possible way he could resurrect himself without hugely disrupting Katherine's life and exposing the fact that both her parents had lied to her. The longer the simmering secret was kept, the greater the reaction and possible damage it would potentially cause, if ever exposed.

Knowing where Katherine lived in Kensington and where she worked, he felt the overwhelming urge to go to her and tell her the truth, but he knew he could not do that. He would have to speak to Elsie first as she was the one upon whom he had placed the burden of his supposed death. She was legally still his wife and he wondered about writing to her. He sat down and drafted a letter, and another and another, which all ended up being thrown in the fire. As he watched the flames leap around his feeble attempts to explain himself, he felt those very flames engulfing his soul and leaving only self-pity and deep regret. He knew he had painted himself into a selfish and unfulfilling corner.

At the time he had written that letter to Elsie, he was a POW and his youth had denied him the foresight to realise that Katherine may be his only child. As a consequential reward, Elsie had experienced all the joy of bringing up their daughter. Over the years he had often played out scenarios of arriving unannounced to see Katherine and introducing himself, but he always feared total rejection. He wondered if Elsie still had the letter he had written. If not, he thought of denying all knowledge of Katherine's birth, thus making Elsie despise him more than he would want or believed he deserved.

Whatever happened in the future, he knew he may not get to know his daughter, but he was determined that she would inherit from him. He had no one else to leave his fortune to. He immediately made up his mind to contact his lawyer to lodge his will, together with a letter explaining his actions, their respective timings and his untold regrets.

Luke felt disheartened that no matter how successful he was in business, nothing seemed to bring him true fulfilment. He had seen and envied the joy that family brought to his friends and colleagues.

One of his neighbours in Houghton had recently been widowed and his young single son had moved back to the family home to keep him company and help him out during his mourning. Luke had no one to turn to other than his staff, and although he did not question their loyalty, they had their own families and private lives to lead. What he really wanted, was to have people around him he cared about, and who cared about him in a small way. The elusive family.

Luke recalled his happy youth with his parents and sisters around him, the simple things they had all enjoyed: the lively discussions around the table at meal times, the long horse rides with his sisters, how he had wanted to emulate everything his father was and did. Instead of having the privilege of watching him growing older, he had had to hurriedly bury him in a shallow grave before the British attacked them again during the fighting. He would never know if his mother and sisters ever found out that Luke had survived the POW camp. He still carried such guilt that his mother and sisters had perished in those awful cruel camps, and they did not even have individual graves where he could pay his respects to them. He wished his mother had taken all the money she had left him and managed to save herself and his sisters. Instead, she had seemed to have been more concerned about him and his survival. How could she have loved him so unconditionally? This may be an emotion he would never be privileged enough to feel. Despite all her sacrifices and plans, real happiness had eluded him.

He decided to take a walk in his large garden to try to clear his head and break the emotional downward spiral into which he was rapidly sliding. His garden was a picture and he had instructed his gardener to plant a large bed of red roses that, in his own mind, he called 'Elsie's rose garden.' Red roses always reminded him of the roses that grew outside her cottage on St

Helena, and of those she had worn in her hair on the day they were married. He remembered that he had even made a feeble attempt to paint red roses on the wooden box he had made for her. Had Elsie kept the box in which he had delivered the letter that changed all of their lives? It now seemed that his letter to her had only brought him unspoken and unrelenting grief. He would need to explain his decisions very carefully in the letter he intended to write to his daughter one day. Only at this later stage of his life was he beginning to acknowledge the importance of being true to himself. Suddenly, his own self-importance and self-aggrandisement seemed to hold no ground.

Next to the pond he had had white arum lilies planted. They reminded him of those that grew in the valleys on St Helena which he and Elsie had admired during their secret meetings. Some thirty years had now passed and yet he remembered all the details of his time spent there as though it was yesterday. How clever she was, knowing so much about the fauna and flora of the island. She had read many wonderful books and their discussions were always lively. He fondly recalled that they had laughed a lot, something that he rarely did now.

He sat on a bench in his garden and listened to the serenading birds at the end of the day as they called to their mates and made their territories known. The leafy suburb attracted many birds, including the large noisy glossy ibis birds and there were a few on the lawn looking for insects in the grass. Their iridescent feathers shone in the late afternoon sun. The crested barbets trilled their calls and the yellow weaver birds were making the last adjustments for the day to their hanging nests over the pond. If only Luke had someone with whom to share this beautiful garden.

Chapter 24
The Departure

Katherine had worked her last month at the sanatorium and the maternity hospital and had started packing up crates of their belongings that were to accompany them on the boat to England. She felt terribly sad at leaving the work she so enjoyed and the friends she had made there. Although she had spent all those years studying medicine at university, she somehow felt that the delivery of babies and even saving their and their mothers' lives when complications set in could not have been more rewarding and fulfilling. She was taking a huge leap of faith in following her husband to England in the hope that she would find a similar position at the Royal Haslar Hospital. There had been times when not all the patients were very happy to have a lady doctor in attendance, but the nuns always stood up for her and in the majority of cases, the women would agree to have her look after them. Katherine often wondered why some patients could not accept that women were as capable as men in the medical world. She assumed it stemmed from a lifetime of living in a mostly male-dominated society. This made her all the more grateful for the powerful and strong women that she had been fortunate to encounter during her own formative years and the fact that they had unconditionally believed in her abilities. Mostly of course, she was grateful to her beloved mother, wondering how far Elsie could have gone had she had the opportunity to do so.

Norman had been very helpful making wooden crates to secure their furniture and kitchenware. Those very same trunks that had belonged to Elsie's parents were packed up with their household linen and clothes.

Fortunately for Norman, Katherine had managed to secure him a job as a handyman at the Kensington Sanatorium and it came with a small bedroom on the premises so that he would always be on standby in case of an urgent repair. Katherine and Elsie felt as though they were leaving a member of their family behind, but they knew that he would be respected by the nuns and doctors for whom he would be working.

One evening before they departed, the three of them and Michael all sat around the kitchen table enjoying a farewell dinner. They realised that they were each of very different heritage, going as far as congratulating themselves for defying the racist laws that South Africa was imposing on its citizens. Furthermore, they appreciated that they had escaped lightly, with not having been reported to the police by the neighbours for cross racial relations. Maybe their tolerance stemmed from the fact that Katherine was a doctor, who could not possibly be breaking the law and, after all, one never knew when a neighbouring doctor may be needed. It truly was now time to go and start a new life without having to hide Elsie's identity. They toasted each other with the last of the sherry and promised to write to Norman.

Michael, Katherine and Elsie set off on the train from Johannesburg to Cape Town, where they would be meeting their ship. Again, Elsie was not permitted to travel as a first-class passenger and had to travel third class. This infuriated both of them but, as ever, there was absolutely nothing they could do about it.

When they finally arrived in Cape Town, they had a chance to visit Marie in District Six, as well as the nuns at the convent, before they took the voyage to England. Elsie stayed with Marie, and the newlyweds spent a brief honeymoon at the Mount Nelson Hotel.

During their stay, they enjoyed a visit to the famous Kirstenbosch Gardens and hiked to the top of Table Mountain on a lovely sunny day. They walked past the Woodhead Reservoir, Table Mountain's first dam, built to assist with the increasing demand for water in the city below. Michael remembered his father telling him that it had been built with a series of porters literally carrying all the building material for the dam wall.

The view from the top of the mountain was breath-taking and they shared some of the picnic that the hotel had provided with the Cape Hyrax which the locals referred to as 'dassies' (Swahili for 'rock rabbit'). They watched an eagle soar way up in the thermals, rising up the sides of the mountain with such ease and grace, which enhanced the stunning view across Table Bay. They could see some ships moving about in the harbour and Robben Island in the distance. Michael pointed out the Twelve Apostles Mountain Range extending from the majestic Table Mountain towards Hout Bay. Katherine identified the white sand of Camps Bay beach she remembered visiting as a child.

Michael told Katherine that he had heard a folklore reason for the name of Devil's Peak which sits next to Table Mountain. Apparently, Van Hunk, a pirate, was smoking his pipe on the mountain one day when he met a man who challenged him to a smoking contest. It turned out that the man was the Devil, and the belief is that every time the mountain is covered with the 'tablecloth' the two are battling each other.

Michael had invited some of their Capetonian university friends to join them for a belated celebratory wedding dinner at the Mount Nelson. It turned out to be a wonderful impromptu party. Sadly, Michael's family made the choice not to see him and this, in fact, confirmed that they were disowning him because of his marriage to 'that Coloured girl'. The fact that they felt like this about Katherine, and that they believed themselves more superior to her, deeply saddened Michael.

On the last night he had spent with his parents, he had implored them to rethink their racial views and explained that, being a doctor, he was unable to see the difference between people despite their heritage, colour or religion. He assured them that as far as he was concerned, everyone is the same on the inside and their blood runs as red as the next human. However, this only seemed to infuriate them even more and caused them to question why he bothered to operate on the lower classes. He soon realised that his fury at this statement would go nowhere positive and so he walked away from his family with deep disappointment and loss in his heart.

Yes, it was time for Katherine and him to start afresh in a place where there would be no history of their previous lives haunting them; or at least, this was his hope. He had written ahead to the Royal Haslar Hospital advising them that his wife was a doctor specialising in obstetrics and minor surgery and that she would be joining him on his return to England. He expressed the hope that, in time, there would be a position for her at the hospital. The reply had come back to him that there was a possible chance of a vacancy and that there was also an allocated doctor's house for married couples in the grounds that would be available for them to move into on their arrival.

This was thrilling news for all of them, although Elsie could not help but express her concern about being accepted there as Katherine's mother. She said that she planned to sort out the house for them and knew she would enjoy cooking, baking and caring for them; possibly she would even get involved in the local church? Hopefully she could join the library and read all those books on her wish-list. Additionally, there was the challenge of her completing her cookery and household tips book which she dreamed of publishing one day.

Katherine reminded her mother that, since 1918, women over the age of thirty had the right to vote in the United Kingdom and they might enjoy the novelty of going to vote together when the next election came up.

They all visited Marie, who had grown much older and stooped but continued to run her little jam and pickle making business successfully, with a little help. She was delighted to meet Michael and wished the couple every happiness in England. Mother Superior too was thrilled to see them all and sweetly said that, when Katherine had come as a small girl to board at the convent and be educated, she was like a little rosebud, and here she was presenting herself now as a beautiful rose in full bloom. It was easy to see that Mother Superior was happy to take some credit for Katherine's achievements, although she would never ever admit it, and the obvious pride on her face shone through.

The day soon arrived when the ship was scheduled to sail. Michael had booked them first-class cabins and refused to enter into any discussion when Elsie objected to the unnecessary expense. He reminded her that she was now his mother too and that, despite his father's recent lapse in respect, he had taught Michael that one can judge a man by the way he treats his mother. Elsie did not really have an answer to that, but tearfully thanked him and said how blessed she was to have him as a son. What Michael had not revealed until they sailed, was that the ship was due to stop at St Helena Island to pick up supplies, mail and a few passengers. He thought it would be a wonderful treat for Elsie to visit there again, and for Katherine to see where she had been born. The boat was only due to stop at St Helena for a couple of days, but he too looked forward to discovering the island with his wife and mother-in-law.

Michael made the announcement to Katherine and Elsie over dinner as they left Cape Town.

"I have great news for both of you. This ship is due to visit St Helena for a couple of days in about a week's time." Looking very pleased with himself, he went on to say, "I thought that it may be an opportunity to visit the grave of Katherine's father? Perhaps… also the graves of your parents, Mum?"

At the mention of this, Elsie went an ashen colour and excused herself from dinner. Katherine hurried after her and Elsie claimed to be feeling seasick. However, it had not gone unnoticed that her mother did not seem pleased to be visiting St Helena. Katherine decided to take this up with her later. She did question Elsie when she appeared better, about why she did not seem keen to visit the island again, and least of all Luke's grave. By this time, Elsie had prepared her answers and said that she believed Luke may have died on the boat on the way back to Cape Town. Katherine felt sure that there would be some record of him, either in the museum, the church, in the archives, or maybe noted somewhere in the port authority's documents. Elsie immediately went on the defence and said that Katherine should leave the departed in peace and questioned why she would want to poke around in the past.

Katherine found her mother's attitude strangely aggressive but nevertheless, she respected the possibility that her parents' relationship had not been as happy as she had always wanted to believe.

Elsie seemed to grow increasingly subdued as they approached St Helena and Katherine wondered whether she would even disembark the ship. However, when the ship started approaching the island, Elsie was on the bow exalting the view and noting the few changes she could see from a distance. She pointed out the weathercock on the spire of St James' Church – which was a fish, Jamestown that sat snugly between the high and forbidding walls of rock, the slopes that had treacherous looking paths cut out of jagged sides, and Jacobs' Ladder on the right side leading to the top from the harbour. The Heart Shaped Waterfall was just visible in the distance up the hill. She noticed that there were now more dwellings creeping up the slopes. Elsie realised that she really wanted to walk amongst those buildings again, find her old home and the school she had lovingly arranged to be rebuilt. She wondered if it had stood the test of time and hoped that the termites had not returned to nourish themselves on the wooden panelling.

Were the minister and his wife still there?

She felt the need to see all this at close hand overruled her reasons to hide Luke's secret. After all, she had married him in St Paul's Cathedral and their marriage certificate was in the small wooden box he had handed her.

So, what did she have to fear?

Only that there was no record of his death. Surely no one would even remember what happened some thirty years ago, and least of all care?

Katherine and Michael were pleased to see that Elsie

seemed less daunted by the prospect of visiting St Helena again, and decided that they would let Elsie show them around on the first day and they would go their respective ways the following day.

Elsie was highly animated, telling them stories and remembering happy times as she explained how she used to come down to the docks as a little girl to listen to all the foreign voices and watch the frenetic activity. Following the short crossing in a rowing boat from their ship that was anchored in the harbour, they walked up through the arch to the main square while Elsie continued her commentary, recalling memories for them as they walked through the town. They commented on how free they felt as a family here on the island, where ethnicity did not matter. Elsie showed them the schoolhouse in the gardens next to the castle, which looked almost the same as when she had left. The old school was now painted cream on the outside and appeared to be private residences and no longer a school, which saddened Elsie.

They made their way up to Napoleon Street to the little cottage where Elsie had lived with her parents and where Katherine had been born. Sadly, the house looked uncared for and there was an old man sitting on a chair outside. Elsie approached him saying that she used to live there and that she would love to show the house to her daughter and her son-in-law. The old man smiled broadly and told Elsie that he remembered her and when she had bravely left with her baby. He had been one of the local guards at the POW camp and he asked Elsie if she ever found that man that got her up the spout. Elsie was deeply embarrassed and mumbled that he had died. The man replied that he thought Elsie was too good for one of those Boer POWs anyway.

They quickly looked around the neglected cottage and

part of her was relieved that there was little left to remind her of the love she had received and given there. The one thing that did remain was the rack of hat hooks on which she had once hung Luke's hat. Also, the red rose was still growing next to the front door. It did look very woody and had clearly not been pruned for years but there were a couple of red blooms and Elsie felt the need to pick one, to which the old man agreed. She planned to press and dry it, and later place it in the little wooden box amongst her other memories of St Helena.

They stopped for a cup of tea at the Wellington Hotel and Elsie was again recognised, this time by the owner of the establishment who brought in some of the neighbours to see her. Katherine and Michael made their excuses and decided to walk up to the Heart Shaped Waterfall. It was a beautiful spot and Katherine thought how wonderful it must have been for her mother and father to have courted on this picturesque island. Little did she know that this was the very spot where she had been conceived.

They hired a man with a horse and trap to take them to St Paul's Cathedral, where Katherine knew her parents had been married. There were no motor vehicles on the island, and they felt like they were stepping back in time.

Katherine was a little nervous heading up the steep incline with the almost sheer drop. On arrival at the cathedral, she and Michael were surprised at how simple the building was, surrounded by an extensive graveyard, almost like a field of the dead. They entered the cool cathedral with its rather stark beauty. The walls were white and had a number of inlaid memorial plaques. There was a very high roof supported by dark wooden arched struts, and a bell tower with the ropes to ring the bells next to the entrance.

They held hands as they walked down the aisle and

Katherine felt, or perhaps imagined, a strange connection to this holy place where her parents had been married.

They decided to walk back to the landing stage to meet the tender boat that would return them to the ship for the evening. Before descending Jacob's Ladder, they paused to admire the beams of sunlight escaping through the clouded sky, creating golden pools on the calm sea.

Back on the ship, over dinner that evening, Katherine had endless questions about St Helena and Elsie's life there. Elsie said that she wanted to visit the graves of her parents the following day and Katherine and Michael would like to join her.

The next day they made their way in a hired horse and trap to St Paul's Cathedral and, on arrival, Elsie went straight to the gravestones of her parents. The headstones were looking very neglected and she knelt, trying to hastily weed and tidy the surroundings.

Michael and Katherine left her there to try to find a grave keeper and to pay him to keep the gravestones in better condition. Elsie hardly noticed them leave as she was so engrossed in memories of her beloved parents and the wonderful childhood, they had given her. She found herself having a whispered conversation to them about why she had returned to the island.

Michael and Katherine thought they would knock on the door of the nearby rectory to see if they could find anyone to assist them. A very elderly minister answered the door and, when they explained who they were, his face lit up as he remembered Elsie and eagerly followed them to meet her again.

Fortunately for Elsie, both Michael and Katherine hung back to let Elsie meet the minister again on her own. The minister explained that his wife, Jane, had recently passed away. He also enquired if Elsie had met up with Luke in South Africa as he recalled that Luke had written to him to get Elsie's address in Cape Town, and they had put him in touch with Mother Superior at the convent. Elsie was clearly distressed at the conversation and quietly explained to the minister that she and Luke had not been reunited. Elsie whispered to him that Luke had requested that Katherine be informed that her father had died, and she still believed this to be the case. Luke had thought it easier because he could not have acknowledged Elsie, being Coloured, as his wife in South Africa.

The minister appeared very concerned and said that he believed that the mother superior in the convent in Cape Town had also been in contact with Luke, which stunned Elsie to her core. He reminded Elsie that, should Luke still be alive, he was still her husband in the eyes of God, and that Katherine deserved to know the truth about her father. Elsie agreed that one day she would have to tell Katherine but, as she had kept the truth from her for so long, the lie seemed too large to overcome. What if Katherine never forgave her for hiding the truth about Luke? The minister was adamant that Katherine needed to know the facts and reminded Elsie that Katherine was now a grown woman and capable of making up her own mind.

Elsie was overcome with grief at seeing her parents' graves again and hearing the hard-hitting truth that the minister was insisting she had to reveal to her daughter and her husband too. On hearing that Mother Superior may well have been in touch with Luke over the years and never mentioned this, Elsie felt quite confused and deceived.

Elsie told the minister that she felt that she would have to choose her moment to speak to Katherine, and the minister suggested that she not leave it too long. He emphasised that it was time for Elsie to unburden herself of the deception that she had been carrying all these years. In fact, the minister's words to Elsie were, "The burden of this secret must feel as though you carry a wet mattress on your back." Elsie agreed that that was exactly what it felt like from time to time.

Respecting Elsie's privacy, Michael and Katherine remained at a distance so they would not hear the conversation. When the discussion seemed over and the minister stood, saying a prayer for Elsie's parents, both Michael and Katherine joined them. Michael offered to make a substantial donation to the church in order that the head stones of Katherine's grandparents could be maintained. The minister said he would ensure one of the local men did so.

It was a warm day and Katherine suggested that they visit the Heart Shaped Waterfall again as it was such a picturesque spot. Elsie immediately felt panicked at the thought of returning to the spot where she and Luke had made love for the first and only time. She declined their offer to join them and instead decided to take one of the nature walks that her father used to take her on. During her stroll towards Longwood House, where Napoleon had lived, she spotted a wire bird and felt sure that it was a sign from her father that he was still there in spirit.

Michael and Katherine agreed that Elsie was behaving a little mysteriously but decided that there were probably many conflicting memories that she was having to deal with right now.

They made their way to Plantation House, the official residence of the governor and home to Jonathan, the famous tortoise. Here, one of the gardeners showed them the old tortoise, who was believed to have been fifty years old when he come from the Seychelles in 1882. The gardener gave them some vegetables from the kitchen garden to feed it.

Making their way back to the docks, they admired the views and Katherine wondered what would have become of her, had her mother not taken the brave step to move to Cape Town. They discussed what Katherine's father may have been like and Katherine decided that she would make a point, when the time was right, to ask Elsie more about him. She had always respected her mother's wish not to discuss him, but she hoped that visiting St Helena again may have settled some sad and possibly difficult memories. She really had a burning desire to know more about her father, having now seen the island where her parents had fallen in love and married.

Michael enquired if Katherine had ever tried to find any of her relations in South Africa, as surely her father would have had family there? Katherine had thought about it but dismissed the idea, as it would have meant either hiding or revealing Elsie's ethnicity.

Chapter 25
Luke's frustration

Luke had been to see his lawyer who seemed somewhat surprised to learn about his marriage to Elsie thirty years prior, and about a daughter that he had only seen from a distance over the years, although he had secretly financed her keep and education. Luke admitted that he had insisted on receiving copies of Katherine's end of year school reports from the convent, which had always been a very private source of great pride. The lawyer was even more intrigued when Luke informed him that he would be leaving eighty percent of his estate to his daughter and the balance to his wife, Elsie. He had decided not to mention that Elsie was a Coloured person as he thought that may complicate matters and possibly even make the marriage illegal, although this had not been the case on St Helena.

Luke had also given the lawyer a sealed envelope containing the letter he had written to Katherine, apologising and explaining his absence as a parent and emphasising his deep regret at not having been part of her and Elsie's lives.

He was constantly thinking of both Elsie and Katherine and found himself once again driving across to their home in Kensington. He thought he would park nearby in the hope of seeing either of them. He was most surprised to see a dark-haired lady emerging from the little house pushing a pram. He immediately knew that this was not Katherine and so got out of his car to ask the young woman if she knew where the doctor, who used to live there, had moved to. The young woman replied that she had never met the doctor, as she had moved out a few weeks prior to her moving in with her husband and baby, but she had heard that she was moving to England. Luke thanked her and, feeling rather shocked and deflated, realised that he was now even further away from his daughter than before. He wondered where Elsie was. Had she gone to England too?

Luke had childishly kicked at the tyre of his car in frustration before climbing back inside to drive home. He contemplated whether he should try to find them in England, but where to begin?

Now more than ever, he had an overwhelming desire to contact his estranged family, regardless of the consequences. He was in his fifties and becoming concerned that he may not have many years ahead of him to get to know them; besides, Elsie may not be very willing to allow him into the family fold, and she would have had every right to feel that way. Katherine too, may well reject him for abandoning her as a baby. He knew he had dealt with complex situations at his mine with workers' disputes, but there was no 'family' involved in these cases, and so he was always able to stay emotionally detached and remote.

Perhaps now that his lawyer knew of his circumstances, he could try to trace where Katherine was living and working in England. After all, women doctors were generally few and far between.

Luke also wondered if his lawyer may somehow be able to get access to the passenger lists of some of the recent ships that had departed for England from Cape Town. Yes, he would use his contacts to track them down. His need to know where they were suddenly became a burning obsession as he realised that prior to this, he had mostly always known where Katherine and Elsie were living. Having secretly paid for Katherine's education, and knowing she was living in Johannesburg had given him at least a sense of comfort and even slight control when she was younger.

Now that Katherine was with her husband, Luke felt that he may well have lost her forever. He would not only have to try to win Katherine and Elsie over to see his point of view, but there was now also Michael, whom he doubted would take kindly to him or his tale of abandonment of mother and baby all those years ago. He had somehow always believed that he would, one day when the time was right, be able to make things better between them, but now he felt he may have lost the small grip he believed he once had.

Luke was still sending a monthly money order to his blackmailer, Dan, in Cape Town. It riled him every time he had to post it. Then, one day, two of the envelopes were returned to his address unopened. He became anxious that Dan may have moved and would decide to report him to the authorities. He made a long-distance phone call to the residential hotel that he posted the monthly money orders to and asked the person answering the phone if Dan was still in residence.

"Ag man… no, he died. He seemed to come into some money and took to boozing too much. I am the manager of this place and one day I found him in his room… choked to death on his own vomit. Still owes me a month's rent too."

Luke felt a great sense of relief and prayed that Dan took his knowledge to the grave with him. He could not help feeling that he got what he deserved.

Chapter 26
Voyage to England from St Helena

The rest of the voyage for Elsie, Katherine and Michael was uneventful but extremely enjoyable. The three of them dined like royalty and enjoyed each other's company. Elsie spoke a little more about her time on St Helena and shared many of her childhood memories; however, she always became extremely guarded and uncomfortable when it came to mentioning Luke. Katherine had had so many questions about her father burning inside her for years. She did not even have a photograph of him. Elsie had told her little else other than he had had blonde hair and striking blue eyes, the very same shade as Katherine's. She boldly asked Elsie one night, after a glass of champagne, if she was hiding a picture of her father in the little wooden box beside her bed.

Elsie had sarcastically replied that photographs had been somewhat of a luxury that was not readily available in those days. The truth was that she had often wished that she had a photograph of him when he has younger, as she had almost forgotten what he looked like. She had only had the briefest glance of him that day a few years ago when she was outside his home in Houghton, and he drove up the driveway whilst she was talking to his gardener. She also had a few press cuttings of him looking very distinguished. Did Luke ever wonder what she looked like now? Moreover, did he ever think of or care about her or Katherine? She had been rather astounded to learn from the minister on St Helena that Luke had been in contact with him and possibly Mother Superior in Cape Town.

Why would Mother Superior have kept that information from her?

Was it an oversight or deliberate?

Perhaps Mother Superior had made the judgement to protect her and Katherine. Elsie was becoming a little unnerved as she realised that the secret of Katherine's father still being alive was beginning to unravel. This made her angry inside as she was the one who had been left with the burden of the untruth and Luke had taken no responsibility, not even in faking his own death to his daughter. A cowardly copout! What would his business colleagues and fancy friends in Houghton have thought about his actions, let alone his marriage to her?

Hopefully, this was all behind her as she could now start a new life in England, where no one would question her past or, in fact, care. Leaving South Africa had somehow enabled her to dismiss Luke, keeping him locked in that little wooden box, even if it was still safely tucked into her hand luggage like some prized possession. She thought of throwing it overboard into the Atlantic Ocean but could not quite bring herself to do so.

There was great excitement on the morning that the ship approached Portsmouth Harbour. They passed the Isle of Wight, which looked like an interesting place to visit and they all hoped to go there one day. Then, looming ahead were the very impressive Palmerston Forts. Michael informed them that these forts were engineering wonders that had been built in the middle of the Solent in 1860. At the time, the English were concerned about the strength of the French Navy and the perceived threat of their invasion of England at Portsmouth.

There was a yachting regatta taking place at the far end of the Solent, and the sails made a beautiful and welcoming picture with the backdrop of the Isle of Wight.

Luke pointed out the large Royal Haslar Hospital in Gosport on the western side of the entrance to the harbour. On the eastern side was Southsea Castle and the Hot Walls on which many people were standing and waving at them as they came past. The tugboats came alongside and guided them in through the narrow entrance to the harbour. There was a band playing the national anthem as they moored up against the dock. The sun was shining, and a light breeze tugged at the flags and bunting draped around the boat. They stood and watched the skilful sailors throw the ropes down to the men on the side of the dock. Catching the thinner rope with the monkey's fist at the end, they looped the ropes over the giant capstans that slowly winched the heavy ropes in and very carefully drew the ship towards the mooring. There was a slight, familiar feel of Cape Town to Portsmouth, although Table Mountain was much larger than the Portsdown Hills in the distance.

Elsie recalled the day she and Katherine had arrived in Cape Town, having travelled from St Helena. Their journey had been far less comfortable and Katherine as a one-year-old, had struggled with motion sickness. There had been no one to meet them, and the hard realisation had hit her that she would have to live life in South Africa with the burden of being a Coloured person. None of that had mattered in St Helena, and Elsie was holding high hopes that in England, things would be much the same. As they came down the gangplank, there was a man from the hospital waiting to meet them with two vehicles, one for their luggage and one for them. He informed them that their furniture and boxes would be delivered to their home later that day.

In the meantime, he drove them to the Queens Hotel in Southsea, an area within Portsmouth City that overlooked the green common and the seafront. They stopped here for a light lunch before they went on to their new home in the hospital grounds. The hotel was a very stately building in the Edwardian baroque style: brown terracotta with ornate stone-carved balconies adorned with countless neoclassical decorative flourishes. How grand they felt ascending the red carpet on the stairs of the entrance, into the high-ceilinged dining room overlooking a formal garden. The gentleman who had met them at the dockside turned out to be the medical officer in charge of the Royal Naval Hospital in Haslar and he briefed them about their accommodation and working arrangements. Katherine would be working in the emergency and outpatient department and Michael in the orthopaedic department. They would be expected to start work in a week's time, once they had settled into their new home and explored their surroundings. Elsie would be allowed to stay with them in their home and it was suggested that she may like to volunteer for some of the projects available, like needlework or flower arranging for the chapel.

After lunch, they were chauffeured around the harbour past the ancient Portchester Castle. The medical officer pointed out Cams Hall, where Lord Nelson and Lady Hamilton were believed to meet. Next they drove through the quaint market town of Fareham that had an amazing brick viaduct crossing the estuary where many swans were elegantly gliding across the shimmering water. The road meandered back down the western side of the harbour towards the Royal Haslar Hospital in Gosport. On their arrival there, they quickly unloaded their bags, and the medical director proudly gave them a quick tour of the extensive grounds and explained the layout of the hospital.

They came across a beautiful rose garden next to the sisters' mess where Elsie would, in the future, often sit and remember the rosebush at the front door of her little cottage on St Helena. A very attractive water tower had been built in 1885 and was some 120 feet high with two 125-ton water tanks, each holding 50,000 gallons of water needed to supply the hospital with the vast amount it needed daily.

There had been an ambulance tram car that brought naval patients off the ships from the Haslar jetty to the arcade, where the patient receiving room was situated. These trams had been hand-propelled and only the rails remained. This method of transporting patients was certainly unique and interesting for its time.

The architecture of most of the buildings in the grounds was impressive; the history was remarkable – where else could one care for patients in a ward once used by the wounded from the Battle of Trafalgar?

The medical director pointed out the views of the Solent, where the nautical activities seemed unceasing. He explained that the medical staff could find solace in St Luke's Church in the grounds, where the organist often played soothing music and one could pray for the patients and ask for strength to carry on in what surely was a very demanding doctor's position. The saint's name of the church did not go unnoticed by the family, who gave each other meaningful glances.

There was a zymotic block where patients with contagious diseases were cared for. All goods were passed through a purpose-built hole in the boundary wall to prevent cross-infection. Patients admitted to zymotics were bathed on arrival and their clothes washed in Lysol.

These were thought to be the perfect grounds for convalescing, and sea-bathing was encouraged as well as taking in the sea air.

There was a lovely wooden pavilion facing towards the Solent that was used on occasions by staff, patients and their families. Inside the pavilion was a plaque that read:

'This shelter was presented to the hospital by the Ladies Needlework Guild 1917 – By the Lady Adelaide Colville and Lady Welch, 1921.'

Lady Colville was the wife of the Commander in Chief Portsmouth, who was to become Aide-de-camp to King George V.

Benches and seating were scattered in the grounds in the form of various pavilions and follies. There was the long Admirals Walk lined with pollarded trees and perfectly manicured grass tennis courts at the medical mess. The large hospital laundry had a water tank on the roof and on having been given a quick tour, Elsie was acutely aware that all those doing the heavy manual work in the laundry were White people. In fact, she was yet to see a Coloured or Black person in Portsmouth.

There, surprisingly, had been a medical, natural history and ethnographic museum in the grounds which had included a specimen of a four-footed duck. The Haslar Hospital Museum had been founded in 1827 until 1855. It had contained thousands of natural history specimens which were sent back to Haslar by expeditions. These specimens had been used as tools in the education of naval surgeons, servicemen, and explorers.

Michael, Katherine and Elsie were allocated one of the houses on The Terrace in the grounds of the hospital. It was a three-storey terraced house, and they were delighted to have been given such a wonderful, large home. Elsie immediately started settling them in and organising the home, much to Michael and Katherine's pleasure, as they had no time to think about home-making themselves with their new jobs to settle into.

Within a couple of days, Elsie had found a local grocer and butcher where she immediately set up accounts and arranged for them to deliver to the house. The shopkeepers seemed to assume that Elsie was the housekeeper to the two new doctors at the hospital and she thought it may be easier to leave them thinking that as it really was none of their business.

She was determined to stay as anonymous as possible, but she knew that her father, James Baker, had been born in Portsmouth and did wonder if she had any relations living there. In some of James' old papers, she had found his family address. It was the address that she had written to when he passed away.

Elsie decided one day that she would go and look for the house and knock on the door to ask if anyone knew of any members of his family who might still be alive. She found the house and it was a rather nice looking home off Elm Grove. Elsie plucked up courage and went to knock on the front door. A stern looking woman answered and Elsie nervously began to explain.

"Good day, ma'am, I was wondering if you could give me a minute, please?" The woman grunted a consent. "You see…" continued Elsie nervously, "I am the daughter of the late James Baker, who moved to St Helena as a teacher many years ago and I was wondering if you knew what happened to his family?"

The lady looked Elsie up and down and said, "But you are a Coloured woman. Touched with the bit of the old tar brush, aren't you? We heard he had married some local Coloured woman down there. No, no, no… I think it best you go on your way and don't come back here worrying us and looking for handouts. Go on off to where you came from! Away with you," she shouted, dismissing Elsie from the doorstep.

Elsie hastily retreated and was hugely saddened to realise that race discrimination was also alive and well in Portsmouth. In the future, she would certainly keep to herself and her immediate family and forget about finding any possible distant relations.

The small garden at the rear of their terrace home had a damson plum tree espaliered against the south wall, and a healthy-looking apple tree in the centre of the lawn. Elsie immediately started planning to make jams and puddings for her family. Some of the neighbours came to introduce themselves and they seemed a little taken aback when Elsie was introduced as Katherine's mother, but far too polite to question the skin colour difference. Both Katherine and Elsie had been very relieved at their reactions and felt that they were getting off to a good start with no evident or obvious discrimination. It was hoped that once they had commented to each other on the skin colour difference of the mother and daughter, that they would stop noticing or feel it necessary to remark any further.

Once Elsie had unpacked and organised the home and was in a routine of preparing meals for the family around their long shifts in the hospital, she found time to work on her recipe book.

Michael and Katherine were given a few days leave and the three of them took the train to London where Michael showed them some of the sights. They even went to stand in front of Buckingham Palace! They wandered through Hyde

Park and took tea in Fortnum and Mason, and it was there they visited the new Sports Department, where customers were taught the art of how to ski on their own miniature ski-slope. Having never seen snow before, this was truly fascinating. Michael promised to take them to Europe to try skiing one day. That evening, they went to an Elgar concert at the Royal Albert Hall to hear the London Symphony Orchestra perform in the round. The building was an extremely impressive design and they were interested to learn that the red bricks used to build it had come from the Fareham Brick Works near their new home.

London was all and more than Elsie and Katherine had ever dreamed of, and they felt very grateful and privileged to have visited this elegant and exciting city. Michael had proved to be the most perfect and well-informed guide.

Both Katherine and Michael enjoyed the challenges of their new work environment and felt that they were learning much from their colleagues. Katherine did miss the delivery of babies and only seemed to get involved when there were severe complications during a birth, as most babies seemed to be delivered at home by the local midwives.

Chapter 27
A new arrival

Despite Katherine's obstetric and medical knowledge, she unintentionally fell pregnant. She initially did not identify the pregnancy symptoms as she was working long hours and often felt exhausted. Before they were married, she and Michael had agreed that they would not have any children and took precautions. She toyed with the idea of organising an abortion, but knew she had to discuss this with Michael first, before making such a huge and possibly dangerous decision.

Once evening, she suggested that the two of them go for a walk along the seafront immediately after work. It was at sunset, but there was a stiff breeze whipping across the Solent. Katherine had prepared her speech and her justification for the abortion, but when she finally plucked up enough courage to broach the subject, she was overcome with emotion and simply started to cry. Michael put his arms around her and asked her what was wrong. She began to sob and was quite unable to speak for a while. They sat on a nearby bench overlooking the sea and Michael begged her to compose herself. She took some deep breaths before she told him what was troubling her.

"I don't know how to say this, my darling... but... I am pregnant!" she announced.

"You are? That is the very best news I have ever heard. Oh, I love you so much, Katherine. That is terrific news, our lives will be so complete with a child."

"No, no, Michael! This was not meant to happen... we agreed to have no children because of my mixed-race blood. We cannot take the chance... can we? What if the baby has dark skin like my mother?"

"Katherine, darling, we live in England now. Please, let us have this baby. Mixed-race is far less of a problem here and certainly not against the law. After the birth, you could even return to work as I'm sure that your mother would love to look after her grandchild."

"But... I thought I should have an abortion."

"I *know* you should not!" Michael quickly interjected. "I'm confident that we will be wonderful parents together."

They walked back home and broke their now joyous news to a more than delighted Elsie, who immediately started making plans, much to the amusement of her daughter and son-in-law.

Aside from the initial morning sickness and tiredness, Katherine had a reasonably easy pregnancy. She found the experience extremely beneficial in terms of her work in obstetrics, as male doctors cannot know how it 'actually feels' to be pregnant. How could they understand mood swings and food cravings? She would now have huge empathy for pregnant women and a far greater understanding of what they were experiencing. Having been taught obstetrics at university by male lecturers, she concluded that there was really nothing like going through the trimesters oneself. Once she had accepted the fact that she was pregnant, the privilege of having a baby developing in her womb was a true miracle and delight. She found that giving birth was both terrifying and empowering, experiencing polarised emotions she had not really thought about until her own personal experience.

Katherine and Michael's little boy was born with bright blue eyes and very blonde curly hair. His skin was a beautiful pale olive colour. They named their son Christopher Luke and hoped more than anything that he would pass as European in this cruel judgemental world. He was a healthy, happy and content little boy and Katherine stayed at home with him for some six weeks before returning to the hospital to resume her duties. Katherine loved her work, and Michael agreed that she would work shorter shifts than before to allow her to spend quality time with Christopher Luke.

Elsie was overjoyed to be the doting nanny.

Chapter 28
Luke's Quest

It had taken Luke's lawyer well over a year to gather the information about Katherine, Michael and Elsie, and their exact whereabouts in England. The South African Embassy in London's Trafalgar Square eventually agreed to assist in locating Katherine and her family when they were informed by Luke's lawyer that there was potentially a rather large inheritance for the family.

On discovering that the Clavering family was living and working at Royal Haslar Hospital in Gosport, across the harbour from Portsmouth, Luke immediately started planning for his business to be run by his management team in his absence, whilst he undertook an extended trip to England. He said he was hoping to look for potential investors there as well as visit London, which he had always wanted to do. He too had to travel to Cape Town by train from Johannesburg and get a passenger liner to England.

Luke booked himself a luxury suite on the Union Castle Line that travelled from Cape Town to Southampton. The journey seemed like a good idea at the time, but once Luke had set sail, he began to question how wise it was. He still had no idea how he planned to approach his family and announce himself. He played out every possible scenario in his head and realised that he only had a script for one person in this scene: himself! It terrified him to think that the family may reject him outright. He thought that perhaps he should just visit London and tour the United Kingdom and go back home.

Whatever the outcome might be, he decided that he would travel to Royal Haslar Hospital and take a look for himself, even if he decided in the end not to approach his family.

On arrival in England, he booked himself into the Dolphin Hotel in Southampton for a few days, before making arrangements to travel east to Portsmouth.

Chapter 29
Walking on the foreshore

Most afternoons, if it was not raining and the wind not blowing a gale, Elsie would take baby Christopher for a stroll in his pram. She would walk out of the front entrance of the hospital and along the Haslar foreshore to enjoy the sea air and the view across the Solent to the Isle of Wight. Baby Christopher nearly always fell asleep with the sound of the sea. Elsie felt very at home hearing the waves breaking and swooshing on the stones with the seagulls squawking overhead. She felt the same inner peace and joy she had experienced as a child on St Helena, taking long walks with her dear father. Baby Christopher had brought such happiness and contentment to her life, and she absolutely doted on him. She felt honoured that Michael and Katherine were happy to have her care for their son.

One day, she noticed a man sitting on one of the benches looking out to sea with a scarf almost completely covering his face so that only his eyes were visible. She thought it a little strange, but perhaps he was unwell or had toothache? She felt that this gentleman was staring at her and began to feel slightly uncomfortable under his unrelenting gaze.

As she passed the bench he was seated on, the man stood and approached her, "Good afternoon Elsie," he called out to her in a strong South African accent.

Elsie immediately recognised Luke Viljoen.

She was at a complete loss for words at this shockingly

unexpected meeting and only just managed to utter the word, "How…?"

"How… What… Elsie? Is this our grandson?"

"Luke? Is that you? How did you find us?" Elsie hesitated as she took in Luke, standing before her, now some thirty years older than when she had last faced him, as was she for that matter, she fleetingly reminded herself. Smoothing strands of her now very grey hair that had been teased loose by the wind, she noted that he too, now had a full head of steely grey hair. His eyes were as blue and piercing as she remembered them to be when he handed her the box with his letter and money.

Gathering her thoughts, she aggressively asked, "What do you want, Luke?"

"A chance to please explain, possibly make good and hopefully get to know Katherine and our grandson here?" he replied confidently, peering into the pram.

Thirty years of anger surged through Elsie like molten lava, and it felt as though she would choke. She stood staring at Luke in utter disbelief and then, in a low voice that did not even sound like hers, she calmly replied,

"We were not good enough for you when Katherine was born and now for some reason it suits you to acknowledge us? Your audacity astounds me!"

"Please, Elsie, give me a chance and deliver this letter to our daughter. Let her decide if she would like to meet me."

"You asked me to tell her that you died. How can I now explain that I have deceived her all these years?", exclaimed Elsie.

"Please, Elsie, I am begging you to give her this letter from me. Let her make the decision." Luke tucked the letter down the side of the mattress next to the little boy, taking another long hard look at his sleeping grandson.

"No, Luke, no! You ask too much. Too late. You are dead to us!"

With that, in shock and blind panic, Elsie started walking swiftly away from Luke, pushing the sleeping Christopher in his pram back towards the hospital entrance. She stepped directly into the street without looking either way. A large shiny black car was heading at speed towards her and the baby, and Luke, having run after them, launched himself at Elsie and pushed her and the sleeping baby out of the way of the fast-approaching vehicle. Elsie screamed as the pram sped across the road and she went sprawling along the ground; she heard the dreadful thud behind her of a body connecting with a vehicle, and she saw Luke flying through the air and landing some twenty yards away.

"You are dead to us!" she heard herself whisper again.

And suddenly there were people shouting and rushing towards them. The driver had leapt out of his vehicle and was loudly apologising and saying that the woman had run out in front of him without looking. The accident had taken place almost at the entrance to the hospital and some of the nurses and a doctor immediately came running to assist at the scene and attend to the casualty, who was lying motionless on the ground. Elsie too lay still on the ground, but was seemingly only badly grazed, winded and in shock. Baby Christopher was awake in his pram which had come to a halt against a tree, and he appeared completely unharmed. Luke, on the other hand, seemed to be in a bad state when he was assessed where he lay, and was soon carefully moved on to a stretcher to be carried in haste into the emergency area of the hospital.

A nurse, who recognised Elsie as Dr Katherine Viljoen's mother, helped her into a wheelchair, once it was established that nothing was broken. Another nurse was checking over baby Christopher, who was crying at the shock of being woken, as his pram collided with the tree, mercifully having somehow remained upright.

The nurses insisted that Elsie come into the outpatient area for her grazes to be cleaned and dressed, and they went together with baby Christopher to be checked by a doctor.

Katherine, who had been attending other patients at the time, heard that her baby and mother were in the outpatient area, after somehow being involved in an accident in which a pedestrian had been knocked down by a motorcar immediately outside the entrance to the hospital.

On arrival at the emergency department, baby Christopher thankfully looked very content, playing with one of the nurses. Katherine immediately took him into an examination cubical to establish that he was indeed unharmed. She asked where her mother was so she could check on her also. Elsie was having her severe grazes dressed and appeared otherwise unharmed, apart from crying uncontrollably at the shock of what had just transpired. Katherine spoke to one of the other doctors in the department and it was decided to admit Elsie for observation as a precaution.

Katherine took baby Christopher home in his pram, where she enlisted the help of one of their neighbours to temporarily look after him until she returned home after her shift, which was due to end in a couple of hours. When she lifted him out of the pram to change him, she discovered an envelope addressed to herself, tucked down between the blankets and the mattress. She slipped the envelope into her pocket to open later and quickly packed an overnight bag for her mother.

When Katherine's arrived back at her mother's bedside in the ward, she found her mother still sobbing and in an almost hysterical state. The matron in charge suggested mild sedation to which Katherine agreed. Katherine was handed all her mother's personal effects, her small handbag that had been retrieved from the road after the accident and her jewellery which included a gold chain with a crucifix, and the little key hanging from it.

Katherine immediately knew where the lock for this key was and fleetingly wondered what secrets her mother had hidden in that box close to her bed. She had a moment of temptation to take a peep inside it later that evening, as this may be her only opportunity to discover what had been hidden inside for all these years.

She placed the chain with the crucifix and key around her own neck in order not to lose them, and went to place her mother's small handbag safely in her personal locker. Whilst in the doctors' private area, one of the other doctors was there having a break and enjoying a cup of tea. He asked after Katherine's infant son and mother and mentioned that he had been put in charge of the man who had been knocked down by the car. Katherine asked after him and enquired if there was any explanation about what had happened. The other doctor said that no details had yet emerged, but that the police were currently investigating the incident; however, his patient was still unconscious and appeared to have severe head and back injuries, with a possible cracked pelvis, which would all be confirmed post a number of x-rays. Then, as Katherine was leaving the doctors' lounge area, her colleague mentioned that the injured man had had his passport in his pocket and strangely had the same surname as Katherine – he was a Mr Luke Viljoen.

Katherine had to steady herself on the doorpost and suddenly felt quite faint herself.

Who was this man?

Could he be a family relation?

Why was her mother involved?

Had she known him?

Why was her mother so hysterical and upset?

This all seemed too coincidental and strange. She knew she would have to deal with these questions later when she had finished her shift and checked on Elsie again, before going to collect Christopher from their neighbour. Michael was operating at the time, so she would have to wait for his return home later that evening to try and piece it all together.

When the end of her shift came, Katherine went to see Elsie and found her settled and in a deep sleep. The matron showed her the medication records and explained that Elsie had been quite heavily sedated to calm her down. She gently took her mother's hand and whispered to her that she loved her and that they would need to have a long talk about the events of the day, and what had occurred before the accident. She kissed Elsie on the cheek and left the ward, leaving instructions that she should be called for if her mother woke upset again.

Katherine rushed to collect Elsie's belongings and her own handbag from her locker, into which she had placed the envelope addressed to herself that she found earlier. She collected Christopher from the neighbour and returned home, needing to prepare the evening meal, as Elsie normally had this in hand by the time she and Michael returned from the hospital in the evenings.

Christopher was fractious and hungry when Katherine collected him, and she wondered how Elsie managed to cook dinner, feed and bathe him and have him ready for her to spend time playing with him before he went to bed. Everything looked so easy and calm by the time she and Michael arrived home for dinner in the evenings, and it was usually before the little boy went to sleep for the night. Katherine was shocked to realise how much her mother did for them all and that she had no idea how she would have coped as a full-time busy doctor and mother, had Elsie not been there to care for Christopher and keep house for her and Michael. No wonder the university in Cape Town suggested that woman doctors should not marry and have children. The demands were too great and either motherhood or her career would have suffered without the sort of support that Elsie afforded them.

Between feeding Christopher, a spoonful at a time of scrambled egg, Katherine managed to make a meat loaf of sorts and popped it into the oven. Elsie had already shelled the peas and peeled the potatoes that morning, leaving them in water on the side before she had taken Christopher for his walk along the seafront. There was an apple pie on the cooling rack with a lovely golden crust and custard made up in a jug. Katherine marvelled at how organised her mother was. She was deeply puzzled and concerned about Elsie though, and wondered why she appeared so hysterical and in such severe shock after the incident that afternoon.

Katherine was bathing baby Christopher when Michael arrived home and he happily joined the fun as bath time was always a joy with their little son. He was such a contented little boy. His parents knelt beside the bath and watched him playing and splashing in the bathtub with pride.

Michael had heard a little about the earlier accident through the hospital grapevine and had checked on Elsie before he came home, though she had still been sleeping. He mentioned that he would be seeing the gentleman who had been knocked down in the morning. His medical colleagues had reported that he was apparently still unconscious, but stable.

Michael mentioned the strange coincidence that a South African passport had been found in the man's pocket and that his name was Luke Viljoen, but commented that 'Viljoen' was quite a common name in South Africa after all.

They put little Christopher into his cot, and he soon settled after a bottle of milk and his fun bath time with his parents.

Michael and Katherine sat down to their dinner at the dining room table that Elsie had also managed to set earlier that day, before she and Christopher had gone for their afternoon walk. They both realised that they needed to show their appreciation even more.

Katherine mentioned that her mother had been badly grazed from her fall and that she had no idea whether Elsie had tripped or jumped out of the way of the motor vehicle. Katherine explained to Michael that her mother had been so hysterical that she was unable to get any sense out of her at the time, hence the reason for her sedation.

Later that evening, there was a knock on the front door and Michael went to answer. A couple of police detectives asked to come inside and discuss the events of the afternoon. They advised that, from an eyewitness account, it appeared that the gentleman, Mr Viljoen, must have seen the motor vehicle heading towards Elsie who appeared not to have checked before crossing the road. He had rushed forward and pushed Elsie, who was pushing the pram, out of the way of the vehicle which had then hit him and sent him flying some distance before landing on the roadside. Both Michael and Katherine were surprised and somewhat horrified that Elsie had pushed their baby into the road without checking first and wondered what had distracted her, causing her to be so careless, something which was truly not in her nature.

The detectives wanted to know if either Katherine or Michael had any information about Luke Viljoen and whether he knew Elsie? Katherine explained that Viljoen was a common South African name, but strangely had also been the name of her late father. Before departing, the detectives asked Katherine and Michael to contact them should they think of anything further to report. Michael did mention that he was an orthopaedic surgeon and was due to examine Mr Viljoen the following morning to assess his injuries and consider whether surgery would be helpful. He advised that Mr Viljoen had still been unconscious earlier that evening when he had left the ward to return home.

Katherine remembered the sealed envelope addressed to her that she had found tucked next to the mattress of Christopher's pram when she had brought him home earlier that afternoon. She went to retrieve the envelope out of her handbag and explained to Michael where she had discovered it.

They sat down together on the sofa. Katherine carefully prised open the envelope of very high-quality bond paper, on which in a sweeping and bold handwriting was penned:

My dearest Katherine,

I write this letter with the faintest hope that you will continue to read on when I admit here and now that I am your father. I am alive and well and here in England.

You have no reason to read further or even accept my explanation about why I have been absent your entire life, but I can no longer live with myself knowing that you are out there and now married with a son.

Yes, I did marry and then abandon you and your mother on St Helena Island when you were a baby. I want you to know that I truly loved your mother, but our relationship would not have been accepted on any level in South Africa because of her skin colour. I admit that I did ask her to tell you that I was dead, as I believed this to be the best decision at the time, but please, Katherine, you must know that I have deeply regretted it ever since. I tried to support you as much as possible by paying money for your keep, for your school and university fees over the years. This was only possible with the help and total discretion of Mother Superior at the convent in Cape Town.

I have worked hard and become quite successful in South African, cattle farming and latterly in the gold mining sector. I did marry once but had no other children and soon divorced as I realised that, whilst I still love your mother, it has always sadly been an impossible love.

Now that I am older and finding no satisfaction in business success or indeed friendship, I have realised how much I have regretted that decision. I have cut off my nose to spite my face. I have a family that, up to this moment (at the time of your reading this letter), does not know that I even exist.

I appreciate that this letter and my admissions will be a

huge shock for you. Please forgive your mother for not telling you the truth, as this was wholly at my request.

If you have it in your heart to forgive me a little, please can we meet?

I promise to answer any questions you have about this horrid untruth.

I am deeply ashamed that it has taken me so long to contact you, but I feel you may understand that I have had to summon up enormous courage to do so.

I am staying at the Dolphin Hotel in Southampton.

Please, give me a chance to explain?

Your father,

Luke Viljoen

Katherine and Michael both sat in silence for a while with many thoughts and questions whirling in their heads. Tears started to flow down Katherine's cheeks. Michael took her in his arms and simply let her cry.

There was so much to take in and discuss and, with them both in a state of shock at this revelation, they were unsure where to begin.

Katherine eventually managed to compose herself and felt that she now understood why her mother had been so hysterical after the incident. She realised what a shock it must have been for Elsie, not only to see Luke here in England of all places, but also her fear that the truth was about to be disclosed and it was beyond her control. They both realised that Elsie must have been so panicked at seeing Luke that she had rushed away and across the road. What if Luke had not pushed them out of the way and Elsie and baby Christopher had been run over by the motor vehicle? It did not bear thinking about.

Katherine made a phone call to the nurses' dorm in the grounds of the hospital and asked if one of the off-duty trainee nurses could babysit Christopher the next day. They all knew the cute little fellow and one of them immediately volunteered to help.

Katherine and Michael finally got to bed that night, both feeling quite shattered by all the events that had unfolded that day. Katherine could have lost both her mother and son in an accident and now she suddenly had a father that she had always believed to have died when she was a baby. Bizarrely, as a result of the automobile accident, there was a chance that he may well now die anyway, before she even got to speak to him.

After the babysitting trainee nurse had arrived the next morning and Katherine had given her the instructions for the day, she and Michael left for the hospital, promising to meet in the doctors' lounge for morning tea and to update each other on the unfolding events.

Katherine changed into her white coat and joined the doctors' early meeting for her department, to be updated and get the schedule for the day from the matron. Matron immediately reported to Katherine that her mother was awake and a little drowsy, but still very tearful. However, physically she seemed fine and could probably be discharged after a further examination. Her bruising and grazes would need to be checked regularly for possible infection, but it was thought Katherine could do that at home.

Michael made his way to see his father-in-law, who was still unconscious and looking very poorly. He had been placed in a neck brace and traction for his back injury. His right arm had been broken and was set in a splint. Michael uncovered Luke's feet and pinched his toes sharply. There seemed to be a slight reaction which was a good sign. Michael stood there looking at him, in his professional capacity as a doctor and then, as his son-in-law. Whilst he wanted his patient to get better, he was also extremely angry to have discovered that he had deserted a mother and baby all those years ago. As a doctor, he had to put those feelings aside and do his very best for his patient - Mr Luke Viljoen. He asked another doctor to assist him with the diagnoses and treatment as he realised that he may well now be related to him by marriage. Ethically and for objectivity reasons, he felt he should not be treating a family member without the assistance of another doctor.

Katherine came to Elsie during her rounds. She kissed her mother on the cheek and cheerfully told her that Christopher was fine and being cared for by one of the nurse trainees. Katherine advised Elsie that she was to be discharged shortly and that she would arrange for her to be taken home at lunch time, when Katherine could accompany her. It was thought that Elsie would be rather stiff and sore, but that the grazing should heal well if kept clean and no infections occurred.

Elsie looked deeply into Katherine's eyes and whispered,

"I am so, so sorry," as her eyes welled up. Katherine squeezed her mother's hand and replied,

"We will talk later."

Elsie noticed that the chain, crucifix and key that normally hung around her own neck was now being worn by Katherine. Had she opened the box last night? What if she had? Elsie realised that it was time to share her past with her daughter and she did not know whether to feel relieved or anxious.

Elsie watched her daughter, Dr Viljoen, as she continued her round on the ward, and could not help but feel a huge sense of pride. She cut rather a glamorous and stylish picture with her slim figure and blonde hair perfectly cut into a neat bob.

Katherine and Michael met for morning tea in the doctors' lounge and exchanged updates on Luke and Elsie. Michael reported that Luke had briefly regained consciousness but had not yet spoken. He was due to have an operation, carried out by one of Michael's colleagues, to pin his pelvis. The plan was that they would leave him in traction for his back injury and continue to monitor his nervous system, as he seemed to have some feeling in his feet. They were hopeful that the spinal cord was not too badly damaged in the accident.

Michael had suggested that they talk to Elsie together later that evening, as this was a huge revelation that should be discussed as a family, and a family decision was to be made. Katherine was grateful to Michael for being so level headed and understanding, as she was dealing with quite polarised and mixed emotions and still reeling at the news.

Upon her discharge from hospital, Elsie was slowly and carefully escorted home by Katherine. Whilst they waited for the replacement trainee nurse to assist with Christopher to arrive, Elsie declared,

"We have lots to talk about, Katherine, my dear." To which Katherine replied that they would do so when she and Michael were home later. Elsie felt a little relief and respite at not immediately having to face the fact that she had lied to her daughter her entire life about Luke. She assumed Luke had been killed in the automobile accident as she had heard that terrible 'thud' as he had landed on the road after the impact with the automobile, but she thought it inappropriate to ask Katherine if he had survived or not.

Elsie spent a tormented afternoon not knowing how much Katherine and Michael knew at this stage. She tried to subtly ask the trainee nurse if she knew the fate of the man who had been involved in the accident, but she replied that she had been off duty and not heard any reports from her colleagues; besides, she was forbidden to talk about patients to non-medical staff.

Elsie believed that Katherine had overreacted by getting the young nurse trainee to stay with her and baby Christopher for the afternoon, but found herself soon feeling exhausted and wanting a nap. She really felt quite physically, and emotionally, bruised and battered.

She realised that no matter how much Katherine and Michael knew about Luke, it was too late to try and cover up the truth for a moment longer. In a strange way, Elsie began to feel a huge sense of relief that the truth was emerging, although she was terrified that her daughter could choose to disown her for keeping the truth from her about her father. Why had she remained so loyal to Luke's request? He certainly did not deserve her loyalty. Could he not have warned her that he was planning to visit and write to Katherine? Elsie remembered that Luke had tucked a letter addressed to Katherine into the side of Christopher's pram. She struggled on her stiff and aching legs to check the pram in the entrance hall, but the letter was nowhere to be found. Elsie was slightly hopeful that it had blown away during the commotion of the accident.

When Katherine and Michael returned home that evening, they all sat down to a dinner prepared by the trainee nurse under Elsie's direction. Baby Christopher was all smiles to see his parents and had already been bathed and fed.

Clearly, the elephant in the room was the subject of Luke and how he was, and no one seemed to be able to bring themselves to mention his name for a long while. Eventually, Michael took charge and announced that they needed to have a family discussion about Luke Viljoen.

Elsie felt as though her dinner might instantly return and

forced herself to keep swallowing and remain calm. She twisted her fingers in her lap and watched herself doing so, unable to make eye contact with her daughter or son-in-law.

Michael spoke in a measured tone as though he was in a doctors' meeting, reporting that Mr Viljoen was still in a serious condition and in extreme pain. He was suffering from concussion but seemed to be lucid from time to time and was able to enquire about Elsie and the baby before he slipped back into a semi-conscious state. He had had an operation to pin his pelvis and remained in spinal traction. There was no definitive reason to think he would be permanently disabled, but it was too soon to know for sure.

Rather sternly Michael addressed Elsie directly,

"I think, Mother, you owe your daughter and me an explanation about what happened to cause the accident."

Elsie started to cry but dabbed her eyes with her lace handkerchief and tried to tearfully explain.

"I was pushing Christopher along the promenade next to the sea for our usual afternoon walk and noticed a man sitting on one of the benches. He was muffled up in a scarf against the stiff breeze and I only recognised him when he walked toward us and spoke. I was in shock, and angry that he should be so audacious as to assume that he could give me a letter for Katherine explaining his absence for her whole life. After all, I had carried that burden of his secret at his request, and now he believed and hoped he could just walk back into our lives."

Elsie started crying again and continued through her sobs, "I am so sorry for what has happened and for putting little Christopher in danger. I was angry and panicked. I reminded Luke that he was dead to us and rushed to get away and that was when it happened! You know the rest and I am assuming you found his letter too?"

Katherine put a comforting arm around her mother.

"If only you had told me this years ago, Mother. I am not a child, and I would have understood. I too am now angry and confused and wondering how many other secrets you may have in the little wooden box from St Helena!"

Elsie replied,

"The box is next to my bed, and you can open it now if you wish as the key is with you. There are no more secrets. I kept newspaper cuttings about Luke when I found them in Johannesburg. There is also the original letter he gave me when he handed me the box that he had made before he left St Helena. There is even a small piece of the caul that was on your head when you were born. I discretely sold pieces of it to some of the seamen at the harbour, as it was believed that if one had a piece of caul in one's purse, one would never drown. The money I got went a long way to pay for our passage to Cape Town."

It took days of questions and explanations for Michael and Katherine to begin to understand the logic of Elsie's secret. Elsie knew that her daughter and son-in-law were disappointed in her for not having been honest about Luke in the first instance and she even got to the point that she offered to leave them and return to South Africa, which would not be entertained by her family.

Luke made very slow progress and, when he was fully conscious, Katherine went to visit him. He tried to explain his own point of view to Katherine, but everything he said seemed feeble and pathetic. She stood at his bedside with mixed feelings of anger, concern and indifference.

Katherine asked him why he did not bring her and Elsie to England all those years ago, where there was surely much less racism and where they could have lived as a family? There was no good explanation and Luke knew that there was little chance of her ever truly forgiving him.

Luke had gained some use of his legs but was unable to walk unaided. There was a new physiotherapy department at the hospital, and it was recommended that he should visit there daily in the forthcoming months.

Chapter 30
A Family?

During the period of Luke's recovery, Michael and Katherine made the very generous decision that he should move in with them, as they had a spare ground-floor bedroom and bathroom in their home. This would mean that he could easily be collected in a wheelchair to attend his daily physiotherapy.

Elsie was somewhat shocked at their decision but realised that it was probably not her place to object. How strange that in her fifties she and her husband, for the first time, would be living under the same roof.

There were awkward and strained times with a relative stranger in the house. But the atmosphere eased as the weeks went by and everyone felt less like they were stepping on glass when they encountered each other.

The truth of many situations can sometimes be multifaceted, like a kaleidoscope that can be swivelled to change an image and, in a similar way, so the family members each interpreted the events that had led to them being separated for so long. But now they were thrown together by some partially orchestrated event that led to the accident and resulted in their having to face up to long hidden truths and new emerging images.

One evening, after dinner when they were all enjoying a coffee, Katherine decided to tackle the fact that her parents had hidden the truth of Luke's existence until now. Firstly, she turned to face Luke and, looking deep into his blue eyes that matched her own in perfect tone, she asked,

"Father... Dad... both these words still feel strange on my tongue. When was the last time you saw me before coming into our lives here in Portsmouth?" She held his gaze and observed the colour drain from his face.

"No more lies or cover-ups. Please, I need to know the absolute truth from here on."

Luke glanced nervously from Katherine to Elsie, and shifting in his chair replied to his daughter, "I was at the back of the hall for your graduation. The reverend in St Helena and then Mother Superior and I had remained in contact over the years. She had written to tell me that you were graduating. So, I made my way there and watched both of you from a distance. It was one of the proudest moments of my life, as well as one of the most painful. From then on, I realised how alone I was and how selfish I had been, as there I was, in flesh and blood, but merely an unknown ghost of a father. When you were a baby and I wrote that letter to your mother on the island before I left, I was young and foolish and certainly didn't understand the long-term implications. I suppose I believed at the time that I could forget both of you and thought it would be easier for you if you were told I had died."

"Would you have sought us out if you had had another family?" asked Elsie.

"Don't really know about that... but, probably... yes, as it has been some thirty years of wondering and imagining how different life could have been."

Elsie scoffed and, folding her arms defensively across her chest, said, "Really, Luke? What fun we could have shared in South Africa as a mixed-race family. I can't believe you came spying on us at Katherine's graduation. What were you hoping to gain? We were better off without you, Luke. Still would be!"

"This is not helpful, Mother. You are just as guilty for not telling me the truth. I am not a child and yet, you chose to keep lying to me about my father. I had a right to know and make up my own mind. You are as selfish and guilty as each other."

Katherine paused and dabbed her eyes with her hankie.

"The problem is that I love both of you and strangely understand that your reasons may have been to protect me, as well as yourselves. I want Christopher to know his extended family and possibly his paternal family will one day come around too."

When Luke and Elsie were by themselves, Elsie made no attempt to hold back the anger that had been simmering in her for years. Luke tried to explain his position, but Elsie barely heard him; however, they were as civil as possible to each other in front of the family and slowly the atmosphere between them began to thaw. Baby Christopher was always the icebreaker and was enjoying all the attention from both his grandparents. Luke was obviously delighted to learn that he was named Christopher Luke.

Another evening, Katherine asked if Elsie would mind if they opened the box from St Helena together and looked at its contents.

Luke was surprised that Elsie still had the box and explained in an embarrassed manner that he was a poor carpenter and that was the first and last bit of woodwork he had ever attempted. He laughed at his attempt to paint the red roses on the front of it. He reminded Elsie that they used to grow around the front door of her cottage and that she had worn one in her hair the day they were married. Elsie revealed she had a dried bloom in the box from the bush that she had picked when they had stopped at St Helena on the way to

England.

Katherine commented that her father had carved her initials on the lid and was a little saddened to learn that 'KGV' was really the abbreviation for 'POW' in Dutch.

And so, she carefully unlocked the box and took out the slightly musty smelling contents, one at a time. There was her parents' original marriage certificate; the heart-breaking letter that Luke had handed to Elsie as he left St Helena; the piece of caul from Katherine's birth in a small leather pouch; neatly folded press cuttings from the Johannesburg newspapers about Luke; Luke's Johannesburg address written on a small card; and a dried red rose. Elsie said she had no need to ever lock it again, as the truth was now out and free. She laughed, declaring that the box from St Helena was the longest serving POW, holding all those secrets.

Luke was getting stronger by the day and able to walk a few steps unaided at home and in the garden, but he still needed to be pushed in a wheelchair for longer distances. He decided that he would like to retire near his family and buy a house that had recently come up for sale overlooking Stokes Bay, which was close to the hospital. It was a very grand house and not dissimilar to his home in Johannesburg. He went about buying a car and employing a chauffeur, so he could become more independent. He asked Elsie if she would help him to choose furnishings for the home and assist him with the employment of a housekeeper and gardener. Initially, Elsie was not prepared to help, but she slowly warmed to the idea and could not help getting involved. When he was stronger, Luke moved out of Katherine and Michael's home. Elsie was initially pleased that he was not around all day and enjoyed having little Christopher to herself once again. However, she found that she did miss their good spirited and lively conversations. Luke often invited her to bring baby Christopher over for visits, which she did readily.

There was an ongoing, underlying tension between them though. Luke had become more aware of it, the more time he spent with Elsie. One day, when they were on their own in the Victorian styled orangery attached to Luke's home taking a little sherry together and watching the stunning sunset over the calm waters of the Solent, he braved the question…

"Elsie, I know I have hurt you immeasurably over the years, but I feel of late that there is something really bothering you; in fact, I have felt a few times that you have wanted to say something to me. Maybe it has not been the right time? However, circumstances have brought us together again and I would like to clear the air, if possible."

Elsie was caught a little off-guard, even though she had practiced this conversation with Luke a thousand times in her mind should she ever get the right opportunity. It was now or never.

"Yes, there is a very personal issue that has haunted me since we were on St Helena together."

"Elsie, I know how wrong I was and if only I could turn back the hands of time, I would have made very different choices. Again, I am so sorry I abandoned you and Katherine."

"Actually, as I said, Luke, this is a *very* personal matter."

Luke raised his eyebrows and drained his sherry schooner, never imagining what was to come. "Please continue, Elsie."

"When we were intimate all those years ago at the Heart Shaped Waterfall…" Elsie took a deep breath. "You were very rough with me and, to be honest, I have often felt that you took me forcefully. Perhaps you even raped me?"

"No, no, Elsie! It was never like that. I loved you. And still do." Luke began to shake and reached for Elsie's hand which she pulled out of his way. "Oh, Elsie, I cannot deny that I was completely inexperienced and was driven by my passion and had no previous experience at all. I am so sorry if I hurt you, but even more distressed that you have felt this way for all these years. Oh my God. I am so sorry."

"You did not even look at me. I have always wondered if… Was that because of the colour of my skin?"

"Never, Elsie! I loved you and was so upset when I woke to find you gone without having had the opportunity to tell you so." Luke took a few deep breaths. "It deeply pains me that you have thought all these years that I just used you, when in fact, in my mind, it was all so perfect. We men are so different to women."

They sat in silence for a long time and Luke whispered. "I left you with our child but, worst of all, I left you thinking that I had perhaps… raped you? That simply is not true and hearing that from you is like a twisted dagger to my soul."

Elsie began to whimper, and the tears welled up and rolled down her cheeks. She had not shed a tear for Luke since the first time she read his letter – that letter of abandonment. She had vowed never to shed another tear over him and now here she was, crying in front of him.

"Luke, you were everything to me after both of my parents died and I had believed, back then, we were friends, slowly learning to like and perhaps love each other. I had to face the disgrace of being the school mistress left with a child. That is one of the reasons I left St Helena. To save face, as the locals all believed I was going to meet up with you and we were to live as a family."

Elsie began to laugh through her tears. "What you did give me was the strength to start a new life. I developed a core of steel and became determined to give Katherine the best opportunities. Oh yes, you indirectly supported her with finance, I know that now, but I was there to love and guide her. You missed out on that. I almost feel sorry for you, Luke. You denied yourself that greatest gift of parenthood."

Luke had not ever seen this side of Elsie before. He hated himself for so many things, but to see her cry was so painful for him. "Can you ever forgive me, Elsie? This is far more hurtful than I ever realised. I am so, so sorry. I wish there was something I could say or do to make you believe that you are the one I have always loved. You have haunted me ever since I left you. I even planted a garden of roses which I called Elsie's Rose Garden."

Elsie stared long and hard at Luke.

"Elsie, please try to forgive me. I understand you have held this anger in your soul for too long. Punishing me may well have felt like the answer over the years, but I speak from experience when I say that revenge is like swallowing poison and hoping the revenged person dies."

Could she ever believe that he truly loved her and always had?

Was it too late for them?

Elsie began to realise that, by putting everything aside that had happened and not happened between them, she really did enjoy his company. They continued to discuss politics with great passion and read the same books. The garden was a great source of joy and they shared ideas and cuttings.

When Michael and Katherine were not working at the hospital, they would often visit Luke, and all take walks together. They were now a family, appearing like any other, who strolled along the sunny seafront with the breeze playing with their hair and clothing. They looked across to the Isle of Wight and Katherine commented that they should take a family holiday there sometime soon, to which everyone agreed.

Elsie pushed Luke in his wheelchair whilst they had long conversations, and the tension between them seemed to be easing. He was also starting to walk short distances on his own and his recovery was looking promising.

Katherine and Michael each held one of baby Christopher's hands as he toddled between them. Every now and then, they swung him up in the air and he would squeal with delight.

How bittersweet it felt to be a family at last. There was still so much to understand and so many personal demons that needed to be laid to rest. However, they so nearly never found each other. Now together at last, perhaps family was all that really mattered?